Praise for "20 and Still a Virgin!!!

hello ankur,

Well this is joy from m.p.(jabalpur). "20 and still virgin" is one of its kind and the way its been presented is delicious to all the readers. The Language been used is simple and easy to understand That was phenomenon dude. Regards

—Joy Bose, Executive Engineer, Tata Automobiles

Dear Ankur,

I just finished "20 and Still a Virgin". I would like to congratulate you for writing an amazing book. Every page of your book completely gripped me and i could not keep it down till i finished reading it...... Cheers..... Keep writing.

—Aniket A Bhalerao

Hi Ankur,

I read ur Book....it's really awesome.... Ur book somehow relates to our story also i.e. me and my friends... The way u wrote this book it does nt seems that it is ur first book.. Thks & regards

—Umang Gupta

---

hi bro.. m rahul poonia from hisar.. m too a jat... yes i acc. read ur novel 20 & still a virgin... this is my 1st novel & its really grt. i m really a big fan of ur,s.. tc & have fun bye

---

Hey...Ruturaj here. 4m nagpur.

Lemme tel u i just luvd it...awesum work man... superb n ma so called "department of brain" have ths much words only to describe ur mindblowing work[;)]...add me in ur fanlist bro...aftr a long (since 5.sum1) i hv got sumthng new to read... Everything is just perfect...... tc

---

Hi, ankur,

i am himani. actually i would like to congratulate you for your first novel. i really liked your book. its something unique. all the characters are friendly. i found all the emotions. it made me laugh on friends joke. it made me cry also. I really liek th character Rehaan. thanks for giving us such a lovely book regards

—Himani

Hellooo dear

With full hope that u will b fine with ur first rocking novel. Ankur usually I don't read novel, reason being I don't get ample of time 2 read it.But really I read ur novel in just 3 nights waiting 4 next day 2 read the wt fuck is going to happen next. Ur novel really remind me of my school nd college days. nd thanks 4 nostalgia of mine. Ther r lots more question and comments but not 'ek dam' All the best

—Naveen Dhingra

Hi Ankur,

I'm Aarsh, 17 from ahmedabad.I just finished reading your novel and you can bet that there is a tear in my eye right now accompanied by a smile..... The best part is,..... you've capture the spirit of the young india. I've read five point someone and believe me your book was actually better..... your book was a more serious kind..... yet didn't really lose its humorous touch!!

Thanks dude, for such a lovely and awesome book....... thanks for giving us an insight into the world of girls...... how these weird species of girls live,eat,think and breathe. And thanks also for the beautiful way in which you depicted the friendship of the three guys in the book. Best of luck for all your future ventures and congrats for the commendable perfomance of this book!!!!!

Thanks

—Aarsh

THE #1 NATIONAL BESTSELLER

20 And Still a ~~Vergin~~ Virgin?!!?

A NOVEL

BY

ANKUR DAHIYA

gbd books

New Delhi, India.

20 And Still a Virgin

First Published, August, 2009
Second print, September, 2009
Third print, November 2009
Fourth print, January 2010
Fifth print, October 2010
Sixth print, February 2011
Seventh print, July 2011

www.AnkurDahiya.com

This book is a work of fiction. Names, characters, places and incidents either are products of the author's imagination or are used fictitiously. Any resemblance to actual events or locales or persons, living or dead, is entirely coincidental.

ISBN: 978-81-88951-46-8

Published by
gbd books
I-2/16, Ansari Road, Daryaganj,
New Delhi - 110002, India.
generalbookdepot@yahoo.com
www.goyalbookshop.com
Ph.: 9810229648, 9312286851

Distributed by
General Book Depot
1691, Nai Sarak, Delhi-110006
Ph.: 23263695, 23250635

Composing & Cover Design
Atul Kumar

Printed at
Radha Press, Delhi - 110031
radha.press@yahoo.co.in

This book is dedicated to my Parents

&

Aayushi, Ankur Hooda,

Deepak and Manu

PREFACE

The insect of writing a novel was born in my 'Department of Brain' way back during my graduation days. I was sitting outside a shopping mall in the evening with my friends Ankur, Deepak and Manu. On the third sip of the coke I declared that I am going to write a novel. God knows if people would consider my written crap a novel. Ankur Hooda wondered if the beer that I took last night still has some impact on my mind or it's just my upcoming semester exams which are screwing me like this. Manu on the other hand already started testing if something is wrong with the poor cold drink or it's yet another all time high scoring poor joke of mine. And Deepak declared that the place is not suitable to sit; the guy thinks that the problem is with the aura created by the pathetic music being played by few new learners of guitar.

A month later I started writing. The journey of writing was not that easy as I used to think. I had written few pages but thought them irrelevant after few months. I then restarted writing from the beginning and the story repeated many times like this. When I somehow was able to complete the first five chapters, my fate brought me good news email one morning 'Hello Mr. Dahiya with due apology you are hereby informed that your laptop is not working'. The poor hard disk was no more. I think my gaming tortures were solely responsible for this. That way I lost whatever I had written. It made me lethargic to start the project again from zero, but the fire of writing this stupidity never died in me.

Then one day an angel came into my life; her name is Aayushi or to be more correct Dr. Aayushi. I met her on some online community and found the only person on earth taking interest in my world of poor jokes. It was just the starting of our friendship, but my 'Department of Heart' suggested me to share the idea of writing a novel to her. One night over the phone I said.

"Yaar Aayu I want to write a novel." I then told her the tale of 'The Lost Five Chapters'.

The next day she gave me a schedule and also a new unique kind of reward & punishment model designed especially for notorious asses like me. I have to write minimum five pages and maximum eight pages daily. If I do that the reward would be increasing the target for the next day. But if I failed to write five pages in a day, then after listening to my article of 'Ankur and his 1000 excuses', Aayushi would give me a long lecture. Those days I also considered writing another novel on 'Aayushi and her 1000 ways of screwing a person's mind through her long boring lectures'. At last after listening to her lectures almost all the days, I somehow completed my work. She also critically edited the novel. Hats off to you dear Aayushi.

The story and characters are fictitious and any resemblance to any real place or person will be just a coincidence. So all those girls who came into my life, who are still in my life and are planning to come into my life there is no need to run after me with sandals and *chappals* in your hand. I am innocent.

Well the novel is not carrying any money back offer so there is no use declaring it as crap after reading it...... although it is a crap. *Kahani main hero hai, heroine hai, pyar hai, villain hai, dhokha hai, dosti hai, maa hain, bauji hain, emotions hain, fight hai, hindi gaane hain aur aakhri main..... kyun bataun aakhri main kya hai.... khud padh lo.*

Happy reading.

— ***Ankur Dahiya***

ankurdahiyarocks@yahoo.com

# Acknowledgements

The idea of writing a novel came to my mind on aannn..... I don't exactly remember as I was drunk that time. Forget it. So for this my sincere thanks to myself and all my functionary organs for their sincere support. Thanks to my laptop for sitting on my lap continuously for hours and hours. Thanks to my mobile phone for not ringing most of the time while I was writing. Thanks to my bums for trying their best to maintain good relationship with my uncomfortable chair throughout. My sincere thanks to the tube light of my room which worked continuously for 4 months before getting fused. Thanks to my fan for its not so cooling attitude, my glasses of milk which waited to be drink up by me. Thanks to my pillow & bed which during many sleepless nights enjoyed their not so expected holidays. Also thanks to my alarm clock for never giving me even 5 more minutes to sleep. I wonder how this damn thing works as it always start annoying me right at the right time being set on. I think this is what Engineering is.

OK, on a serious note: This is all because of blessings of my parents that my work is seeing the light today.

Now coming to few creatures, which exist in almost everybody's life *i.e.* friends. My special thanks to my friends Ankur Hooda, Deepak, Manu and Surbhi. They are the ones because of whom this not so happening story exists.

Thanks to Vikram, Gaurav, Pawan, Hans Vivek and Sonika, who also contributed intentionally and unintentionally. Also thanks to Kiran and Jyoti.

In my graduation days in IMSAR, one of our professors Dr. Daleep Singh was the one who opened the blocked doors of intellectual rooms of 'Department of Brain' of students of my class. Thanks to Dr. Rishi Chaudhary, my Finance teacher, his words really motivated me. Thanks to the Director of my Institute Dr. Ajay K. Rajan, who gave me many management assignments, which helped me in my work. Thanks to Dr. H.J. Ghosh Roy for inculcating the habit of writing in students of my class in graduation days. Also thanks to the other teachers of my institute and school. My sincere thanks to all those professors and lecturers for never listening to my extraordinary creative excuses and throwing me out of the morning classes for coming late.

My sincere thanks to Kaushal Goyal, of GBD Books for agreeing to publish this book in our first meeting only. He has also helped me in editing & proof reading. Thanks to Atul Kumar (the computer incharge) for giving warning near the July end, the warning goes like this..... 'This is the fourth time I am doing corrections. If I find more then two mistakes on any pages in the 5th printout, I will commit suicide.' God is great; Atul is still alive.

My debt to my dear friend Aayushi is immeasurable; but for her unflagging faith and encouragement, this novel would not have been possible.

— ***Ankur Dahiya***
ankurdahiyarocks@yahoo.com

20

And Still

a ~~Vergin~~ Virgin?!!?

1

Beer, Girls and Flashback

Life was never easy to me and neither this present situation is. Losers have their own advantages, at least they are always ready for the worst. Moreover, having best friends like Rohit and Aadarsh; I do deserve a bravery award. Thanks to Rohit, today we have decided to make a night-out, as according to him, it will introduce another chapter of adventure to our lives. Sometimes I wonder, why Rohit never participates in those idiotic reality shows, at least they suck less than Aadarsh.

It is around 10 p.m., we three are sitting in the top row of the stadium, with beer bottles in our hands. We call this place '*Shanti Sthal*' (peaceful place), the reason is not to be questioned. Aadarsh is about to finish his second bottle, declaring that two poor beer bottles have failed to make any effect on him and his condition is still the same, as it was before. But his trembling legs are stating a different story, altogether.

On the other hand, poor Rohit is struggling with his first bottle. Half done but drinking the rest of the half for him is like cracking the CAT exam in the first attempt with preparation of just one month.

Lastly, myself Rehaan, the average student, who finished his first bottle, enjoying the warmth of it inside my body.

"I miss my school days." Rohit said, while putting his half finished bottle on the floor. Thank God CAT test is now postponed for some time.

"Me too. We used to have fun at that time." Aadarsh answers and somehow manages to sit next to Rohit. I think he at last noticed his trembling legs and finally became convinced that he is drunk.

"Especially Aarti, Kamana and Nandini." Rohit says. Both of them start looking at me expecting me to take part into their world of women talks or at least appreciate their views. This is the common problem with boys, majority of them are suffering with JTS (*Janani Talk Syndrome*) i.e. after consuming alcohol, many of them start behaving like girls. They start crying or else start cursing their life, like a looser.

It's not a new thing for me, as every time Rohit drinks, he has only few things to discuss about—school, Nandini, Kamana and Aarti. And for that Aadarsh and I, are his worst victims.

"That period taught us many things. We are different persons now, all three of us." Here comes my philosophy.

Fuck man, we have to pass our time, not for an hour or two, but for the whole damn night. Trust me if there was any topic which is capable of making us pass our time, then of course, Rohit is on the right track.

So the three of us travelled to the most constructive part of our lives—where we realized the power of stupidity within ourselves—the 10th class.

2

Dreams, Introduction and the Black Sheep in the Herd

I am lying on a not so comfortable bed in a dilapidated or ramshackle room. Cigarette smoke is all around and nothing is visible. My left hand is resting on one side of the bed with a burning cigarette and smoke rings surrounding me all over. I am constantly looking at not so clearly visible stationary aged fan, which seems like moving at its maximum. A girl is lying with me under a blanket with her face hidden under my arm. She is grabbing my vest with her hand, in which she is wearing a cute thin golden bangle. My right hand is moving back and forth on her back for making her feel comfortable. I crushed the half burned cigarette on the table nearby. I then kiss her cheeks again.

I woke up suddenly. Damn! The same old dream, which I have seen two-three times before also. What does that signify? 'Stupid dream, it can't mean anything. It is just a dream.' I told myself.

Wow! it's seven already and I need to get ready for the school.

In the mid of tenth class, I used to think myself as the most insignificant asshole in the whole world. I considered myself to be a unique kind of species, until I met Rohit and Aadarsh. After that things never remained the same.

Aadarsh, by his name any layman can imagine his image. He seems to be "muma's boy", a gentleman who is a dream of every average Indian girl and her parents. A boy who stands first in the class, talks softly and gently to everybody, one girl man and has a perfect life. An idol of every young child in the family. These were the interpretations of his mother while assigning the name to our devil. With due apologies, he scores zero out of ten in each of the above mentioned fields. Aadarsh is a guy who is a specialist in gaining weight. His oversized tummy can drive any girl away from him. He is the one who spends all his life in search of the answer to the well renowned question i.e. 'For what reason is he surviving on the earth?' God is great as he has blessed him with one damn talent and that is—whenever he smiles, it's a matter of research for our great scientists to find out, where his eyes get disappeared?

Rohit, if you see his face then surely you will conclude that he has a moral right to get arrested. His face resembles many anti-social elements but in reality I bet my whole landed property, if he has ever hurt a single mosquito, even. His peaceful attitude has a capacity to bring tears to the most non-violent person of India. He is blessed with a rabbit sort of a face—with messed up hair and an imperfect denture supported with incisors coming-out making a perfect smiling face. He belongs to that group of retards who score above 90% and then scream at their fate, as to why it is only them who score so low. They also struggle to get admission into IITs and IIMs. My heartiest sympathy is always with Rohit. In short you can call him, the eleventh wonder of the world or the most pathetic ass of 21st century.

Lastly myself, I wonder if I have done anything right in my life till now. Neither do I expect anything out of myself in future. My life revolves around certain things like—dreaming all the time, poor mathematics, higher expectations of parents in academics, girls, and of course how to overcome my lovely bad luck. My friends in previous classes, teachers and my relatives, always considered me as a useless person, who could never do anything constructive in his life. People call me with different names—'looser', 'jerk' 'an idiot' and some even prefer 'an asshole'. But I still consider myself as a born stud. You may call it a drawback of positive thinking. I have two things in my life—my dreams and a fire in my belly to achieve them.

There is one thing common to all three of us and that is stupidity. You can trace various kinds of stupidities. We are considered to be the most eligible 'Samples for Psychological Testing' to discover the brainless species existing in the human world.

Being a student of tenth class you notice certain changes. Suddenly you come out of the world of videogames, except a few like Rohit—who still keeps a record of his high scores of Video Games, collects pens of different kinds in his girly geometry box, and competes with other younger chaps in collecting Tazo and Cards, which are given free of cost with packets of chips.

With time, a drastic change was noticed in Aadarsh. The guy who once used to keep track of the abusive words of mine and Rohit, now starts and ends each of his talk with fuck you, thanks to Aarti. Aarti is around 5 feet, a not so cute girl, religious by name only. If you ask Aadarsh about her, he will entertain you by mentioning a couple of qualities of her, of which Rohit is still unable to trace even one. The dude introduced the concept of love for the first time in our group and guess what? Aarti likes Aadarsh so much that even if he is the last man remaining on this earth, she would still prefer to marry an animal instead. But Aadarsh has got his own views regarding that matter, thanks to our democratic rights.

Anyway, Rohit and I are happy with his one-sided love story, at least we have something to laugh at.

Oh! how can I forget to introduce you all to my best friend—my mother.

"Where were you when God was distributing brains?" My mother asks me.

"I guess, in the washroom." I laugh.

"Shut up, you know my elder cousin brother was saying that our family is known as a genius in mathematics. So how come Rehaan, is weak?" My mother says in a deep tone, trying hard to create an aura, as in all *saas bahu* serials.

Well I belong to a family, where everybody is a top scorer in mathematics. But in my case, mathematics and I are like the two poles of a magnet, which by nature repel each other. I think the problem lies in the concept clarity. In the first class, I was confused that why 2+2 is 4 and not 5, and hence as I moved on to higher classes this problem started growing bigger in size. I think this was all the fault of my nursery teacher, as she failed to make me comfortable with the concepts of mathematics. You can say that I am 'a black sheep in the herd.'

"But Mom, none of the fingers of our hand is similar in size and shape, and the task of one cannot be done by the other one. It is the law of nature that no two individuals are same, everybody has his own distinct qualities." Sometimes I really feel proud of myself. May be one day I will be a great philosopher, till then let me carry on with my defence mechanism.

"I agree but why you always choose to be the smaller finger, why not the bigger one?" My father says. In this way another soldier teams up with my mother. This is not a fair fight as now two grown-up soldiers are against a teenager. I wonder when I will be in my 20's and another soldier, my wife joins me for my rescue. But who knows, may be my wife will also prefer to join my parents and not me, as my bad luck never disappoints me.

"I think you are right. Well then, it's a promise I will try my best and show you the results." Sometimes it is better to show the white flag at the right time for your survival.

"OK. Then go and study." My mother says in a winning tone.

Well my mathematics text-book is open in front of me and I am not reading, as my concentration is on the 'Glamour World Magazine' inside the book. I am trying to identify my future aspects of becoming a model someday, as I am quiet influenced by this glamour world. Well every time I look in the mirror, I see the reflection of a Super Model. My friends call me slim but I call it maintenance or that they are just jealous. Life has always chosen good things for me, but I prefer the flip side.

3

Love, Nightmares and Mathematics

Model School, Rohtak
Mathematics Class

Mrs. Khanna, our mathematics teacher is drawing some ancient historical figure on the board, which according to Rohit is a 'Hyperbola'. On the other hand, Aadarsh is drawing his own kind of figures in his notebook, which according to Rohit is Aarti's face. I am sitting between them with fear, waiting for some miracle, that Mrs. Khanna doesn't point at me to explain the so called hyp..erbo..bol, whatever.

"Who will explain this to the class?" Mrs Khanna asks. This results in a couple of raised hands. Let me tell you that there are some students in every class who have a habit of raising their hands, no matter whether they know the answer or not. There is some manufacturing defect in their wonderland, that for every question they have an instant reaction of a raised hand. Guess what? One is sitting right next to me, Mr. Rohit.

"No, not the intelligent ones. Rehaan, you come here and explain." She says and I wonder if I had ever teased her daughter. Why me always, even after being aware of the fact that if I could ever solve even one equation, that day would be recorded in golden words in the history of mathematics.

Now I am in front of our class blackboard, or you can say the battle field, and the gun (chalk) is handed over to me by our

Madam. My task is to beat the unbeatable enemy, remembering it's name is yet another mystery for me to crack. So I adopted my age-old strategy—the white flag strategy.

"No. Go and stand up on your bench. Anybody who can explain this?" She says angrily and starts looking at the class. I am standing on my bench and making my class eye-catching to the outsiders; at least I am good in something.

In the recess, the three of us are standing in the basketball court, eating the cheapest stuff available in the canteen, cursing our pocket money.

"Hey, I heard these days you are talking to some girl of our class." Rohit said, side-by-side sharing tomato sauce with his white shirt.

"I think you are talking about Sneha. Actually, I consider her to be my sister."

"Are you really a jerk or just in the habit of making every second girl your sister." Aadarsh said in a taunting way, staring at me.

"Exactly, every second girl, not the first one. This is called 'Networking Among Girls', dude. I don't go directly for the beautiful girl. Instead I make her best friend my sister and the rest of the workload is shifted on my dearest sister."

"Oh! Girls are still an unidentified territory of my life; rather, I prefer textbooks to spoil my time." Rohit explains his view-point while noticing the modern art on his shirt.

Mrs. Sehgal is taking the next class after break. We call her 'encounter specialist', a postgraduate in giving 'corporal punishment'. Sometimes people bet that there is existence of emotional junk present in her personality. If you somehow want to survive in her class, just follow three basic rules—always say yes to whatever she says; always maintain your homework notebook as per Rohit's notebook. Last but not the least, during the class tests, always maintain good relationship with Rohit (by following the principle that book-worms are always right).

"Let me distribute your test papers. I will call your name one-by-one. Only that fellow will come whose name is called by me. Clear?" Mrs. Sehgal commands. Everything she says is always crystal clear in our minds. Of course, who wants to have historical traces of Mrs. Sehgal's fingers on their cheeks. She started calling out names, and one by one the sword starts hanging on everybody's head and lastly stops on one lucky contestant.

"Aditya only 2 out of 25, come here." She says angrily. Everyone sitting was well aware of the fact, as to what is going to happen. Some of us even started praying to keep his soul in peace—you can call it our moral support.

The encounter is carried out in a specified process; I call it a 'Sehgal's 2 on 3 on 5 Respond Model'. It is a simple model which is operated on responses given by us. First she pulls your ear. After that you notice her rubbing it, so as to encourage you to respond. While waiting for your first response, she will adjust her hands in varied angles towards your cheek. After the 1st response about 'why she should let you go', she chooses the best angle of slap for maximum damages. The first response leads to the second step i.e. 2 slaps. Then it depends on the quality of your 1st response which decides whether she will proceed with the third one or not. With the second unconvincing reason or response your cheek will be hit with another slap, making a total of three. Well here comes the break-even point—almost every girl and some boys also, burst into tears. This third illogical and unconvincing response will reap you fruits of two more slaps making it to a total of 5.

There are some like Aditya, who always reach up to the score of 5. I wonder why she never goes beyond 5. It's not that my class lacks in giving further mind-blowing responses, I think her violence model underestimates the capabilities of samples taken into for study (i.e. the students of my class). There are also few diplomat retards like me who save their lives even with their 1st effective response.

Well, Aditya receives 3 consecutive slaps this time, which makes it a total of 13, including slaps of previous encounters, crowning him the 'King of the Ring'. After the encounter he comes back and takes his seat behind me and starts singing a melodious song for this encounter. I heard few of the lines of his song which goes like "@#%$!@#$#&^$#!%."

After school, we decided to tease the 'King of the Ring' who scored 13, making him on top of the list, i.e. Aditya, nick named *Saand* (bull).

"Hey *Saand*! How was the third shot?" Aadarsh laughs at Aditya. Look, 'the King of Fats' himself is calling the other guy a *Saand*. At least he is not eligible to call Aditya a 'motu' but thanks to the freedom of speech.

"You want to taste that also. Let me do the favour." Aditya says in an angry gesture. Take this on a serious note—never tease a bull when he is in the mood of testing out his horns.

"Wow! Relax dude. At least you scored more than anybody else in the class." I replied giving him a friendly gesture. On the other hand Rohit, the significant non-violent insect is busy observing Aditya and Aadarsh's overburdened bellies. He always prefers to be in his small world of observations and bets his money on Aditya's heavy frame but I think Aadarsh is more fatty.

"Ha ha, thanks." Aditya says while trying hard to make his pathetic smile stylish. This is the way—make somebody proud of the thing about which he is ashamed of, and he will be on top of the world.

Like this our life is going almost smoothly. Aadarsh is busy in trying to figure out his future relationship with Aarti and waiting for the right time to approach her and side-by-side screwing up his scores in the tests. Rohit keeps on justifying his new purchases of text books of foreign authors and on announcing his high scores in video games, in the hope that one day he will gain respect for that. My life on the other hand is going Perfect—perfect lectures by my parents on why I should study hard, perfect innovative punishments by Mrs. Khanna and lastly my perfect change of my Mathematics tutor for the fifth time in the hope that one day he/she will make me understand the 'Mysterious World of Mathematics'.

Many a times I have dreams about Mathematics and Mrs Khanna. I find myself attempting only one question in three hours and even in that giving a wrong answer. In some nightmares, I do not even reach in time to my test centre. The most favourite of them all is the one in which I visualise a boxing ring in which I am on one side and on the other is Mrs. Khanna. I find myself attempting to give-up the match even before starting it.

My days were tolerable until that day in November, when everything changed—10th November 2002, 'the most amazing and the worst day of my life'. For me it's a usual day to start with. Mrs. Khanna is taking her not so happening class. We three as usual are sitting together, hoping that today Mrs. Khanna will change her diplomacy towards me, putting an end to the cold war.

"As our syllabus is almost complete now, so let us have a quick revision. I guess by now all of you must have mastered your text book." Mrs Khanna says. Sometimes it feels great when you fall in a category where at least you are assumed to be mastering in something, which you always know that you cannot even do in your next life.

"To start with, let me ask you a simple question." Saying this, Mrs. Khanna draws a right angled triangle which seemed like a love triangle of any B-grade Hindi movie, thanks to my movie knowledge.

"So who will explain Pythagoras Theorem to the class."

"Yes, Madam." The students say in a jingle, and the usual seven students including Rohit raised their hands. But this time an unusual hand is added to the figure of seven, making it a total of eight. Let me introduce you to this upcoming talent, Rehaan. Oh yes, that's me. Mrs. Khanna always ask those students to answer the question who don't raise their hands. So this was nothing but an attempt to save my own ass. I thought by raising hand I would easily escape from the current crisis namely 'Pythagoras'.

"Rehaan, nice to see that you have started studying. OK. Come and explain it to us. Please clap for him." Mrs Khanna says and a round of applause starts. Gosh! Why always me out of the 60 renowned asses. Why not this fatty king 'Aadarsh' sitting next to me who always keeps on justifying his love story on his notebooks.

It feels special walking among the students who are clapping for you. It's like a movie award function where I am about to receive an award for the best actor.

"So, here is the chalk, come on." Mrs Khanna says, while handing me the same old companion who never coordinates with me.

"I am afraid....... I think I just forgot it. I really read this twice, day before yesterday. Trust me Madam." I said.

This leads to an instant movements in upper and lower jaws of Mrs. Khanna. My defence mechanism leads her to clench her teeth inside the layer of her cheeks, especially the crushing of molars in a set order.

"Mr. Rehaan before I slap you hard, get out of this class and stand outside till the class is over. It's enough now, I want to talk to your parents" She says angrily.

Tring tring the match is on—on one side we have five times Champion in Mathematics Olympiad, Gold Medallist Mrs. Khanna and on the other hand we have not-so-popular, not-so-interesting, not-so-intelligent but good-looking Rehaan.

"But, Madam...." before I could complete my sentence, I am spell-bound.

"Madam, may I come in?" An Angel asks for permission.

She is about 5'5" in height, having short wet hair spread all over her shoulders and cheeks. She has a cute round face. Even the worst dress of the world 'school dress' is looking pretty on her. When she smiled at Mrs. Khanna, I noticed a cute dimple on her left cheek. Something is special in her, I thought I know her. I don't know how? Her sweet voice seems familiar to me. The first thing which came to my mind was—Who is she?

"Yes, you may." Mrs Khanna replies, while giving a break to her mouth yoga tactic, allowing her teeth to relax for a while. I can see her face from a close angle, as I am standing next to Mrs Khanna. I find an instant enthusiasm in my left side of the chest; I think my spare parts also approved her.

She informed Mrs Khanna for a meeting, and with every single word of hers, the efficiency of my engine in terms of heart beat increased.

"Knock-knock anybody home." Rohit asks.

"Yeah the door is open. What's up?" I replied sarcastically.

"Are you OK. I mean why you raised your hand when you didn't know the answer?"

I explained him the whole story about my brilliant idea of rescuing my ass. But I didn't tell him my newly invented wish regarding 'The Angel'. I didn't want to make her an issue. Neither I wanted any love-rain in my life, already seen a useless case of Aarti and Aadarsh.

"Sometimes you are really strange." Rohit says and keeps his hand on my shoulders. A kind of sympathetic gesture from Rohit, invented specially for situations concerned with Aadarsh and Aarti.

"So what, any ways Mrs Khanna was going to choose me." I concluded the discussion.

For the whole day I was unable to stop myself thinking about the girl I saw in the morning. She was attractive, so it was obvious that at least for a short span her thoughts encouraged me to know about her. I think I have other things to worry about—the board exams are approaching and I have to take care of my scores, especially in Mathematics. Thanks to the newly bought mattresses, I fell asleep making an end to my worthless queries.

I am in a classroom standing near the blackboard and at the same time watching my Angel. One of my classmates named Sandhya comes to me. I start talking to her.

"Hey, Sandhya"

"Hi Rehaan, how are you?"

"I am fine and you?"

"Same here"

"Hey, do you know her?"

"Who?"

"That girl, who is sitting alone on the second last bench in the first row"

"Yeah, her name is Kamana."

"Kamana" I shout and wake up. It's 6:45 a.m. and time to get ready for school.

Oh, that was a strange dream. Man what is happening to me. I just saw her yesterday and already started dreaming about her. What was her name? Kamana; I have never heard such a strange name.

Today, I arrived at my school half an hour earlier and to pass my time am standing near my class and watching the beautiful things, 'the girls' and praying to God, that Mrs. Khanna won't come to school today.

"Dude, what's up?" Abhi asks and shakes hand with me. Abhi is my classmate. I wonder, why all the boys having name 'Abhishek', have a nick name 'Abhi' always?

"I am rocking, as usual." I answered and continued with an obvious question "So how is your preparation going on for board exams?"

"Fine, not sure about Hindi but for other subjects, I am about to finish the syllabus. What about you?"

"Well starting with my favourite subject Mathematics, you already know that I am a genius. Talking of Science and Social Science, these are the easiest of all, as if you master one, you have mastered the other automatically. For example, if I prepare for Science then just by adding the word Social, I will master the other and *vice versa*. You know me, I believe in smart work. Talking about English, well I will be having a tuition class for it in the near future. Regarding Hindi, what say—it is my mother tongue, so I won't waste my precious time in knowing something that I already know. Last but not the least IT, as it is an additional subject, so passing and failing in it won't matter. Therefore you can say that I have almost finished my preparations." I explained

"Funny, right? Board exams are approaching, so just be serious." Abhi says in a pathetic tone.

Gosh! The same girl I saw yesterday, is in the basketball court and going towards the Arts room.

"By the way, do you know that girl? The one in the basketball court." I pointed towards my so called 'Angel'.

"Hmm yes, her name is Kamana. She is in 10th B.

Life is full of surprises, but this is extra-oridinary. How can I know her name in my dream? Either my dream is Real or it's an Omen trying to tell me something; Whatever it is, I think I should talk to her. Rest my fate will drive the car of my life ahead.

In the recess, I am sitting in canteen with Aadarsh, while Rohit went to buy something to eat. After a few minutes Rohit joins us with three burgers in his hands.

"Ding dong, if you don't want to eat it, let my tummy do the honour then." Rohit says while waiting to handover my burger to me. I am still lost thinking about my dream and Kamana.

"Oh no. How could I be so harsh to your tummy. Let me face my hurdle on my own."

"Fuck man, where is the tomato ketchup? Why people eat more of the ketchup than the food stuff?" Aadarsh shouts while continuing his search and rescue operation of ketchup.

"Because it is available free of cost." Rohit has a point. Sometimes I find boys and girls eating their lunch (which they bring from their homes) with canteen's tomato ketchup.

"I think I like a girl." I declared.

"Yeah, good joke." Aadarsh says.

"I am serious."

"Dude, I even forgot how many times you fall in love and for how many days you stick to that girl. Don't worry; you would be fine in a day or two." Rohit says while gulping the bigger bite of his burger, even bigger than his mouth.

I told them the whole drama of my first encounter with Kamana and about that dream.

"Ha ha, I told you that he sucks and something is wrong but you never bothered. Hey there is my tomato sauce." Aadarsh laughs and moves to the table in front of us, and picks the bottle.

"Excuse me, I need it." Kamana says to Aadarsh. She is sitting with her friends on the table on which Aadarsh identifies some traces of tomato ketchup in the bottle.

"After me, honey." Aadarsh says and without listening to her take away the bottle. She was left staring at us.

"Crap, that fatty ass gulped up the whole stuff out of the bottle. So, you were saying something about Kamana and your dream. Show me the lucky chick?" Aadarsh asks while sharing the few drops of ketchup with us.

"That 'same fatty ass' is Kamana, you asshole, from whom you just won a battle of tomato sauce."

"I thought she is some new teacher in a school dress." Aadarsh starts laughing and continues "Moreover she also has an added advantage of being ugly, too."

Rohit also joins Aadarsh's strange laughter with a bite of the remaining burger in his mouth.

Now this is the problem with people. One fatty uncle is abusing a girl of his own community. She is not fat, you can call her healthy, instead. Thanks to the right to express, Aadarsh is free to express his views. But what about my human rights?

"So, what next?" Aadarsh asks me.

"I don't know,? I think, I will talk to her. At least I won't screw myself, as you are doing for Aarti." My counter attack.

"I will do something, let the right time come. Question is not about me, but about you. You don't know her. How will you approach her?"

"Network bro, 'Network Among Girls'."

Its evening and I am still trying to identify my so called available networks, suddenly an error occurred.

"I am talking to you, Mister. There is a calculation mistake." My father says.

After giving chance to five mathematics tutors, who failed to answer my highly professional queries, in the end I preferred my father to identify the deep route cause of the problem. My father at his time scored 197 out of 200 in mathematics, which my mother always uses as a negative motivator stimulant, to motivate me. I call it 'Those Days and These Days' phenomena.

"Look boy, the problem is not with your mathematical concepts, but with your silly calculation mistakes." He says while rounding up another one and continues "This could be corrected only when you stop reading mathematics book and start practicing it on your notebook."

"Yes, I will do that, Papa." I said, while minimising the windows of 'Networks' & 'Kamana' in my brain and concentrating to each and every word of his. Never argue with authority—authority is always right, especially when you know it's your fault. It's better to surrender, remember my 'white flag strategy'.

"Always keep in mind 'Mathematics is all about practise'" saying that Papa finishes with today's class.

After he left the room, I again re-opened the minimised windows and continued working on the concept of 'My Networks Among Girls'.

Children of my age are busy in preparing for their board exams. Rumours are being spread that Rohit saw Aadarsh carrying some text books and notes to the library; I call it a hallucination of Rohit. I am busy with my nightmares of Mrs. Khanna and Mathematics, and trying to search alternatives to approach Kamana through the concept of 'My Networks Among Girls.'

4

Network Among Girls, Few Other Nerds and Board Exams

Sometimes I wonder, why all girls fantasize the concept of 'Prince of My Dreams.' Every girl thinks that one day the prince of her dreams will come on a white horse (mare) wearing a black superhero kind of dress, to take her along. Firstly, the guy needs to come in a special black dress (black hat, black-night-suit kind of clothes, black goggles made up of cloth and black shoes—the brand depends on his economic condition) on white horse (mare) and propose her. For the marriage the poor chap needs to repeat the process with a few witnesses in the name of '*Baraat*'.

The thing which is horrifying me now a days is—as Kamana is also a kind of the same girly stuff—that the concept 'Prince of My Dreams' applies on her also. Firstly, how difficult is it to arrange for the white horse (mare), then bargaining for the hire (curse my pocket money), further figuring out shops selling that black dress, is worth cracking a nut. Also at the time of marriage, managing the speed of the horse to cope up with the speed of baraat and those cheap musical instruments with a low-paid singer adds to your embarrasment further.

"Hi." A sweet voice interferes my 'Prince of My Dreams' concept

"Hey, ignoring such a beautiful girl like me is really worth appreciating." Tinu says in a monotonic tone.

Girls and their misconceptions. Beautiful! I call her a 'Aunty Stuff'. Tinu is the biggest rival of Sneha and thats why I don't feel like talking to her. As she is a so called sister of my school friend Sagar, I have to tolerate her sense of humour. Once I shared the concept of 'Networks Among Girls' with Sagar and the next day he comes up with this new sister named, Tinu.

"How can I dare to ignore you? How is your life going on?" I asked, but what I meant was, why don't you leave me alone?

"Well it's like a scratched CD, trying hard to run smoothly without stops." She explains.

So why don't you throw that CD into the dustbin, I thought. Actually recently she had broken off with her fourth boyfriend.

"Oh! Everything would be fine. Don't worry, give yourself sometime." I said. Nothing would be fine with a girl like you, as I know the fifth boyfriend is already on her way of processing.

"So how many girlfriends do you have, huh?"

"Who wants to live a life of a domestic dog? Girlfriends are BBS—brain and bank account sucker." I said. In reality, I too wanted to be one. Hey, why don't you make me your fifth boyfriend, I thought.

She starts laughing at my poor joke. Sometimes I encourage myself to write a book of my poor jokes. I have traced at least one buyer of my book, Tinu.

"Wait a minute. Are you in B section?" I asked, giving a break to my philosophy. My machinery called 'Department of

Brain' calls off its strike, which was going on for last few days, because of lack of availability of 'Networks in the Kamana region'.

"Yup"

"Do you know Kamana?" I enquired, even after knowing the fact that she is the 'Daily School Gossip Magazine'.

"Kamana. Yes I know her. She is in my class. Mr. Rehaan, if I am not mistaken, you were explaining your BBS theory to me a few minutes ago." Tinu smiles, as if I have proposed her and her answer is yes.

"No, nothing serious. I just want to know her better, and feel like talking to her."

Talking,....... if things work accordingly, I will even marry her.

"Hey I am joking. Don't you worry, I will talk to her. You just relax." She says, while giving a break to her poor jaws.

At last I traced some network connections in the remote area of Kamana. Let me pray for my success.

"Hi Kamana" Tinu waves her hand.

"Hey, hi Tinu"

"Do you know Rehaan? He is in E section?"

"No, I don't know him. What happened?"

"Actually Kamana, he proposed you through me for friendship."

"Not interested." Kamana replies.

"Common Kamana, at least just talk to him. He is a nice guy."

"Who is he? I don't know him. Tell him to keep away from me. I don't talk to roadside Romeos." Kamana says with a bit of an attitude.

"Fine, I will convey your message to him"

After school I am desperately waiting for Tinu in front of the playground. Throughout the day I was on a trip of 'Day-Dreaming' about my future plans with Kamana. The planning process started with a 'yes', followed by excitement of meeting her, talking to her with my hands locked in hers, plans of managing my pocket money in a way to give her chocolates every alternate day and introducing her to Rohit, Aadarsh and all my other friends. Going to college singing a couple of Hindi rain-songs and love-making scenes, followed by marriage. I was about to give names to my would be son and daughter, suddenly my bus of 'Day Dreaming' got punctured.

"Kamana is not interested in talking to you." Tinu explains the whole story like a host of a cheap suspense thriller serial.

"OK. By the way, thanks for the favour." I said and left for home. I also sold my bus named 'Kamana Dreams'. My poor daughter and son failed to register their names because of their would be mother—my heartiest sympathy is with them.

As I am a stranger to her, it is obvious to have a 'No' from Kamana, my first ever 'No' from the world of girls. I just wanted to talk to her but great Tinu said to Kamana that I wanted to be her boyfriend—girls and their art of over presenting things: She should have done only what she was told to do. May be this is the end; the end of my short lived 'I want to talk' story. Now I should try to patch up with my old girlfriend i.e. Mathematics.

Life never goes on your decided path, so mine also didn't disappoint me. My board exams are approaching and instead of giving appointment to my subjects, I am in the habit of a new so called 'Eye Chancer.' All the time, I am curious to see Kamana—her face, her cute smile with a dimple, her walking style, her way of talking, her hair style, the list goes on. This includes my automatic and non-intentional head movement towards Xth B.

On 16th February Rohit, Aadarsh and my other friends got an approval from the 'International Community of Kicking Assses', to kick my bum in the name of 'Birthday Bumps.' The bastards got a chance to take a revenge for some of my past doings.

Birthdays usually start with some unwanted annoying mid-night wishes, where people compete to be the first one to wish—may be out of expectation of getting a larger piece from the free-of-cost cake—their misconception. In the evening my birthday was celebrated by an over-budget treat to friends and giving justification to my parents at night. Hence the day ends up with a lecture from parents on the value of money and with some late night wishes where some people who actually forget to wish, justifying themselves, by making it their intentional strategy 'Dude my wish is unique being the last one'

I am held between the earth and sky by my friends and doing some mathematical calculations by using the theory of probability of their chances to eat more and expensive dishes which would be a burden on my black money (the money which was given by my father to buy some text books). I am also keeping a track of the number of kicks and its intensity per individual. For which Aadarsh is scoring quiet high. Maybe I am paying for the disapproval to Aadarsh's way of love for Aarti and his 'Right Time' formula.

All my friends are busy in checking out the prices of dishes in the menu. I, on other hand, am trying hard to console my ass for the excesses made on it. Another victim of the act is my back-bone; retards don't even know that 'Birthday Bumps' are meant for the bum and not for the back. But out of excitement of kicking, sometimes your back also come into kicking range.

Let me introduce some other nerds to you.

Starting from Manas, who strongly believes that behind every successful man there is a woman. The dude falls in love with every single girl who comes in his life, although always ends with a one-sided love frustration. He belongs to the same species, likes of Rohit and has an ordinary face. Once we used to be of the same height, but as time passed, our mother nature didn't justify with his height factor. He always cries for his short height. Many a times I gave him example of many celebrities possessing short height, but thanks to my lack of good convincing skills, he never understand. Whenever Manas and Rohit meet, they discuss some mathematical figures and formulas, which is an enemy territory for me. What else you expect from intelligent Aliens or persons belonging to unwanted population.

Next is Prashant, a guy with 5'8" height, broad shoulders, perfect biceps, triceps and an over broadened chest, which I call breasts. I have my own explanations for that. He has a round face, with uncombed hair, calling it a rugged look. He is a true tube-light or you may call him a brainless creature, just like me. He is considered as a stud until he starts speaking. He is habitual of passing unwanted and unnecessary comments, still girls give him a chance to speak, which further raises questions regarding their choices.

The next entry is Vicky. I am unable to figure out why people think him to be cool. If one considers his dressing sense then that fellow will seriously think about bringing some revolutionary changes in our Fashion Industry. He is something like a 'Jugaad'. A person interested in only two thing in life—one is machine and the other is he, himself. His face is full of scars and some other marks which looks as if he got them from a freedom struggle of some poor country. But he got them from his own struggles. Right now he is justifying a punch mark on his eye to Prashant.

Mr. Aadarsh is checking his shoes, as if my poor ass by mistake has hurt his prestigious branded shoe.

"So, who is Kamana?" Manas asks and I prepare myself for a brain storming session.

"Well she is in my school and I just like her." I started my 'I Love Kamana' story, which took about twenty minutes.

"When a person sinks fully or partially in love then the wastage of time is equal to the time spent in knowing her." Manas explains a new kind of scientific principle, what else would you expect from a geek.

The war is on between Lovers and Anti-lovers Associations, I wish the man with Aarti theory would join me. While Mr. Rohit on the other hand is struggling hard to register his new neutral association.

"Let us see, how Kamana looks like?" A voice rises from the 'Anti-Lovers Association'.

"I will show you on our last board exam of Mathematics." In this way my birthday got a happy ending with a discussion about my girlfriend 'Mathematics' with whom I have thought about breaking up in the 11th class.

Never underestimate exams; they are capable of changing an atheist like me into a religious extremist. Exam days lead me to visit the temple. My progress usually starts with delivering a couple of demands to the mailing address of the highest authority. Now a days instead of demanding some miracle which leads to attainment of love-goal called Kamana, I prefer to acquire certain magical super-intellectual powers to answer those tough question papers. I think due to some congestion in the traffic above, my prayers always remain in the waiting list.

My examination day starts with cursing the lengthy syllabus before going to the centre, and waiting for Kamana so as to see her good-luck face before the exam. But I wonder if her so called good-luck face has done any wonders yet. With some unwanted best of lucks, which hardly make any difference in the performance, survival is the only strategy to be strictly followed.

The poor question paper always fails to make positive first impression on me. The first encounter with the question paper leads to wondering how come all the questions are out of syllabus. This leads to starting of 'Save Life And Search Rohit' mission. There is no use of bulky answer sheets for me, as I believe in short and sweet, so all my answers require seven to eight pages of parking space.

The ringing bell declaring the end of time leads to passing common statements to the public, that if only five more minutes were given to me, then I would be the one who appears on the front page of newspaper amongst the toppers. Generally I pass low profile statements of cursing the education system and its impact on youth thereof. Then promising myself that from next year I will start studying right from the beginning.

The thing which sucks the most is that it's always Rohit's answers which pass sarcastic comments to my poor low profile answers. After all, my answers also have some self-esteem that should be respected.

The one positive thing which gives a dumb like me a reason to smile is—whenever Kamana passes me she looks at me continuously for quite some time. Thanks to my lack of guts, I wonder about the evolution of passing smiling technique in me. Life is going fine till the stage is set for the last battle. Today is the last exam of Mathematics. The excitement for this paper leads me to four visits to the temple in two days.

"So how is your preparation, son?" My father asks, already knowing the status of my preparation of Maths. Making fun by asking questions on already known area is yet another qualitative skill which my father possesses.

"Good Papa. I am ready for the challenge." I said while calculating probability in my head-office (brain) about getting 33%, i.e. passing marks.

"You should revise your paper after completing it." My mother says while marking redline on my forehead in the name of '*Tilak*' as if I am going to the battle ground.

Facing the mathematics question paper is one thing, attempting it is another and passing the paper is yet the most impossible thing which requires lots of resources that my poor self cannot afford to put on.

For the first time my eyes failed to get any appointment to see Kamana from my 'Department of Brains', as today I am busy in cramping the formulas and shortcuts of Maths.

Seeing the question paper certain formulas of Algebra, Geometry, Trigonometry etc. start dancing around me. I started with the first question; I don't know it, second No. OK, starting from the last one—nope, second last—again I don't remember. I am about to surrender my weapons i.e. pen, pencil, divider, scale, standing in the middle of the battle field facing the huge army of questions, the hierarchy of rank followed with the marks attached to them.

The army of questions is about to conquer my head quarters (brain) by weapons of fear of failure, suddenly I got an '*umeed ki kiran*' (the light from the darkness). Two of the 'six marks questions' are the same my father taught me the day before yesterday; these were defeated by using same set formulas. Being the highest marks questions, I just counter attacked the Major General, itself. This kind of sudden attack proved to be the turning point. After that a couple of three pointers were thrashed away. My highly motivated army attacked the 'two-pointer soldiers' and civilians by couple of air attacks through scale & pencil and with the bombardment of pen marks. At the end by capturing one more six pointer question as a war hostage, I declared my victory over them.

"By the way what's the answer to that fifth question? My answer is 32." Rohit asks, while rounding that particular question on the question paper.

"Hey why don't you carry your ass to that 'book-worm' group standing over there." I said while matching it with my answer. Thank God my answer didn't disappoint me—it was wrong.

Aadarsh is sitting in a sad mood—may be due to after-effects of severe battle or if any incidence of nuclear attack from enemy lead to defeat of Aadarsh's Republicans.

"Hey, what happened dude? Is everything fine? How was your exam?" Rohit asks Aadarsh.

"Exam was fine; I think I will get passing marks. Now I am thinking about holidays. I will really miss Aarti."

Rohit was about to say something, suddenly sounds of unwanted persons interferes.

"So, where is your Kamana?" Prashant asks me while Manas starts playing the game of 'Matching Answers' with

Rohit. Manas and Prashant are from different schools. I never thought that they were so eager to see Kamana that they would just rush over here. After a while Vicky also joins us.

Kamana is standing with her friend Mona under a tree, near the parking place.

"Hey, who is that boy, staring at us?" Mona asks.

"Rehaan. Remember I told you about him." Kamana replies.

"Yeah that Romeo who proposed you, right."

"Yup, all the time he just keeps on staring at me." Kamana says changing the direction of her eyes.

Meanwhile the question is again repeated "Where is our Kamana?" This time the priorities are changed from 'Your' to 'Our Kamana'

"Look there, under the tree, in the parking lot." I said with an innocent smile. I could see her looking at me; some experts may prefer calling it 'staring at me'.

"Who? That three feet creature?" Prashant says in a tone of a stud.

"No, the other one standing besides her."

"What? That African elephant. She is your Kamana?" Prashant says and starts laughing "I think that three feet strange species would justify better. Thinking about making an African elephant domestic, dude you are really unpredictable."

"Kamana, heavy name to the heavy stuff. Hmm! I will give her 3 out of 10." Manas says while finishing the game on a draw with Rohit that means hundred to both.

'What 3? Damn! 1 will justify." Declares Vicky

"What 1..... I am considering the negative scoring aspect." Prashant continues his laughter, with Vicky and Manas joining him. Rohit and Aadarsh are used to it so they are just focusing on other issues like Aarti.

"You bastards! This is not a modelling ramp where you are required to give scores out of ten. Well, I like her so it's your duty to shut up." I said showing 2.83% anger (O! that's my limit of showing anger).

After that 'Aadarsh-Aarti' case is reopened. For Aarti some appreciating comments are passed like 'hot chick', 'nice legs' and some other censored stuff. My poor Kamana is not considered as eligible to be discussed even; Kamana competing with Aarti is like putting your money on a donkey in a race of highbred horses. At the end Prashant and Manas come up with certain conclusions.

"Aarti is a much higher thing to expect. She is the kind of upper level stuff. Look at you and look at her. She is a dream come true for you. Dude dreams are just dreams. So better back of." Manas tells Aadarsh.

"And you Elephant lover, raise your standard. Don't make us feel ashamed. At least, there should be something worth noticing in her. Dude your choice is really questionable." Prashant remarks.

With some more discussions, a few defence mechanism and theories of 'blind love', 'true love', 'this love', 'that love' etc, we end our induction program.

5

Amulya, Seven Days and the Kiss

It is the start of our holidays and I have only one thing in my mind—you know that. In the evening I carried my 6 feet frame for an evening walk to a nearby park. Small kids are the most honest and innocent human beings on earth. They live in their own dream world—no worries, no mathematics—they are just kids. While moving on from the children corner in the park, I take an exit from the kid's dream world and entered the password to the gateway of my own 'Dream World of Kamana.' Then my eyes spot out some unwanted disturbances.

"Hey lover boy, how are you?" Prashant questions me.

Manas and Prashant, are sitting on a bench. Some movement takes place resulting in making a parking space available for my honourable bums.

"Lover boy is good. What about you?" I said while adjusting myself between the enemy bums.

"How is your 'Baby Elephant'? Oops! I mean Kamana." Prashant laughs.

"She is not that big, and I like her, so shut down your dustbin." I said while defending the truth. I promised myself that after marriage the first thing on my list would be to send her to the best health club in the city—damn only if my poor income will ever allow me to do so—otherwise I will send her to a not so expensive health club.

"Dude, it's not the first time. Your glorified history has always questioned your choice. Your past affairs were also noticed to be having 'Three Room Flat' sized figures. My only question is why?" Prashant enquires and starts laughing with a wide-open mouth. I wonder about those fucking flies which are always late for their action at the hour of the need. Gosh! Why don't two or more flies enter into his wide-opened 'Department of Eating and Barking'?

"I know the reason. He is approaching fatty females intentionally, as he himself is thin, so that their children will enjoy a balanced state of figure." Manas's contribution to the ongoing 'Birth-Evolution Theory'.

"Khi khi khi, joke, right. Joke of the year!"

I started my explanation. "It's not how she looks like; I just like her for what she is. I don't have any bad intentions for her. I just want to be with her, as a friend." I noticed that neither of the two students of 'My Moral Police' was mentally present.

When I changed my angle of eyes towards my sincere students, Man I felt as if I got an electric shock of 10 volts(actually my body could manage only that level of shock). A girl about 5 feet 7 inches, one of the best creations on earth, enters the park. She was so stunningly beautiful that if given a chance to see the last thing in the world, I am sure my eyes would pick her up. She was wearing a white coloured T-shirt with a written declaration of 'Hot Girl' on her hilly areas and a low-waste torn black jeans. Her dark brown hair with some light brown stripes and sparkling eyes gave her a 'high society' look.

"Please pinch me, so that I wake up."

Manas, fully exploited the opportunity by pinching my upper arm.

"Ouch! You bastard, this is not the last pinch of your life." I stuck my elbow at his chest, returning full amount of his 'pinch loan'.

"Now that's what is called a '*Totta!*'" Prashant passes a smile, but his poor low profile smile fails to register with her sensory organs. In the meantime I get a punch on my shoulder from Manas—may be a reward for timely payment of loan.

"Oh man!, Who is she? She could make anybody crazy with her power of beauty. She just can't be real." I said while giving a punch on Manas's genitals, making full and final settlement of the deal and of some future loans also. This will make him busy for at least half-an-hour.

"Fuck you! She is Amulya who lives near my house. Her father is a billionnaire. You cannot even afford to dream about her." Manas says in a low frequency, as if somebody turned down his *bass & treble* and poured some water into his speakers.

"I am not saying that I will go after her. You know I like Kamana and even the most gorgeous girl on earth cannot change my priority for Kamana."

"Hey, we are not discussing 'Animal's Natural Kingdom' here, and you failed to convince even that fatty stuff, so Amulya is something far beyond your level." Manas places hands on his crouch, an attempt to provide shield for further expected bombardment on the restricted area.

"Enough. OK, here is a deal. Today is Sunday, starting from tomorrow on the 7th day, I will be sipping coffee with Amulya at 'The Coffee Point'." I said, without even caring about what the shit I was speaking.

"Dude, you have put yourself into great trouble. Seven days, done." Manas and Prashant placed their hands on mine.

The stage is set, I have seven days to do what deep inside I know is not only difficult but next to impossible. I know what I am supposed to do, but I don't know how I will do that. I don't know who she is and why such a stunning beauty will take interest in me. What I know is that I have only seven days.

Day 1

The first day I was full of enthusiasm. My day started with shopping of certain items like a tube of hair gel Rs. 90, deodorant Rs. 150, pair of goggles Rs. 200 and mouth freshener worth Rs. 10, leading to a total of Rs. 450—a major dent on my three months of pocket money and raised my expenditure graph with a steep slope.

I made a couple of rounds around Amulya's house on my little 'Priya' scooter . My scooter is one year elder than me. It is the only girlfriend kind of a thing in my life. Whenever I am on my scooter, people stare at me, specially girls. I think they are jealous, as I have Priya in my life although it's just a machine.

I am sitting in the park in the evening. Wearing a bell shaped jeans, in which—according to my mother—I look like Rajesh Khanna, the Super Hero of 70's. There is nobody to tell my mother that we have crossed 2yk, as she has her own justifications about it. I also bought my first ever white T-shirt, with 'Anti-Social' written, without my mother's consent. I over burderend my hair with lots of gel. Wearing sunglasses in the evening made me an overpaid attraction point for kids and their families in the park.

Unfortunately Amulya did not come that day. Day one gone six more to go.

Day 2

I reached the park at 5 p.m. I am wearing the same old Jeans & Top and sitting at the same bench, praying that my eyes could somehow see her in the park. Again it is a disappointing day without any clue of her. At least my presence leads to an entertainment approach for few 'babas and babies' in the park. Two days gone, still five are in my pocket.

Day 3

Even an overdose of deodorant was not effective in suppressing the bad odour of my clothes, which I am wearing for the third day, continuously. At least this is an effective way to keep away flies and other unwanted companies. 'Babas and Babies' are also busy with their Mummas and Papas may be their sophisticated nose made them realise their mistake, which leads to depression in the newly opened business of evening attraction.

Well, Amulya enters the park, declaring emergency amongst my sensory organs. She was wearing a black T shirt with 'Chick' written on top and a blue denim skirt revealing perfectly waxed legs. She is alone and talking on her mobile phone.

I waited for more than half an hour, praying she somehow notices 'The Attraction of the Park'. Few crows around me are revealing my future career opportunities as a 'Scare-Crow'. She leaves the park without even allowing my teeth to show their brushing struggles. Day 3 gone without any achievement. May be my high class designed outfit is a hindrance to my 'Mission Coffee'. Last 4 days remaining. Please somebody suggest me something.

Day 4

My 'Department of Brains' thoroughly investigated the matter. I think it is my dressing sense which might be the reason, that she did not notice the presence of a 'Future Supermodel'.

After a thorough study of alternatives in my 'Research and Development Department' I chose the best one. I got a cool new hairstyle, as if I had got an electric shock. With my blue school blazer that I put on that too in summers and a formal black jeans, I was yet again successful in catching the crowd of 'babas and babies' and few of my close friends from the crow community.

The day doesn't disappoint me and she comes with the previous day outfit—may be her washing machine is on a strike or something. She is again talking over phone and ignoring the most ideal match for any single girl.

These beautiful girls are behind the many-fold increase in the yearly profits of telecom companies around the world. After a while she gives some rest to her *bak-bak* and start playing with kids in the other corner of the park. After sometimes she left the park with few clicks on her phone, making optimum use of 'giving missed call' technology. End of the day 4, three more days left and what I gained was the knowledge of the taste and preferences of 'babas and babies', and a few not so domestic crows.

Day 5

The earth is round so are my ways of tackling tasks. I am in a frustrating mood as I know that if I have seven years instead of seven days for convincing a gorgeous girl like her, even then it would be like cracking a nut with a piece of paper.

I am sitting on the same bench, wearing my casual track-suit, with more than required hair-oil on my head, giving me a '*Champu*' look. I am struggling with the ongoing case in the court of law, between my decision making hormones and standards deciding hormones. As the decision of the '7 Days Bet' proved to be an unachievable task and above the standards decided for the type of girl for whom I should go for. I am also thinking about how I will justify my worst performance in front of Prashant and Manas. What about my poor Kamana? Well, she will again become a full fledged laughter dose for them. The case is about to be decided in favour of my standards committee, suddenly an outside party interfered.

"Hey little brother, how are you?" A familiar sweet girly voice knocks my ears with some unwanted address of calling me her brother.

"Hey Sarah, what are you doing here?" I replied in a surprise.

Sarah was with me in the same school and was two years senior to me. She passed 12th last year. At that time one of my school friend Sanchit liked her. Being a true socialite, I made Sarah my sister in the hope that I will help Sanchit that way. My act hardly helped him and I felt a guilt of making Sarah, a beautiful girl, my sister.

"Actually my father bought a new house near this park." She says which reinforced my guilt further.

"Hey Amu, look here." She waves her hand towards Amulya, who enters the park.

"Sorry to disturb your wonderful conversation." A not so strange voice interferes.

Before I could understand what was happening, they started talking to each other as if they are the best of friends.

Whenever two girls start talking, they are capable of ignoring anybody who is with them. Girls are genius in explaining even those things which they are not asked for. One thing of which they are born postgraduate, is talking and just talking. Sufferers of JTS (Janani Talk Syndrome).

"Ahm, ahaan, oho." I started creating 'I am also present' sounds.

"Oh, I forgot to introduce you to my brother, Rehaan."

"I know him. He sits here every day playing with small kids, right Rehaan." For the first time Amulya's eyes looked into mine. Wait! She said every day, that means she had noticed me, but when? Wait again! I never played with kids, they play strange games with me. So what if the 'Goddess of Beauty' is saying something that should be universally acceptable.

"Yup, by the way you are very beautiful." Shit, what the hell did I say? What will she think about me passing such an open statement?

"Thank you. You are also good, I mean good looking." Amulya compliments me. Her good-looking statement was enough to justify my dress of 70's.

In this way the three of us went on discussing not so important topics of societal problems—like non-availability of desired pair of shoes or jeans in the market, the colour of Sarah's newly bought Sari, & its non-matching phenomena with the blouse, embrodiery work on Amulya's *Pallu*. I didn't try to change the topic as it was introducing me to some strange territories of girly talks.

"Hey Amulya, may I have the honour to be a friend of the most gorgeous girl I have ever seen." I proposed her finally. Damn! I did it!

"Why not? We are friends from now on." She took my hand. My goodness! The frequency of the electric shock flowing in my body can't be measured even by most sophisticated shock measuring device available. Her hands were so soft that even cotton seemed to be hard.

"Will catch you tomorrow, and by the way my friends call me Amu."

Her words were enough to drive me crazy, and to decide the case in favour of the decision making committee of mine. End of day 5 again proving the effectiveness of my 'Networks Among Girls'.

Day 6

For the whole day I was confused with what I should wear for the evening. I tried to take suggestions from the fashion show channels, but I wonder if somebody wears that kind of stuff with that much amount of makeup, he or she could easily take over my business of attracting 'babas and babies' and crows in the park. At last I settled with my blue jeans and a multicoloured T shirt.

"Hey Rehaan, how are you?" Amulya is right on time. She is wearing pink salwar suit, with untied hair, enough to bow my head to the 'Queen of Cuteness'.

"Fine! How was your day?"

"Not so good. Coaching classes really screw me, especially Maths." She says while signing a friendly treaty for our common enemy, 'Mathematics'.

I think these beautiful girls are not meant for those premium institutes, rather they should set fire on some fashion ramps displaying some 'not so casual wear' trendy clothes.

"Let's go for a walk to some other park." Amulya said.

"Yeah, sure" I can even go to Hell with you.

While walking her fingers clutched into mine. I immediately jumped out of shock.

"What happened?"

"Actually, this is the first time that a girl, and that also a beauty like you, is holding my hand like this." I said in an utterly innocent way.

"OK." She said still holding my hand. This was enough to call the fire brigade, as the act put fire in the asses of many boys, walking and jogging around.

"Amu, I want to say something, but am afraid you might take me in a wrong sense."

"Hey 1st thing is that you are my friend. That means you can share anything with me. Now tell me what happened?" She holds my other hand also.

I told her the whole story about that seven days and the bet of having coffee with her and the reason behind that, 'Kamana'.

"You know Rehaan, you are really very innocent. The first time I saw you, I guessed it right. You are a nice person." She hugs me.

"I know that Kamana would be the luckiest girl on earth to have such a loving boy in her life. Don't worry I am with you. Tomorrow lets meet at 'The Coffee Point' at 5:00 in the evening. Be there in time, allright."

Day 6 gone and the countdown has begun for the final day.

Day 7

It's about 3:15 p.m. and for last one hour I am getting ready for the big day. Couple of creams and decision regarding clothes and hairstyle still demanded further one and half hour. Changing hairstyles lead to declaring an emergency in the areas of the gel bottle, as it was about to finish and my fingers were still on the search mission for last few drops of gel. If for once, somebody could put life into my comb, I am sure it would sue me for mental harassement and physical torture.

I was responsible for finishing up the face cream, so that the dressing table can be accommodated with some new brands. An overdose of deodorant is yet responsible for declaring bio-chemical attacks in few territories of flies and mosquitoes. At least 25 feet area around me is declared as strictly prohibited area.

I am sitting at 'The Coffee Point' in the front row. Manas and Prashant are sitting at a back-side table, so that they can keep a track of my activities. It's around 5:10 p.m. and there is no clue of Amulya. Smile from Manas and Prashant is about to declare me a looser.

It is 5:15 p.m., I am checking out the menu for the fourth time and requesting the waiter to wait. Its 5:20 and I am drinking my fourth glass of water with some dirty looks from the waiter.

Its 5:25 and she is still not here. I think she felt bad about whatever I told her. I stood up from my seat, suddenly two hands grabbed me from behind.

"I am sorry sweetheart; my coaching class stretched a bit today." Amulya gives me a second hug from the front, enough to declare blackout and a wartime silence amongst Prashant and Manas.

"No, it's OK. I was thinking that you felt bad about what I said." Innocence and I are like twin brothers.

The blue denim short skirt, which she was wearing, is eligible to be certified as a 'mini skirt'. She is wearing a Red short T-shirt with fine work of embroidery on it. Her new laser cut hairstyle and shinning lip gel is enough to bring an element of efficiency in the working of spare parts of all the men present at 'The Coffee Point'.

To my further surprise there is a revolutionary change in the behaviour of the waiter. The guy is asking for the order by crossing the limits of humbleness and respect. Now, I am the most awaited customer in the history of 'The Coffee Point'. We ordered two cups of coffee with some cheese sandwitches.

"So tell me, are your friends present over here?"

"Yup! They are sitting at the last seat on the side row on the left." Sometimes I regret that why I didn't carry a camera with me. The photos of Manas and Prashant's looser faces were enough to establish me as a well renowned face in the world of photography.

Amulya and I started talking. We didn't have any clue about what we were talking. We just went on and on and on. At 6:30, Amulya stood up from her seat and to my surprise of the year, came near to my ears and said. "Best of luck dear" She kissed my left cheek and waved at me saying 'Good Bye'.

Being the first kiss and that also from a damn beautiful girl, it took me five minutes to come back into my senses. That too thanks to Manas and Prashant as they came and shook me up.

> *I remember my mother used to tell me that when I was a small kid I was the most lovable boy amongst girls. At that time my cheeks were unnecessarily harassed with kissing and a few statements of 'He is so cute'. Many a times, I wonder why my poor cheeks lost their utility and popularity now and what about my cuteness. Are not grown up boys like me cute and should be adequately paid for their acts of displaying cuteness. Amulya's kiss settled all the past instalments due to my cuteness.*

"Dude I....I... Just, I just......." Prashant is unable to express his views, being an eyewitness to an impossible act, the act now became a barrier to his process of communication.

"How, how did you do it?.... How could it be possible, she kissed you, what....?" Manas 'the book worm' who had read the stories of 'Stud' and 'Playboys' in books and cheap literature is now surprised to see all that bookish stuff becoming real.

"Gone are the days, when you used to have a right to bark. It's my day, so just pay attention to my words, note it in your diary and always remember in your life."

"What's that?" Both Manas and Prashant ask at the same time.

"Never ever teach your father how to fuck."

6

Expectations, Results and the Blame Game

I am sitting in front of Television, watching trailers of not so popular Hindi movies. It is a non effective way to divert your concentration knowing the fact that today is the result day. I am trying to ignore the same fact and those unwanted panic thoughts of 'What if I fail in Mathematics?', 'What if I fail in any other subject?', 'How will I tolerate Mrs. Khanna again in 10th class?', 'How will I face my parents and other people?' and the most important. 'How will I face Kamana?'

When I reached the school to see my results, students had already formed few groups.

'We scored above 80% and 90%',

'We got average marks',

'At least we got passed in all subjects.'

Last but not the least. 'Dude, what is the procedure for rechecking and reappearing.'

Rohit scored highest amongst us-84.2% and Manas-81% (100/100 in Mathematics) and hence belonged to above 80% group. I scored 62.6% (45 in Mathematics) and proudly honouring the average group with 70% of Prashant. Aadarsh with 58% (35 in mathematics) formed his newly registered group 'If I had studied hard......', but I consider him in 'at least we passed in all the subjects' with Vicky who also scored in 50s.

There was no limit to my happiness as I scored first division. I am crossing the school gate, suddenly Kamana comes on my way. My heart started demanding more fuel with increase in the product input.

"Hi, Kamana" I said instantly.

"Hi Rehaan" She replies with a smile.

"How was your result?"

"Hmm, I got 91% marks. What about you?" She asks.

"I am just going to check it out." There are times in your life when you realise if you changed your priorities in the past to studies. I never wanted to reveal my 'average boy' image as my first impression.

"OK, best of luck!"

"Yup same to you. No, I mean thank you." Man, I didn't know what I am talking about and what I should say. Her presence ruined my thinking capabilities.

"OK, bye." She smiles at me and leaves for her home. I am on the Seventh sky.

I am joined by Rohit, Vicky and Aadarsh. Aadarsh is busy in writing an essay on the topic 'My Aarti', who is standing near the parking lot with her friends.

Reaching home I realised the true status of my average marks through 'blame games'. I told my marks to my father. He is happy with it, he has always been in favour of my marks, which he thinks are never capable of judging the real capabilities of a person. The moment my mother heard something 62 from my mouth, she came up with some statistical graphs and tables of the achievement and marks of my neighbours and children of my uncles and aunties.

"What just 62%?" My mother gets the shock of the day. May be her expectation engine is getting over-heated.

"No, not 62 Mom, 62.6%." I corrected the figure.

"Only 45 in Mathematics. How come you score so low marks? Don't we provide you sufficient facilities for studies. I know you are not such a dumb boy to score just 62%." My mother who is three times world champion in inter-mother's blame game championship.

"Mom its 62.6%" I corrected the statistical data again.

"Shut up. Your .6 is not making any difference. If you had studied hard, you would have scored much more. "

Now this is the problem—if you are an average student you will be taunted by everybody—your parents, your family members, your neighbours and by teachers, why? Let me tell you, every time my parents and others see my result, they feel that if I had worked hard, I would be easily in the creamy layer. They forget one simple fact that 'Mediocre is always at his best.' Always remember that good result comes with side-effect of future expectations of further improvement—so it's better to stabilise your performance.

I then told her the result of my friends starting with Vicky, Aadarsh, Prashant, Manas and Rohit in the last.

"By the way, which stream are you going to opt in 11th class." My father asks me.

"Commerce and that too without Maths, for sure." I stated. My words are enough to declare emergency among 'the army of words' of my mother, which were resting a while for few drops of water. But thanks to my father, I won in the end.

"Always remember son, that it does not matter whether you are an engineer, a doctor or a lawyer. What matters is what you are from inside." My father concludes.

In the evening Aadarsh, Vicky, Manas, Rohit and me are sitting together in a park with the statements of the participants of the blame game. We are the judges to decide who would be the winner. First chance is given to me; I provided them with the statements of my mother. Hence the big start is from my mother's side.

Then comes Vicky's father who stated "I think I am wrong at my decision to see you as a scholar one day. Better you should start ploughing the land in the village, and give some rest to bulls and buffalos, who are more sensible than you." This is something we already know, so it hardly made an impression on the judges' mind.

The dice comes in the hands of Manas. Manas's father stated "Not good marks. Rima in the neighbourhood scored above 90%. I warned you earlier that Rehaan and Prashant are spoiling you. Its better you should study in 11th class right from the beginning or else you have to face the consequences."

The time came for the most awaited statement of Rohit's father. His father said "You call this a result. I had expectations from you, but you as usual disappointed me. It's all because of that fellow Rehaan. His company spoiled you and your result is a proof of that. This time I am going to talk to his father. I know Rehaan will not achieve anything in life. Keep the company of intelligent students of your level." As being his favourite, uncle's statement seemed biased, that leads to some negative markings by the judges.

Last, but not the least, Aadarsh's mother presents her own expert fact and figures after post-mortem of the issue.

"My son used to be very intelligent in his previous school. His new friends and this school are solely responsible for his poor performance." Actually his mother's data is based on, that once upon a time when Aadarsh was in the first class, he stood third in the class of nine students, amongst whom one was reported to be absent.

Aadarsh's mother's statement is enough to change the face of the competition, by making it one sided. After a few formalities in the shape of discussions for declaring the results of Blame Game, we all voted in favour of Aadarsh's mother. Hence she is the new 'World Champion of Blame Games' for this year.

I am about to go to school for our registration, opting stream for 11th class and to deposit next year's admission fees.

"So you decided that you will not listen to anybody. Neither me nor your cousins, and you will do only what you want to do by opting for Commerce." My mother is struggling to change my opinion either to Non-Medical or Medical stream.

"Yes mom, I will take Commerce only and that too without Maths." I finalised my words and leave for school.

I am sitting in the school office on a not so strange sofa. I still remember, when I was a small kid many a times my father brought me along with him for depositing fees for my junior classes. It is this same sofa which is there for the last 10 years.

"So you completed your form? Show it to me." Receptionist demands my form. I hand over my admission form to her.

"What have you written on it? You are going to 11th class and look at your handwriting." She shouts.

"Blah-blah-blah." I whisered.

"So you are going for Commerce stream and that too without Mathematics?" She asks by rounding of my subjects written in the application form.

"You read it right."

She was looking up for something in the already submitted forms. In that I saw Kamana's application form and noticed that she had opted for Medical stream. The moment my eyes went for further investigations to look for her phone number, she noticed me looking at Kamana's form. She keeps the application form back to the drawer. I thought for a while and said.

"I will go for Medical stream."

"What? You have opted for Commerce, I think."

"Yup, now I will go for Medical stream."

"No way. I have already completed all the formalities, I won't change it." She adjusts the specs on her nose. Suddenly my joy ride came to an end.

"Listen lady to go for Medical stream in this school, one needs above 60% marks and I have scored 62.6%. Your job is to do whatever I am asking for. So are you going to do it or I call my father?"

"Who is your father?"

"He is an advocate." I gave her a one sided smile with sign of sarcasm.

"Let me see, but at least tell me the reason for changing your decision." She adjusts her specs again.

"That's none of your concern, lady." My taunt's impact could be noticed through sudden change in the position of her specs again.

My decision was greeted at home with delicious food prepared by my mother. At least for some days I am going to be treated like 'Prince of the Kingdom'.

"I think you were opting for Commerce stream." Rohit asks me.

"It's not so brother. Right from my childhood I dreamt of becoming a doctor one day and serve humanity. It is the only mission of my life." I never ever had such a dream.

Aadarsh changed his school, because he wanted to pursue a career in Medicine and was not eligible in our school. Manas opted for Non-Medical (Engineering side, i.e. Physics, Chemistry and Mathematics). Vicky and Prashant went for the Commerce stream. Rohit went for the combined subjects and hence opted for Biology, Mathematics, Physics and Chemistry (the toughest stream of all).

"Aadarsh are you nuts? Why don't you take Commerce. You know Medical is not that easy." I questioned.

"All three of my sisters are doctors and my parents want me also to become a doctor. What's there in Commerce? I think it's you not me, who declared his interest in Commerce a decade ago." Aadarsh justifies his decision by indirectly targeting my stand.

"It's because of Kamana that I changed to Medical."

"So you put your whole career on stake just because of a girl. Dude, are you in your senses or what?" Rohit joins Aadarsh's brigade.

"I don't know. I just....want to be with her. I think it's a small amount to pay to be in her class." I look for appreciation for my love-stand.

"At least you got what you desired. My condition is worst of all. I wanted to be an Engineer but as my father wants me to be a Doctor, so he himself filled up my application form and puts me into this trouble of the combined stream."

Rohit's views are always a laughing material to Aadarsh and me.

7

Couple of Wrong Decisions, 2nd Attempt and The Code of Conduct

It's 18th time that I am standing in front of the mirror, according to my mother. The excitement of the first day of my 11th class and that too in Kamana's class is covering all restricted, civil, defence, private, religious, public, national, international, red light and all other remote areas of my brain.

I am the one guy, who can go for detailed explanations about difference between three identical white shirts. I am now checking out the fourth white shirt. Thank God, I never had that much choice available amongst my pants. My over-polished black shoes are telling a different story of their independence struggle from colonial polish brush.

It's an overcrowded class of 65 students, amongst whom only eight are boys and rest are the material capable of driving any boy crazy, our favourite creature 'girls'. This class is eligible in all aspects to being seriously considered as a 'Dream Class for Boys'

Kamana came to the classroom half an hour early. I am busy in watching her but she has not noticed me yet. After some time Mr. Gupta our new class teacher enters the class. He is of small height with dark complexion.

"I am here to teach you Chemistry. Before I start I have to assign certain duties to two students, who will be monitors of the class. One would be a boy and the other a girl. Firstly from the girl's side—who wants to be the Monitor?"

About eighteen girls raised their hands with one idiot from boy's side also; his eagerness to become class monitor crossed the limits. Kamana didn't raise her hand; she seems to be in a 'not interested' kind of mood.

"OK. You will be the monitor from girl's side. What is your name?"

"Shreya." She says and starts looking as if she is about to receive her most awaited Doctorate degree.

"Now from the boy's side, who wants to be the Monitor?" There is a sudden reaction as all the eight boys raise their hands. What a response? I am also struggling hard from the last bench to make my hand a tough competitor.

"That one, sitting alone on the last bench, what's your name, young man?" He points me out, making the members of 'The Back Bencher Association' to come into limelight.

"Rehaan." I am excited as if a billionaire girl just said yes to my marriage proposal. In the meantime I moved my head towards Kamana and saw her staring at me.

That day many a times we made eye contacts but most of the time she preffered to look at the blackboard.

"Hey Hi, where were you the whole day?" I asked Sneha.

"I am in your class, joker. Didn't you notice. Oh I forgot, that throughout the day Mr. Monitor was busy complimenting Kamana's beauty." She started laughing with a facility of irrigation *via* spitting.

"Do you know Kamana?"

"Yup, she is not a close friend of mine. What's your scene Mr. Monitor *cum* Romeo?" She asks giving a break to her irrigation machine.

"Actually, I like her." I then told her the story about how I came to know her name in my dream.

"Your dream was too mysterious. By the way, she is with me in the Biology tuitions also."

"Sneha, I really like her a lot." I said while Kamana crosses from my right side.

"Don't worry I will help you out. Yeah take this address; we go for our Biology tuitions at 5:15 p.m. I am getting late. Talk to you tomorrow. Bye" She moves her hand through my hair. Damn! my hairstyle, but not to worry as Kamana has already gone.

"Thanks sister. Bye and take care."

"May I come with you Mr. Chocolate hero?" Rohit asks.

"Oh hi, so how was your day?"

"The day was awesome, specially the Chemistry class. I am certainly confused about few formulas. You know water is 2H+O, that means we drink Hydrogen and Oxygen." Rohit expresses his disappointment.

"Sorry dude, I attended only Loveology lecture. Hey guess what? I managed to get the address of Kamana's Biology tuition class."

"Dude, this place is near your house." Rohit smiles.

"Yeah, how come I didn't notice?"

"Because now a days you have only one thing in your mind."

After school me and Vicky generally go to Rohit's house first. Rohit lives near the school in the Officer's Colony. Vicky parks his old bicycle in his house with few other classmates of Rohit. That's nothing but a 'Cost Management Technique' by these future managers, saving parking fees by utilising not so large parking front of Rohit's residence.

Prashant and I went to the stadium to meet Aadarsh and Rohit. Aadarsh had some important thing to talk. We four are sitting, waiting for the so called important thing of Mr. Aadarsh.

"Guess what? I went to Aarti's colony." Aadarsh stands up from his seat and start jumping out of excitement. Prashant and I look towards each others face. Rohit also smiles with his so called smiling face.

"She was playing badminton with a.....wait, who was that boy with whom she was playing badminton?" Suddenly the second attempt of public display of excitement by jumping is postponed.

"He might be her brother or neighbour. Our society is not so open as yet to allow unsocial game of love so openly." An attempt from Rohit's side to revive the spirit of Aadarsh.

"Yeah, you are right. My 'Noni', she is my cutie pie." In the third round of excitement Aarti got a new name 'Noni', the meaning of which is available only in 'Aadarsh's Love Dictionary'.

"Now who's 'Noni'?" Rohit raises a question.

"Damn, I am talking about Aarti. She is my 'Nonu-monu', my 'Cutie Bacha', my 'Nona.'" I am fairly keeping a track of score of 'Name Game' of Aadarsh. With 'Nona' in the end his score comes to 4. By the end of the discussion, Aadarsh somehow achieved a score of 21.

"So this is an important stage for the birth of a child." Our Biology teacher draws something round on blackboard which she calls a 'foetus'.

"In humans it's a stage after eight weeks of fertilization. In later stages foetus is used to test whether the baby is a male or female. Foetus testing is illegal in our country." She says while turning pages of the book.

Now sex is a topic which is capable of catching every single atom of our attention. Being in 11th class, researching sex is our foremost priority. For the first time, I have got something more important in class then counting the eye flicks of Kamana. I think we need some practical exposure in this field. In the meantime few porn movies provide us the platform for writing thesis on the subject.

"Mr. Monitor, meet Shefali. Shefali is a common friend of mine and Kamana." Sneha introduced me to her friend. Shivani is also standing near Shefali and both are eligible to participate in 'Most Bulky Buffalo Contest'.

"You are wasting your time Mister. Kamana will never say yes to you." Shefali starts giving unwanted suggestions. I expected her to talk something about Buffalos habitat, their life, eating habits, sexual orientations towards bulls. But for my surprise she raised controversial issues about Kamana.

"Rehaan, yesterday I tried to talk about you to Kamana." Sneha says "But she got angry with me and said 'Sneha you have to be with me in the same class for next two years. I am not interested in listening anything about that fellow, Rehaan'."

"So it is better that you find some other girl." This time Shivani, the second buffalo participates in the unwanted discussion. I know why she is suggesting me this as I remember once Sneha had asked me for Shivani.

"I am happy with whatever is going around me and don't feel any use of changing my priorities." I replied and ended the discussion with few fruits of disappointment in my bag.

"Fuck this Biology." Rohit shouts while we are going towards his house.

"Yeah for sure you can do that, but to know how to fuck you still need Biology." I stated.

"Man I don't want this. I don't have any interest in it. I want to leave this subject."

"Whether you want it or not, you have to manage some how, as that's your father's wish."

Aadarsh, Rohit and me are sitting in a lonely park, with the company of a dog and a bitch. The bitch is not in a comfortable position with the dog, they are in some sort of an objectionable situation (*aapatti janak halat*). As the dog is climbing on the bitch and moving back and forth, the bitch is making not so romantic sounds. Only Rohit is the keen viewer present here.

"Hey Rohit look, what is going on between these two dogs." Aadarsh starts laughing.

"Rate of change of linear momentum of a body is directly proportional to the external force applied on the body, which always takes place in the direction of applied force. This is a live example of Newton's 2nd law of motion." Rohit states and continues "Force=Mass X Acceleration."

"For your information, they both are not dogs but one of them is a bitch. Don't declare that poor dog to be a gay." I corrected Aadarsh.

Next day our Chemistry teacher is late. Shreya and I are trying our level best to maintain silence in the classroom. Usually I take special care of one bench on which Kamana sits. My special care, couple of times replied with few weird looks of Kamana.

"This is an important news. As this class is overcrowded, so for effective teaching we have decided to shift few students to the other section of the combined class." Our class teacher announced.

"The students who have scored below 75% will be shifted to the other section." He says and I felt numb. I opted for Medical just to be with Kamana, but my bad luck planned something different for me. I stood up and gave my shoulders one more burden of carrying my school bag, the first being moving out from the class.

"Oh my dear, the Monitor himself has to leave." Sir says. Only one girl laughs in the class, and that is Kamana.

"I am happy about it. That idiot is in the habit of staring at me continuously. After all it's because he scored too low in 10th that he won't be able to sustain himself with us." Kamana smiles sarcastically.

“Hey don’t talk like this *yaar*. He likes you.” Sneha says

“Likes, my foot. Now our class can concentrate on serious studies, as it is free from jerks like him.” Kamana takes out her Chemistry text book.

I am shifted to the combined section, so am now a classmate of Rohit. Being with Rohit is somehow compensating to some extent, to the natural calamity that happened to my ‘Kamana Story.’

In the evening Rohit and Aadarsh came to my house and we three on Rohit’s scooter went to see Kamana.

“I don’t know what I will do now. I think......” I was about to complete my sentence but Kamana with her friends came into the scene. She looked at me for a few seconds and moved on.

“I know what to do now. I think my concepts of Biology need some external help. I need Biology tuitions.”

Next day in the evening I visited Kamana’s Biology tutor at 4:00. I rang up the door bell. Around 40 year old lady comes to the door. I revealed my intentions to her.

She smiled at me “Actually I hold only one batch per class, and for 11th class I have already started a batch one month ago. As they have already covered 3 chapters, so I cannot adjust you in that batch.”

“Madam please, I came to you with a hope. When I asked for thc best Biology teacher, everybody gave me your address. I need your guidance to fulfil my dream of becoming a doctor. I am a bright student so don’t worry, I will manage the initial chapters on my own.” I started my old emotional drama. Hurray it worked.

“Okay, start from today. Please come at 5:15 sharp.” She wished me luck.

Many times I had asked my parents for a motorcycle but my appeal was always rejected by the final authority 'my father'. He is a strict follower of law, and it would not be given till I attain the age of 18. So for the time being I had to tolerate the abuses from my legs due to cycling. As my Biology tuition class is not far from my house, it is OK for me.

"Oh it's just 5'O clock. You came so early. I have not seen such a sincere student." My tuition teacher welcomes me. She is right that I am a sincere student of my favourite subject i.e. Kamana.

I am very excited as it is a small class with ten chairs around a small table. I am on a flying machine to imagine sitting very close to Kamana but my fate sends me an e-mail 'my dear Rehaan with due respect and in a state of deep sorrow, today Kamana is absent.' I replied to this e-mail 'fuck you.' Throughout the class I was accompanied with the expressions of 'how come he is here with us?' from Sneha, Shefali, Mona and Shivani.

"So you have decided that you will not change yourself?" Sneha asks after the class.

"Change what? I am here for Biology tuition. Didn't you see me sitting besides you."

"Do whatever you want." Sneha leaves for her home.

For quite some time I am noticing change in Sneha's behaviour. As she is becoming a close friend of Kamana, no doubt she is behaving like this.

"Hey Kamana, you know that Rehaan has joined our Biology tuitions." Mona tells Kamana.

"What? Oh no. That Sample even managed to reach there. I don't know what he wants?" Kamana feels some non-existing kind of trouble.

I reached my tuition class as usual 15 minutes early and at 5:10 p.m. Kamana arrived. She sits on the chair in front of me. During the class I just continued 'My Not So New Constant Looking at Her Face' practice. I noticed for quiet some time that she is trying to look at me in a strange way. She maintained a down face as if she is studying, but sometimes moves her eyes towards my direction. Man it feels great when she does that.

The next day, for the first time, I arrived late for the tuition. The moment I entered the room I received a new e-mail from my fate 'my dear Rehaan without due respect and in not so much state of pleasure, you have got a seat next to Kamana' and I replied 'dude, you are a stud'. For the first time Kamana and me are sitting next to each other. Madam is explaining something about 'Plant Kingdom' but sitting with Kamana, I was lost in my own 'Kingdom of Dreams', where I am the King sitting with my Queen, Kamana. Her fragrance is awesome; the perfume is rightly complimenting her. My heart-beat reaches to its maximum and my engine already got overheated. I have got only one wish in my life and that's to get her and once I get her, I will treat her as my Queen for the rest of my life.

The next day after school Vicky, Aadarsh and I are sitting at Rohit's home playing Video games on his computer.

"Do whatever you want but don't disturb me when I am studying." Rohit is not in a good mood.

"You know, Aarti looked at me two weeks ago." Aadarsh smiles.

"Yeah if you follow someone right from her home, and that too with a distance of a few inches then even an animal would stop and look at you. And that's not looking, it is starring." Vicky says.

"Aadarsh, one thing I want to tell you buddy. I also feel that Aarti is beyond your reach." I gave my opinion.

"You don't worry. I know what I have to do."

"The password you gave us, is not working." I asked Rohit.

"I have told you earlier also that don't disturb me; I have my test in the evening." Rohit says in a not so friendly tone.

"OK. You concentrate on your studies but just for once see why this password is not working. I promise we will not disturb you after that." I requested Rohit .

"How many times have I told you. Are my words not getting to your head? I am not like you. I have to score high. So just shut up." Rohit shouts at me. I saw him getting angry at us, for the first time.

"Fine buddy, I am leaving. I don't have any intentions to disturb you. May you score well." I got up and went from his house.

I felt bad about my best friend's reaction. I never expected this from him. In the Biology tuitions also I sat in a bad mood. Kamana's eyes were also surprised of missing their company today. I am neither interested in looking at her nor listened to the ongoing topic of 'Animal Habitat'. After the tuition, I just moved out of the class before Kamana—usually I remain in the class till the time Kamana goes out. To my surprise Rohit the asshole is already waiting for me for the last half an hour.

"You said your tuition class would be over by 6:15, its already 6:45." Rohit says.

"Today we started late, that's why."

"So what do you want? You want me to say sorry or you would rather go for the golden opportunity of kicking my ass?" Rohit smiles.

"I will go for the second option. What about your test? I think that's for admission to a premium coaching class for IIT preparation and Scholarship."

"I didn't go for the test; I have something more important in my life then IIT and that's you my brother. You are above everything." Rohit hugs me. "I am sorry I shouted at you. I am an asshole."

"Me too, and bigger than you even." I declared. Meanwhile Kamana is passing with her friends; they all stopped and started looking at us.

"He is my brother." Rohit shouts and they all laugh.

After some days Rohit and I are discussing Kamana in a free period.

"I am going to propose Kamana for friendship."

"When?" Rohit jumps from his seat.

"Today, in the evening. I have asked Prashant to give his motorcycle to me. I will go to her alone."

I was coming out of my school with Rohit. A surprise was waiting outside for me. Amulya waved her hand seeing me. I went to her. Seeing the most gorgeous chick standing outside the school, some over-excited romeos were roaming around her.

"Where were you Princess." I shake hands with her. Rohit is about to faint, but somehow managed to stand still.

"Actually I was busy for admissions and all." She smiles, but it was a sad smile.

Seeing me and Amulya talking with each other, students started taking interest on what is going on. They wanted to verify, what makes the hottest girl talking to the biggest unwanted retard of the school? Somebody please dial 101 to call fire brigade.

"Hey I scored 62.6% in 10th class. And guess what, got only 45 in maths." I started laughing, please somebody join me in my laughter. I never forget .6 with 62.

"Don't worry my baby, you will do well in the next classes, I know that." Listening 'baby' from Amu's 'Department of Communication', Rohit declared that he is in some stupid dream.

"Let's go. I will drop you and your friend home." She said.

"But" 'but' is the obvious response from me, as it is for the first time I will be sitting with such an astonishing creation in the world of girls. I am wondering where is Kamana? Let her feel some spice of jealousy. No, I cannot see my Kamana jealous of anything related to me.

"Come with me I want to talk to you." She said. Amu and I start heading towards her car. I was pulling Rohit's hand, the poor chap is trying hard to escape his ass. Rohit has only one girlfriend and that is 'his books'.

Amulya dropped Rohit to his house. Thank God Rohit's father was not there at that time, otherwise, Amu would be accompaning me to Rohit's funeral, the next day.

"So how is your Kamana? Any progress in your 'love battle-field'?" It really feels soothing when people address Kamana as 'your Kamana'. But second question always disappointed me.

"Kamana is good, but she is not good for me. No achievement yet, but I will go to propose her in the evening. Will tell you the whole story tomorrow."

"But I am going."

"OK, will tell you next week."

"I am going for a long time."

"For a long time? Where?"

"I am going to USA for my graduation in engineering. I don't have any plans for coming back to India."

My excitement for proposing Kamana vanished like fumes in the air.

"But...." I stop again on my renowned station 'but'. Who am I to question her and stop her?

"My flight is in the evening. I thought about meeting you for the last time." She stopped the car and looked into my eyes for a second and continued "Best of luck for your Kamana. I know you will get your love. She is really lucky."

Before I could say any thing, I realised we have reached my home.

"Hey I will miss you, dear. Take care of yourself." I was about to open the door of the car but she held my hand.

"Wait." She said and kissed my right cheek.

"Will miss you too, Rehaan."

I step out of her car. I kept on waving to her moving car, don't know why? I will really miss you, Amu. Thank God, her car was with black tinted glasses; our kissing will not be public. As my neighbours are always on the lookout for a 'Sting Operation'.

In the evening I missed my Tuition class and stood with Prashant outside waiting for Kamana. I was dressed up as if it is some party night. This time designer Rohit came for the rescue of falling TRP of my dressing sense and forced me to wear his clothes for the evening. Trust me I am looking awesome for a change. I also wrote a poem for Kamana, which I will hand over to her, when she says yes to me. It goes like this

You are my reason

There are reasons for everything for everybody.
It's not that I am crazy to put my career on stake.
There's a reason.
Every day I dress like the wedding day.
There's a reason.
My eyes all the time, day and night, look for one person only.
There's a reason.
I visualise you everywhere and
in every moment of my joy and sorrow.
There's a reason.
Many a times I called your name unconsciously.
There's a reason.
My talks, my dreams, my gestures and my
life revolve around only one person.
There's a reason.
I have a dream that one day you would be mine forever.
There's a reason.
And you are my only reason, Kamana.

"Hey, there she is. I think tuition is over. Why this damn thing is not starting up." I start kicking Prashant's motorcycle.

"Because this damn thing starts only when you insert it's key into it, which you are holding in your hand."

"Oh man I am an asshole." I started the motorcycle.

"Yeah I know that, now go. Best of luck bro." Prashant gives a brotherly wish.

I stopped the motorcycle besides Kamana's scooter.

"Hi Kamana, I want to talk to you." My heart-beat start giving constant alarms of overheating of engine.

"Yeah........" Kamana says. I thought she would be asking 'Why I didn't come to the tuition or if I am well'.

"Actually I....." Damn I forgot what I prepared last night. I prepared a whole article about what I will say to her. I kept on revising it till the last moment. Her presence with me calls a strike by 'My Brain Department'. I had to say some shit as she was eagerly waiting for my great speech on 'My love Kamana.' I am holding my poem in my right hand.

"I really like you. Would you like to be my friend?"

"No, not interested"

"May I know the reason? Is there any family problem, regarding girl and boy relationship."

I don't know what to say and what to ask. I am not in my senses, asking whatever is coming to my mind.

"Listen Rehaan, I am telling you peacefully. I am genuinely not interested in you or in your so called friendship. So stop annoying me." She says with a couple of fake smiles. In the meantime her friend Mona reached there. The poem which I wrote for her fell from my hand.

"Kamana what happened? Is he troubling you?" Mona the small creature with small features asks Kamana by giving me an angry look.

"Oh no, the poor fellow wants to do friendship with me." Kamana laughs.

"Even if you try a hundred times, Kamana will never say yes to you. It's impossible, you idiot."Mona laughs and leaves with Kamana.

Heinsberg's Principle of Uncertainty in Physics says that 'if you keep on pushing the wall, then there is a probability in billions of billions that you can cross that wall, even'. It's just about convincing a girl and I had made only two attempts, yet. I motivated myself and went back to meet Rohit and Aadarsh.

"Hmm, so this is the story." Rohit says while eating his Samosa. "To every action there is an equal and opposite reaction, Newton's Third Law of Motion says. So her 'No' is not a big deal."

"At least now she knows about you. Who you are and also that you like her. So in the future when she needs a loving and caring boyfriend, you would be her first choice." Aadarsh grumbles while ordering the fourth Samosa, on the other hand me and Rohit are still struggling with our first one. The hungry bull then jumps on Rohit's Samosa, the poor chap had taken only two bites, the rest was not in his fate.

Exam clouds are thundering above our heads. Throughout the term and my tuition classes, I mastered only one subject and that is 'My First Love Kamana'. But unfortunately the poor subject failed to register itself in the CBSE syllabus pattern.

I got a superb result in first term exams. I failed in Chemistry and Physics, but somehow managed to pass in other subjects due to some external environmental advantages. Aadarsh scored more than me by failing in all three Physics, Chemistry and Biology. Rohit and Manas scored good marks in Physics, Chemistry and Mathematics; Rohit also did well in Biology. Vicky sets his own kind of record in Commerce stream. He did a blunder in Economics by scoring only 3 out of 100. Prashant manages something around an average.

"How was your result, Kamana?" I asked her. She is sitting with Shefali on the stairs near her class.

"I got the worst result. *Aur Rehaan ab tu yahan se dafa hoja* (Rehaan get lost from here)" She shouts at me. She had failed in Physics and Chemistry.

"So what are you going to do now?" My mother asks me after scoring her new all time high score in blame games.

"I will go for Commerce, now." I declared rejecting constant appeal of considering Kamana and Biology tuition by 'My Heart Department'.

"Are you sure?" My father asks.

"Yup with each and every word of it."

My father is the only person who is having tremendous faith in me that one day I will became something big. After heated discussion with my mother at last my father won the battle for me. I love my dad.

After 1st term results, we corrected many of our wrong decisions. I took Commerce stream with Economics, instead of Mathematics. Rohit after a long struggle with his father's ideologies and expectations somehow on 1st September celebrated his independence day in the restaurant by getting rid of Biology. Now he is also a Non-Medical student like Manas.

Fed up with our screwed life, we met at Rohits place to cement our friendship for life. After a detailed discussion, I, Aadarsh and Rohit come up with something like this.

The Tripod

- That friendship would be our first priority.
- That we are not only friends but brothers also.
- That if any of us like a girl, she would be respected by all and considered as 'bhabi' by the rest of the group.
- That we will cross our limits to help each other to find his dream girl.
- That we will respect every '*Ashique*' (the person who is in one sided love) and accept him as a the member of '*Ashique* Community'.
- That we will never hide anything from each other. Trust would be the sole base of our friendship.
- That we will plan and do our operations with mutual consent. We will hear other's point of view but ultimately do whatever that person himself wants to do.
- That it doesn't matter if our friend is right or wrong, we will cooperate with him. We will never leave him alone in his bad days.
- That we will act fearlessly in bunking the school and in dealing with any person entangling with any of our brother. (Proposal by Vicky, which was somehow passed in the parliament of three of us.)
- That Rehaan, Rohit and Aadarsh are the permanent members of this group; others will come and go on their own sweet will.

- That our friendship and our brotherhood comes first before love, girlfriend or any materialistic thing. We will leave our girlfriend (love), in case we have to choose one among our girl and our brother.

VERIFICATION

Verified that this agreement has been made by Rehaan, Rohit and Aadarsh without any fear, pressure, or any other external force.

Sd

Rehaan Rohit Aadarsh

8

THE HEROINE, THE VILLAIN AND ENTRY OF THE HERO.

For me it was an ordinary day. I have been shifted to Commerce section—new class, new weird looking students with a couple of unwanted questions 'Dude, why have you opted for Commerce now?' My reply was 'Dude why you opted to be an asshole?' It's recess time and I am standing with Rohit in front of my old class. But today there is no clue of my 'Kamana'. I just saw Sneha passing by.

"Hey Sneha." I throw a hello to her.

"Hi." She replies

"So you opted for Commerce now?" She asks. Rohit is patiently listening.

"Actually that's the stream I was about to take in 11th class. There's a reason I changed my decision at the last moment, and you know that."

"You really love Kamana a lot."

"Yup! But only I do. It's just a one-sided love story without any future." I said in a low tone and continued "Is Kamana absent today?"

"Rehaan come with me. I want to tell you something." Sneha grabs my hand and starts walking towards the newly constructed empty block near our classes. I gave a signal to Rohit 'give us a minute'. She sits on a bench in front of me and starts speaking.

"Actually there is a serious problem going on in her home. I don't know much about it. Kamana told this to Shefali."

"Oh! What's the problem?" I asked anxiously. My instincts gave me negative signals.

"There is some old property issue between Kamana's father and someone Mr. Pandey. That fellow 'Pandey' is one of the most wanted, cruel and a ruthless killer & gangster." She took a sip from her water bottle.

"Yeah many a times I have heard stories about him. He is very dangerous. He is accused in many kidnappings, rape and murder cases. He kills a person as if somebody is cutting vegetables." I felt some fear in my heart. I snatched Sneha's water bottle and took a sip.

"Eew, what's that in your bottle?"

"Oh, it's 'Jalzeera', I love it, yummy."

"OK, continue with that bloody Pandey." I noticed courage in parts of my 'Rat's Heart'.

"Yup, there is a case of a landed property between Kamana's father and Pandey's younger brother. Pandey wants that Kamana's father, should handover or sell his ancestral property worth millions to Pandey's younger brother for a petty sum. Pandey is in illegal possession of that land and he is not even negotiating.

Kamana's father has moved the court." She goes for another round of drinking her so called 'Zalzeera' and continues her story 'Kamana and Mr. Pandey'. "Pandey is now threatening to kidnap Kamana and her younger brother and kill them if Kamana's father does not transfer that land in the name of Pandey's younger brother. Therefore, her father does not allow Kamana and her brother to go out anywhere, alone." With these words the bell rings, declaring the end of recess.

Some tiny tots who were watching us anxiously as if something interesting is going on among 'bhaiya-didi' leave for their classrooms with disappointment.

The whole day I was mentally trapped in a triangle.

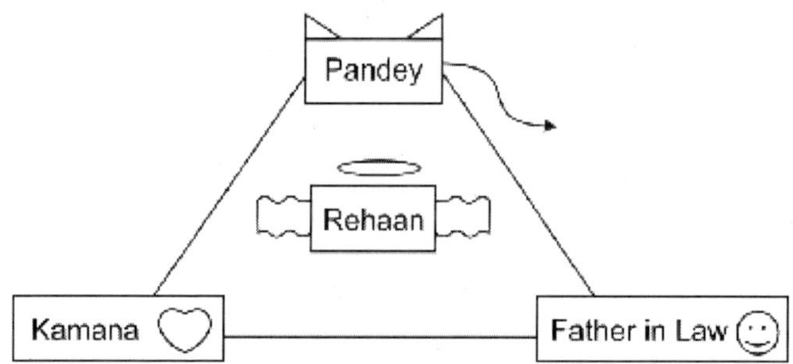

I remember the old saying 'If your father is poor, it's your fate. But if your father-in-law is poor, then you are a fool.' So at least I am sitting with the good news that I am not a fool but am worried with the worst part i.e. 'Pandey'. I am worried that he might hurt Kamana or her family. I am frustrated that being a school boy I have got no power to tackle this sister-fucker Pandey. I am day-dreaming if I was an IPS officer, I would have screwed this bastard Pandey. But the fact is that I cannot do anything in this case. I can just pray for Kamana and her family's welfare.

In the evening I have come with Prashant to Gandhi Book Depot to buy some text books. In this shop books of all subjects from school to college level are available.

To my surprise Kamana arrives there with her father and a policeman (may be appointed by the court for security reasons) and a man aged around 30, who might be her relative. She entered the bookshop and looked into my eyes; I could feel the fear in her eyes. I cannot talk to her as she is with her father. She asked Mr. Gandhi for some books, and looked at me many a times. I tried hard to say 'don't worry I am with you' with my eyes. She took her books, made the payment for them and left the shop.

She was about to enter her car suddenly a Red Omni Van and a Mahindra jeep stopped at the side of Kamana's car. From the jeep three huge ugly looking men came out. Their faces resembled to gangsters in some cheap B-grade Hindi movie. One of them was dark and muscular, and carrying a pistol. The other with long hair and dark complexion pulls Kamana out of the car—her books which she was carrying in her hand, fell on the road.

"Papa help. Papa, please help me." She starts shouting helplessly but they held her tight and threw her into the Van. I am about to run towards Kamana but Prashant holds me back.

After a while two other men came out of the jeep and start beating the policeman who came to rescue Kamana. The one with pistol hit her father's forehead with the pistol-whip. Her relative who was with them ran away seeing the situation, coward. Kamana's father started bleeding. The one with the pistol grabs his shirt, a part of which is now covered with blood and says "You sister-fucker, Pandey Sahib warned you many a times to transfer that land to him, but you did not listen. Now wait and watch what he will do to your daughter." He starts laughing. Kamana's father fell unconscious on the side.

They get into their respective vehicles and drive off from there. Usually in Hindi movies police come late at the site, but even after they left the place there is no clue of any police-jeep with annoying sirens. Meanwhile I freed myself from Prashant pushing him, and ran out of the shop. Fortunately Prashant's motorcycle keys are with me. I thought nothing, just started the motorcycle and followed the gangsters. I have only one thing in my mind i.e. my love is in danger and I will screw anybody who harms her in anyway. How will I do that is the biggest question?

I followed them for an hour and somehow managed to remain unnoticed to them. After sometime, they stopped at an old cottage near a village. It's a kind of messed-up place, surrounded by junk and is situated in a big farm. There are couple of trees around the cottage, on which few vultures are sitting. Four motorcycles and two cars are also parked with not so good looking men with weapons sitting on them. Looks like as if this is the head quarter of Mr. Pandey. Usually in Hindi movies villains use such kind of a place to operate their unsocial and illegal activities.

Time is about to declare call-off for the evening. I parked the motorcycle far from the cottage behind a large oak tree. Firstly, I thought to call the police but mobile technology was yet to be introduced in my life. There was no clue of a STD booth nearby and asking for phone from any of the gangster to call the police is not a good idea for the health of my bones. I didn't want to go back to call the police because I was feeling restless by not seeing Kamana; I wanted to see her right now. Secondly, screw my geography, I forgot the way back. Its night time now. I somehow managed to reach the backside of the cottage without coming into notice of the two men standing in front. I am empty handed and didn't have any plan. I had only one thing with me, my retarded experience of Hindi movies. I have to save my Kamana—how I will do that, I don't have any idea.

Usually in Hindi movies there is always a window at the back side of the villain's place but here there is none at all. There are a few windows but only on the front side. I think like me, they also learned many things from Hindi movies experience. By seeing this location and cottage, I must say Mr. Pandey is quiet intelligent. I think he should go for CAT entrance exam. After passing out from a prestigious MBA Institute, he could earn a million bucks. I wonder why anybody did not give him such a wonderful suggestion. I guess there exists only few gems like me who can give such a suggestion to him.

I didn't have any option but to climb the wall by getting on a tree next to the wall. I wonder if I too have few super powers to climb the wall, by sticking my ass to it. Also in Hindi movies, hero finds out some rope or other means in such kind of a situation. Here I am about to hang in the middle with one of my foot in the hole on the wall and the other on one of the loose branches. I grabbed few bushes in my hand and was about to give up, suddenly few bad thoughts about Kamana came to my mind and I went beyond my limits and somehow reached the top. At that floor the door was locked from inside, but thank God there is a ventilator with a large glass. If I break this glass then again my 'stability of bones' are in danger. Yes, the glass is attached to the iron frame around it with clay. I look here and there and find a small piece of wood, smaller then my palm, even. After half an hour I removed almost all the clay and slowly pulled the glass out.

The size of the ventilator is just enough to allow the entry of my 6 feet frame. Having a slim body has got its own advantages. I slowly-slowly moved down the stairs, with army of few rats around the place. I don't know in what way my poor army of rats is going to help me out, but at least they are giving me courage; I have got somebody on my side. I enter a store-room which is next to the stairs. Yes, from the window here, I could see the room in which Kamana is kept in.

Kamana's hands and legs were tied with a rope, her mouth is also tied with a piece of yellow cloth. I guess usually in movies people prefer white cloth. White cloth needs constant washing, as it turns dirty soon, so it would be just a cost management technique of Mr. Pandey. There is a wooden bed without mattress on which Kamana was lying and 2 broken chairs in the room. There were two men present in the room, the same who kidnapped her. After a few minutes a deadly figure entered.

"Namaste, Pandey Sahib." The two men greeted. Seeing Mr. Pandey I was about to laugh but controlled myself, somehow. I thought that the villain would be a kind of 6 feet with huge muscles, with beard and moustaches, and a couple of scars on his face. Here we have our original Mr. Pandey, who is 5 feet 3 inch something–a bulky stuff, with round face and white complexion and a typical interesting case of hair-fall.

"Namaste, where is she?" A figure came out from behind my misinterpreted Mr. Pandey. Now that's what is called a real villain–6 feet muscular man wearing a white kurta (a kind of men's upper wear in India) and denim blue jeans with sports shoes. He has a broad face with little beard, moustaches and medium hair combed upwards and wearing black Aviator sun glasses. He is the renowned gangster 'Pandey', with a nick name '*Beeru Kasai*' (Kasai meaning butcher), which he got because of his way of killing people——by chopping them with a butcher's knife. I looked back, my army of rats had left me alone.

"Here, lying on the bed, she was shouting too much, so we tied her mouth also." The man says.

"OK, I am giving her father 24 hours to give us his land's official documents. Otherwise, cut this bitch into small-small pieces and parcel them to her father. And yeah you can both enjoy with her before doing that. Here is a bottle of chloroform——use it if she troubles you." Pandey says and leaves the room with the same fellow with whom he came in.

"Just 24 hours darling, then you will be ours." They claim while touching Kamana's cheeks. She started crying. One of them keeps the chloroform bottle on the table besides the bed. The two men start throwing dirty looks at Kamana.

Now it's time to act. But this is not a movie where I will do a surprise entry by crashing through a few not so strong glasses and tackle these bulky gangsters alone. In a movie or in action games generally hero gets some weapon or at least an iron rod, but what I got here is a plastic water pipe. About my fighting skills, I remember once I fought a severe battle with a mouse in my house. In the end the mouse was the 'Last Man Standing'. I had also attended few classes of Martial Arts long back when I was in 9th class. I was the only one amongst the whole batch who was absent on the day of yellow belt test. Hence I remain honoured with my old white belt.

After an hour one of them sits on the chair and starts yawning.

"Hey I am going to buy cigarettes and something to eat." The one who is standing says.

"Hmm." The other is half asleep. After a minute the guy who is standing leaves the room. This is my only chance.

I slowly, without making any noise, entered the room through the window. Seeing me Kamana starts moaning and moves her head side-by-side indicating me not to come.

"Shush" I said not to make any kind of noise. I don't have much time. Suddenly what my Biology teacher had taught me, opened the doors of 'My Brain Department' and I remembered that chloroform is used to make the patients unconscious.

I took the bottle of chloroform and poured few drops on my handkerchief and put it at the nose of the gangster. First he moves his hands here and there but after a few seconds fell down from the chair on the floor. I took a large iron rod lying on the floor and hid myself in a dark corner. I told Kamana to react normally as if I have not released her yet, so that it seems everything is normal. After about 10-15 minutes the second one came into the room. He is the one who had pulled Kamana and threw her in that Red Van. He is the one who touched her cheeks and passed dirty comments.

Now the problem is how should I tackle him? With the experience of losing battle with even a rat, I didn't know what to do? In the meantime the fellow lights up his cigarette and stands in front of the person lying on the floor.

"Hey Ajit wake up. Have a cigarette, dude. Wake up, only few hours left for the honeymoon with this bitch lying on the bed." He shakes him up but no response. I saw a tear trickling down from Kamana's eye, which is enough to make me mad.

The moment he turns around to call other members of his group, I smashed the iron rod on his head with full force by saying "I love you, Kamana". He becomes unconscious and fell down.I kicked him a couple of times.

I then locked the door from inside and started opening the knots of ropes tied on Kamana's hands and legs. Now this is a knotty business for me because I usually prefer elastic in my pyjama because if I go to the toilet then I have to start preparing ten minutes before to loosen the knot of my pyjamas. I took around fifteen minutes to release her and all the time I was in the fear of anyone coming in.

The moment I opened the piece of cloth tied on her mouth, she gave me a hug and started crying by grabbing my shirt with her hands. When she hugged me, what I felt, I cannot express it in words. A mysterious feeling of excitement, I felt in my heart. My heartbeat became very fast. There is a sudden flashback of all my sleepless nights, which I passed wishing that one day Kamana will be mine and I will give her so much love that nobody else can give in this world. But I stopped myself as it was not the right time to think about those things.

"Hey Kamana, don't cry. I am here; nobody can touch you now." I said consoling her.

"Rehaan........Rehaan........Rehaan....." She kept on saying, shivering out of fear. After some time she stops crying, and grabs me tightly.

We heard some sound, as if somebody is coming to this room. I whispered in Kamana's ear and opened the door-bolt saying to her "don't worry". We lifted the gangsters lying on the floor and placed him on the chair. We held up the second one in a standing stance. To my surprise it's Pandey himself and he becomes more surprised than us seeing that the girl is not on the bed. I am afraid, if he starts shouting like in Hindi movies *'Kalu, Raju, Birju kahan margaye sab ke sab* (Where are you all?)'. To my surprise the poor Pandey is weak in general knowledge of Hindi movies. I think he should go for a couple of Masala Movie (hot buzz) magazines. He goes to the one who is lying unconscious on the chair, Ajit and poor Pandey acts according to my plan. The moment he goes near the chair, we pushed from behind the body of the other gangster on Pandey. Without giving any time to Pandey to realise what is happening, Kamana threw the bed sheet over him and I smashed the iron rod two-three times on his head. Pandey fell. To avoid any risk we also poured few drops of chloroform on his nose and also on the other two unconscious gangsters.

Kamana held my hand and we start to move towards the stairs. I stop, went back and take off the black Aviator sun glasses from Pandey's face and wear them on my best asset i.e. my eyes.

"My hero" Kamana says, adjusting the sunglasses on my eyes properly and kissed my cheeks.

It's about 4:30 a.m. now; we took the ropes, which were used to tie Kamana, for going down. When we were about to reach the door, my old army of rats again joined us celebrating my half-done victory. I tried to escape out of the same ventilator, but Kamana pulls me back and opened the main door instead, which was bolted from inside when I came in. This time my Hindi movie experience proved me wrong. Thank God, I had an intelligent girl with me.

We made 4 different knots and were able to make a single long rope. After checking that nobody is there below I sent Kamana down first and I followed.

We managed to reach to that oak tree behind which I had hidden Prashant's motorcycle, but the petrol is not enough in it for our escape. I saw few vehicles in the parking of the cottage and saw nobody standing outside.

"Kamana you wait here, I am going for arranging something." I took a plastic bag and got an idea.

"No, Rehaan, don't go there." Kamana grabs my hand harder.

"Don't worry, I will be fine. If anything happens to me, swear on me that you will run from here." I handed over the keys of Prashant's motorcycle.

I was thinking about pouring some petrol in the plastic bag from bikes standing in the parking. But one idiot had left the keys inside an open jeep.

I took the jeep in front of Kamana. It's morning now, here I am with a green-colour army jeep and wearing black Aviator glasses. With a rugged hairstyle which resulted because of the fight inside, I am eligible for a role of a Hero in a big budget Hindi movie. Kamana steps into the jeep.

"So, you know driving also."

"Can't say that. I remember few months back my father tried to teach me driving in his car. The next day he was standing in a queue for vehicle insurance claims for accident in the Insurance office. After that day he dropped his brilliant idea."

Kamana smiles and says "I am all yours. I am with you, go for it."

It's early morning, so I didn't feel any problem in driving on the clear road, without any other vehicle. I didn't know the area but somehow kept on driving. After sometimes Kamana holds my left hand and rests her face on my shoulder. I can feel her still shivering. After a few kilometres I saw one *Dhaba* (food point, especially for truck drivers). I stopped my jeep there and asked the owner for the telephone. I called the police by dialling '100'. The police located us and arrived in twenty minutes.

We are sitting at the back seat of the police jeep. After some time she keeps her head on my lap and falls asleep. The police leaves us to our respected houses.

The next day my photo is on the front page of every newspaper. All of them had written— 'Pandey, his younger brother and other members of his gang were killed in an encounter by the police. They started firing at the police force when they went there; in counter attack all of them got killed.' My parents were proud of me. Mom is quiet busy in telling the whole story with some additional spice to relatives and neighbours.

Two days later in the afternoon, my landline phone starts ringing. I pick up the phone and it's Sneha on the line.

"Hey Rehaan, meet me at 5:00 in the evening at the Lake Side. It's something serious. And yup dress up yourself well for the evening."

I asked Rohit to take me to the Lake Side.

I am wearing the same dress of Rohit which I wore while proposing Kamana for friendship a few days back. I really look smart in these clothes, I said to myself. Rohit came to me with Aadarsh around 4:35 p.m. We three reached the lake side five minutes before 5 p.m. To our surprise Sneha and Kamana were already there with Shefali and Shivani. Kamana is wearing Orange T-shirt with silver embroidery on it and a pair of blue denim jeans. She is wearing multicoloured bangles, which are looking damn cute on her soft fair hands. Her hair are falling on her shoulders. May be because of Sneha telling her that I like loose hair swaying in the air. With right make-up sense and a shining lip balm, she is the one for whom I can even die for. The gold chain around her neck is complimenting one of the best creations of God. Kamana is constantly looking at me.

"OK Rohit and Aadarsh, you come with us. Allow these loving birds to have sometime in private." Sneha says and continues "So shall we pick you from here after the Biology tuition?"

"No, we will manage to come ourselves." Kamana says.

"From 'I' to 'we', great going." Sneha laughs and they all leave the place. Rohit gave me his scooter keys. Aadarsh and Rohit, my borthers were happy even more than me.

We are standing on a lonely platform over the lake. It seems like it's about to rain. Kamana is standing few steps away from me looking constantly into my eyes. After a few minutes I saw tears in her eyes.

"Rehaan, I love....." Kamana is about to say but I stop her in between. I came close to her, bent down and sat on my knees in front of her. I lock my palms, as if I am praying and then came the moment which comes only once in your lifetime. I proposed her this way.

"I knew that one day all my dreams will come true.
That one rainy day the flowers would also be smiling
a little more and their fragrance will speak on behalf of me.
That one day these birds and trees would be playing
music for me with the flowing water creating the aura.
That one day the sky would be more enriched in
colour as if the stage is being decorated for me only.
That one day the sun will go to invite all for the occasion.
That one day the cool breeze would spread my message to all.
That one day grass, leaves and trees will sway in
the air as if they are dancing for the occasion.

On that day you will be waiting for me only.
On that day I would be looking more special.
On that day I will be dressed like on a wedding day.
On that day everything will go the right way.
On that day my eyes will speak more than my words.
On that day I will let you know what you mean for me.
On that day I will let you know about what you really are.
On that day I will tell you, up to what extent I can go for you.
On that day I will hold your hand in a different
way than any other day.
On that day you will break into tears.
On that day I will tell you that I love you.

After that day, you would become the princess.
After that day, your each day would be special.
After that day, you will never cry and always smile.
After that day, your life would be full of enriched colours of love.
After that day, you will wish to live more than your decided life.
After that day, you will get the reason to live

Today is that day.
I don't know how much I love you,
but I just know that I love you.
I did not love anybody before you and will not
love anyone other than you.
You make me feel special.
Your presence makes the day a festival day.
My words begin with you and end with you.
Whether my eyes are open or closed, I see only you.
You are my thoughts, you are my words, you are my colours,
You are my light, you are my night, you are my days,
You are my girl, you are my love, you are my ways,
You are my dream, you are my life,
You are my beginning and you are my end, Kamana.
I love you Kamana, even more than I love myself."

A drop of tear trickles down on my hand. I look above and see that Kamana is crying.

"I love you too, Rehaan." She picks me up and gives me a hug. She keeps on saying 'I love you' many times over. She gives a slight feeling of love by touching her soft cheeks and nose with mine. She also kissed me while saying 'I love you'.

Generally in Hindi movies after this situation there comes a 'rainy song'. With heroine generally wearing a sari, and hero coming in with an umbrella, heroine then throwing the umbrella away, so that the shying hero also can prepare himself for dancing and few lovemaking scenes. Whereas in English movies the two go for a smooch or a French kiss.

Now arranging for a sari, umbrella and artificial rain, is something out of my budget. If I combine my pocket money with Rohit and

Aadarsh, even then it's a costly affair. So I prefer the English style.

I take her hand into mine, grab her from back and pull her close to me.

"May I?"

"I am all yours." She places her lips on mine and we go for a passionate French kiss till...!!!

My land line starts ringing.

I wake up with some cotton from my pillow in my mouth. Damn that was just a dream. I think it was the result of what I ate last night for dinner and that pathetic Hindi movie with a similar story, which I saw before sleeping. Damn I forgot that I have to buy black Aviator sun glasses also. Kamana's thoughts are ruining me.

I looked at the pillow. My pillow is in a serious condition—it's an emergency case. It was severely harassed with my fighting and few intimate scenes. If somebody puts life into my pillow, it will straightaway sue me for an attempt to murder under section 307 and Rape under Indian Penal Code.

I pick up the phone.

"Hey dude, Rohit here. Aadarsh and me are coming to pick you up in an hour. So get ready, we have got a surprise for you."

9

School Bunks, Not so Porn Movie and the Narrow Escape

"So what's the big deal?" I asked Aadarsh, while we were going to Rohit's 'surprise' place.

"Shut up and relax." Rohit said.

As usual, ask any question to Aadarsh and the reply will come from Rohit and *vice-versa*.

Rohit stops the scooter in front of a building, which hardly registers itself to be called a house—it is an old building of 19th century and seems like it would be the first customer of any earthquake. With a garden-cum-jungle in the front and lots of wild trees, I suspect the surprise could be a habitat of wild animals in domestic area. With iron junk around the house made me confused as if I am standing in a junkyard and Aadarsh is here to sell his scooter which belongs to the revolutionary period of Automobile industry. Two white gates with few patches of rust on it and something hard to recognise as a garage, I think it's the best place that can be hired by Ramsay Brothers, the horror film makers.

"This is Kamana's house." Rohit says.

"Oh! it is a dream house for any person. It is like heaven on earth, best architectural marvel I have ever seen. It is beautiful and priceless."

'Why the hell are you staring at me. Common! Love can make anybody blind. OK. Whatever, after all its my Kamana's house, so what if it seems like a haunted cottage.'

After that life never remained the same. The street dogs near her house got a new company in the face of me.

Life goes on as it was destined to. I bunked the school for the first time with Vicky. The whole day, only one thought was screwing my mind, what if somebody catches me. Vicky for that matter had brought a T-shirt and a pair of jeans, which he changed at Rohit's place, this way to be an expert in bunking makes the difference. For the whole day we played Play-Station at a Videogame shop.

After a few days Rohit also registers himself in the bunking business. We never expected him to do so, but life is all about surprises. Rohit's registration leads to an automatic approval from Aadarsh's side also.

My new class teacher in Commerce section, 'Mrs. Punia', had already started suspecting my declining graph of attendance. It's not that she herself spotted me out on a bunk; I know it's the work of 'touts'.

"There's a new movie releasing this Friday. It's an 'A' certificate movie with few intimate scenes, maknig it the right decision for investing money." Vicky says.

"It's a porn movie! I am not going." Rohit declares.

"It's not a porn movie but an ordinary Hindi movie with a renowned actress. It's about the life of female sex workers. Because of a few bold scenes, it's certified as an adult movie by the Censor Board." Vicky reveals the name of the actress. Being a big fan of that actress, Rohit approves the proposal. Vicky never bothered to ask me as I never learned to say 'No' for such movies. We planned to see the movie next day.

The excitement to see that movie is at its maximum and screwing my sleep too. Being in Higher Secondary School you are now illegally eligible to be introduced to topics like sex, porn movies, porn literature, adult magazines and other mysteries about girls. I remember, I convinced my father to buy me a Personal Computer, by making him count an 'n' number of uses to why a child of my age should have a computer to compete in this cruel rat race. I never used my PC for anything other than listening to songs, Computer Games, pirated Hindi, English movies and few Porn movies. I had not mentioned any of this in my list of 'Why I need a computer?'

After a while sleep knocked at my door.

> We bunked our school. Vicky, Rohit, Aadarsh and I are heading towards the theatre. There is a long queue but Vicky had some contacts with the owner of the theatre and that way we managed our tickets.
>
> We are in the middle of the movie, suddenly few police men and members of our school staff came into the theatre.
>
> "Arrest these bastards." One of our teacher says by pointing us out. We try to run but they blocked us from all the sides. We get caught. Next day our Principal called our parents and suspended us all.

I woke up suddenly in fear. Thank God that was just a dream. But I am having some bad feelings about bunking. I reached the place where we had to assemble for the bunk. We all were about to leave for the first day first show but I held Rohit's hand.

"We are not going to see the movie."

"What?" Rohit, Vicky and Aadarsh said at the same time. I disclosed my dream and tried to convince them to drop the idea of bunking, today.

"No way dude, hell with your dream, I will go anyway." Vicky declares.

"I am also going for the movie. I don't believe in these superstitious things. Nothing will happen with us." Aadarsh says. Rohit is standing without passing any of his so called wonderful statement regarding the ongoing controversy, and that way I managed to have atleast one guy on my side.

"Rohit trust me, I know I keep on screwing you all with my pathetic dreams. But today is a different story. I am having bad instincts about the bunk."

"I am with you." Rohit comes to my side.

"OK then, you two screw yourself in the classroom. We are going for the hot babes in the movie." Vicky and Aadarsh left for the theatre. Rohit and I went to school.

Today many students bunked the school to see the most awaited movie. It's around 9:30 and bell rings for the second period. It's Mrs. Punia's class. My pen fell down, so I was searching for it under my desk when Mrs. Punia comes into the class.

"Enough is enough. Today Rehaan has also gone. He is absent today, right." Mrs Punia shouts.

"Nope, unfortunately he is present today." A voice comes from my desk and I raise my hand with the same pen which I picked up. I stand up and give a smile to my class teacher.

"People and their misconceptions. Sorry to disappoint you Madam." I smiled and she smiles back at me.

"The staff members of many schools have spotted their students near the theatre. A team from each school with few policemen went there to catch them. This time Principal will take strict action against the students who are caught." Mrs. Punia says.

The belly dance by the heroine in the movie is welcomed by a few whistles and cheap comments from the boys. Our heroes Aadarsh and Vicky are dancing on their seats out of their uncontrollable excitement. After a while, few unwanted men, in police uniform join them from one side. Vicky saw them coming towards them.

"Run, it's a raid by the police." Vicky, Aadarsh and other schoolmates of Aadarsh run towards the second exit. To escape, they have to cross another exit down the stairs but unfortunately few of our school teachers saw them and blocked their way. They ran towards the women toilets and locked the door from inside.

"Damn it, what should we do now?" Aadarsh screams.

"Shut up; let me find some way out." Vicky replied.

"If I had listened to Rehaan in the morning, I would have not been in this situation. What if I get caught and suspended or jailed. What will my family do to me........." Aadarsh starts shivering and the virus of shivering spreads in the whole toilet affecting all present there.

"Open the door bastards, otherwise we will break it and screw you all present inside." A voice comes from outside with hard strikes on the door.

"What should we do now? Damn why I didn't trust Rehaan." Aadarsh shoutes again, Vicky also gives approval to his 'If We Had Gone to School With Rehaan'.

The Policemen started striking the door hard . In a minute or two they will manage to break the door.

"We will go from there." Vicky points towards a ventilator above the toilet seat.

"How can we escape from there?" Aadarsh asks.

In the meantime Vicky puts one step on the toilet seat, another on the flush and enters the ventilator by opening it up. As he is slim he escaped easily but fell on his back on the other side.

Aadarsh had no choice but to follow him. Due to short height he needs to take a jump from the flush. The moment he goes for the jump the flush breakes down, but he somehow reaches the ventilator. He just managed to take his face outside, but his bulldozer shaped body blocks into the ventilator. Vicky is pulling his hand from the other side and the other boys are pushing him from inside the toilet.

"Bloody asshole, do it fast, else we all will be caught." A boy inside the toilet shouts, while pushing him hard.

Aadarsh was about to escape from the ventilator, suddenly the toilet door is broken by the policemen. They catch all present inside. One of the policemen catches hold of Aadarsh's leg but Vicky pulls him with his full force from outside. Aadarsh falls on the other side leaving the policeman with his shoe. Aadarsh starts running with only one shoe. His school shirt and inner wears are torn up from many sides in the struggle. His over broad tummy is visible and the present state makes him perfectly suited for begging business at some renowned signal.

Vicky and Aadarsh managed successfully to escaped from the theatre but one of our teacher recognised Vicky on his way out.

Rohit is about to become mad by laughing continuously for last half-an-hour seeing the condition of Aadarsh. Vicky went to Rohit's house to change his dress. Unfortunately now

Aadarsh belongs to a different school, so the poor chap has to carry his 21st century beggar's designer outfit to his home. I kept on laughing the whole day, which raised a few doubts to my parents about my mental health.

10

My Instincts, Seeds of Differences and Rohit's Love Dilemma

Call me superstitious or anything but I believe in my dreams. Many a times I proved them to be reliable also. When I saw Kamana for the first time, she seemed to be somebody whom I knew for decades. She seemed like the person I was looking for. I feel that there is some mystery? She seemed like the closest person to me. Why is that? I don't know! If this is love, then yes I am in love with Kamana.

Believe it or not, something strange is happening out here. Anywhere I go I find Kamana there. For example, yesterday I went to the main market to buy a cap for me and found Kamana there with her mother. Day before yesterday, I was at a petrol pump with Rohit, surprisingly Kamana was also there with Sneha for refuelling. Today my surprise crossed the limits, this time I went for an evening walk on the road behind my house. After five minutes, I find Kamana passing by and looking constantly at me.

I try to convince myself that these are just by chance, but again something happens which proves that Kamana is not a coincidence but my fate. She always says that she is not interested in me, then why her eyes always seems to be looking for me. I remember once I was going with my neighbour for playing cricket, and that time Kamana and Mona were also going somewhere. They were on the opposite side. Kamana while driving looked at me constantly by just changing angle of her eyes towards me. Mona was not able to know that Kamana is looking at me.

Whenever she looks into my eyes, her eyes always say that 'I am yours, Rehaan!' I forget everything whenever she talks to me. When I stand next to her my heart-beat crosses the limits. There is some mysterious kind of joy I feel on my left side. I don't know if she will ever say yes to me, but my love is unconditional. One thing is for sure that one day I will make her realise the true meaning of love.

No matter whether she like me or not, but something deep inside my heart keeps convincing me that Kamana is born only for me. She is the girl who will love me even more than herself, who can go to any extent for the sake of love. She is the one who will hold my trembling hands in my bad days and still love me. It's just that I have to wait for her; for how many years, I don't know. What I know for sure is that nobody in this world can replace my Kamana.

Aadarsh's story is going on the same age-old track with same statements 'waiting for the right time'. Everyday his journey of 'Aarti' starts with his companion Mr. Rohit on the first scooter of the human race. The day starts with following Aarti to her morning Maths tuition class, and then to her school. He comes again after school and follows her till she reaches home. Mr. Aadarsh again waits outside her house in the evening when she goes for her Economics and Accountancy tuition. The poor chap follows her at a distance of at least a mile. Sometimes the dude gets a jackpot when Aarti goes for any function or for a party at night with her family.

Aarti belongs to a rich family. Her car size and model often change with changing seasons. She seems to be a sophisticated girl, out of reach of my poor chap. She is one of the most in-demand girl amongst boys in my school. She is the ex-girlfriend of Anand, one of my class mates.

The story goes that Anand in 9th class proposed Aarti. In the beginning she said no, but her friends somehow convinced her to go for Anand. Anand is one of the boys known as 'Dream Come True' amongst the girls. Sometimes I notice his walking style and gestures resembling girls, and if I trust Sigmund Freud, Anand possesses some gay characteristics.

Anyhow the two, Aarti and Anand fell in love but Anand dumped her after six months without any reason. Often he talks about Aarti by claiming that she has the sexiest legs. Aarti was serious for him and even disclosed about her relationship to her mother. The breakup lead to several restrictions on her lifestyle by her mother. According to reliable sources both are still virgins.

Rumours are that Anand approached Sneha, and got positive response from her. Sneha therefore develops a new enemy 'Aarti'.

In January, i.e. at the end of 11th class, Aadarsh is on a new mission, 'Sacrificing my love for the sake of Aarti' under the world class leadership of Rohit. Objective of this mission is to rebind Aarti and Anand again into the thread of Love. The mission is aborted due to interference of a third power 'Rehaan'. After giving sufficient reasons like 'Anand is now happy with Sneha' and 'Aarti hates him like anything now' and 'You mean nothing to both of them, so why will they listen to you.' Afterwards again under the leadership of Vicky, Aadarsh now wanted to teach a lesson to Anand for what he did to Aarti but thanks to Rohit he stopped.

I remember once in the games period, Aarti asked for playing Table Tennis with me (as both Commerce sections have games period at the same time). I played with her for about an hour; we talked about many things. Her friend Anita kept on looking at me. Some people say that Anita likes me. I thought about talking to Aarti about Aadarsh, but there were many other classmates standing over there so I prefered to keep mum.

In the evening when I told Aadarsh about this he gave me a back stabbing look, as if I married his love, Aarti—orthodox chap. I often interacted with Aarti until she recognised me as Aadarsh's friend, whom she hates the most now a days.

All the time for last 2-3 years, Aadarsh did only one thing, to just follow her. I remember on the result day, he followed Aarti even when he knew that she has come with her mother. Her mother, who looks like a cruel lady of some German literature constantly gave him an angry look. But if somebody asked Aadarsh about this, he would say "At least she now knows who is Aadarsh."

The sweetest part of Aadarsh is that he always wished Aarti on her Birthdays. We managed to know her mobile number. Actually first we noted her address, took her landline number from the phone directory and then one of my female friend asked her mobile number from her mother saying that she is an old friend. Once on Aarti's birthday, Rohit and I went to Aadarsh's house. By chance I opened one of his registers, on each and every page he had written Aarti's name, phrases like 'Happy Birthday Aarti', 'I Love you, Aarti', 'I cannot live without you'. In another register he had written some weird stuff. His English sucks, but those lines really touched my heart:

Nobel Nature

The age of an oak tree is 300 years. Its falls down as dry, drill without leaves withered wood at last.

A flower of lily blooms in the month of May. It spreads beauty, happiness and brightness and fades away the same night. The guy called the Aadarsh. And girl 'Aarti' the flower of beautiness, happiness and my Noni.

The Aadarsh wants to convey that Aarti, the Aadarsh's love is beautiful. We can see and realise that Aadarsh's choice is wonderful. Aadarsh die on her Golu Moluness and noni Adayein. He first see Aarti in my previous school canteen. He was going with his friend Rehaan, the Rehaan told him that the girl walk in front of our both is Aarti. Then the Aadarsh told Rehaan that she is his bhabi. After wards Aadarsh told Vicky to known the address of Aarti and phone number. After this Aadarsh know the address of Aarti and phone number. And then Aadarsh was go to his nonu and watch it. After one and a half year Aadarsh took her photograph from a friend.

Yesterday I went to see the Aarti on Math's tuition. First I went to Rohit's home and take the camera and went to sector in park to meet Rehaan and Prashant. Then both went to see and to take the photograph of Aarti. Then we do not meet with Aarti because of some problem. Then we go 8:45 on tuition we all go to math's tuition and she was outside. Then Prashant and I go to Next Street of where she comes. After passing the street I was ahead of Aarti's scooter and the suddenly Rehaan also take his scooter ahead of Aarti and firstly reach shopping complex and I was go in the street in front of book shop. Then Aarti firstly go in front of the street where we are standing. After that I was chasing Aarti and Prashant take her photograph from behind and I take the scooter in with Aarti, Prashant readies to take her photograph and the scooter jumped due to breaker and Prashant does not take her photograph, and the I and Prashant fall down. ☺

May be Aadarsh's love for Aarti is deeper than even mine for Kamana. People generally tease Aadarsh on his complexion and fattiness and laugh at him when he reveals that he loves Aarti. Everybody would say "Aadarsh have you seen your face in the mirror. Even if you try all your life then also you will not get her. Don't even think in your dreams about her." For Aarti he screwed his studies but she will never understand that he is a great guy and true from heart.

I consider Aadarsh as my brother; I will never let him live in a fake world. Many a times I tried to convince him that his feelings are true but his ways of expressing are not right. Girls will not fall in love by just following them or by trying to take her photograph in public; on the contrary she will start hating you. The problem is that even I don't know the right way. Deep inside my heart I know that Aarti is not his cup of tea. So instead of making him understand the reality, my words had sown the seeds of differences between us.

It's January, the cold weather is at its pick. Today is Sunday, I am sleeping in the day time suddenly my phone rings up. Its Rohit on the other side.

"Dude, I don't know why, and how? But I like Nandini."

11

The Christmas Night, Emerging Competition and a Misconception

Till now I was living in a misconception that at least Rohit was a mature guy who concentrates only on his studies. 'Girls' were considered to be an undiscovered territory of his life, which is expected to remain like this till his father finds a match for his marriage.

Nandini is a cute girl, who once called me her brother in 6th class. Now I know this asshole Rohit can't do anything on his own. In girl's world Rohit is considered as a spoon feeding child who also sometimes tries to eat his spoon. There is only one guy who can help him out; who can bring up the small kid Rohit to the world of materialistic girls, unfortunately his name is 'Rehaan.'

There is a Church near our school. Every year the authorities organise Children Fair around the Church. Kamana and Aarti also visit this church and light up candles on Christmas day. Aadarsh and I are waiting for our girls. Kamana arrives at about 6:00 in the evening with Shivani. They take two candles from a stall outside and go inside the church for prayer.

She comes out after about twenty minutes, but keeps moving here and there looking for something in the shoe rack. After about ten minutes she starts moving towards the exit. By chance my eyes go to Kamana's feet."

"Kamana, where are your shoes?"

"Somebody stole them." She is sounding very low.

"Hey you please wait here. Let me check out."

"OK, its White coloured 'Nike' sports shoes with blue strips."

Aadarsh and I look for her shoes everywhere and in every corner, but there is no clue of it. I get back to Kamana in disappointment.

"Sorry Kamana, I was unable to find them. By the way how much did they cost?"

"Rehaan, they were worth Rs. 6000." She says. My goodness I feel like a king even after buying shoes for Rs. 600. If I get shoes worth Rs. 6000, then instead of wearing them, I will prefer to keep them in a locker.

"Don't feel that low dear. I will buy you a new pair." I am an asshole as I didn't know what the hell I am saying. Even If I sell myself in the market, then also I will not have more than Rs. 6 and I am talking about Rs. 6000—love makes you blind, deaf, dumb and a brainless creature.

"Thanks for your concern, Rehaan." Kamana leaves.

I felt helpless and sad. I cannot do anything for her. I don't have money to buy a new pair of shoes for her. I can't see Kamana in a sad mood. I am ready to sell everything that belongs to me—my bicycle, my books, my cloths, everything—or if Aadarsh and Rohit also help me even then I would reach up to Rs. 1500. I am sorry Kamana your so called lover is a useless fellow.

Sometimes I get calls from girls on my landline phone but the moment my mother picks up it gets disconnected. The call is then declared as a blank call or a call for Rehaan or from a girl (may be Rehaan's girlfriend).

My phone is ringing; I am sitting next to it so I pick it up.

"Hello, is this Rehaan?" The most awaited voice knocked my eardrums. My heartbeat starts receiving power boosters.

"Yup, hi"

"Hi Rehaan, talk to Sneha." Kamana hands over the phone to Sneha.

"Hey Sneha, is that really Kamana who called me up?"

"Yes." Sneha starts laughing.

She talks about 'here-and-there things' before coming to her real business. Sneha now-a-days calls me not to ask about me, but Anand, my classmate and her boyfriend now. Sneha knows my weakness for Kamana and exploited it the full. I can see the future of a bright manager in Sneha. Kamana started talking to me although only hi-hello, but I am happy with it.

After two or three calls in a week from Sneha, with Hi-Hello-Bye of Kamana on my landline, 'My Brain Department' calls an emergency meeting of all my spare parts to discuss the issue in detail. After considering the serious nature of the issue, 'My Brain Department' passed a special ordinance.

"Papa, I need a mobile phone." I requested my father.

"What? Give me a relevant reason why a school boy of 11th class needs a mobile phone?"

I know that the poor clerks of my brain department can't generate even one single relevant reason through it's over costing 'Research and Development Department'. So they prefer their own way. With couple of irrelevant reasons, a little emotional drama and a half-day hunger strike, I managed to get a second hand mobile phone.

Now the question is of the monthly expense on the top-ups and recharge coupons, this further calls for a strike by 'My Finance Department' due to extra pressure on my pocket money. I get Rs. 200 per month as my pocket money, and my total expenses are around Rs. 210. I manage this additional Rs. 10 by overstating the value of my textbooks. That way my pocket money and expenditure graph is evenly distributed.

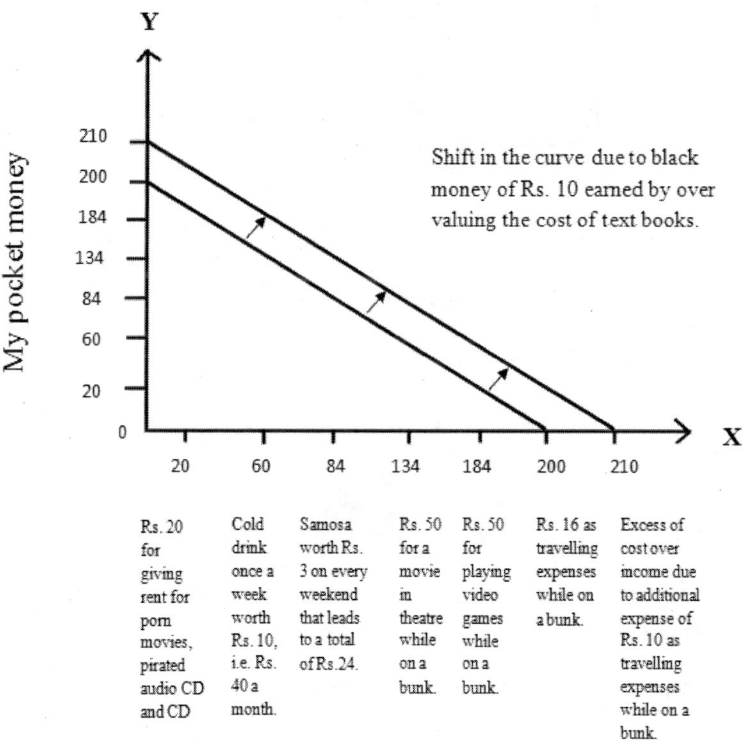

Now the problem is, how will I manage an additional expense of Rs. 100 a month for recharge. My Brain Department, my Department of Finance, Marketing and Personal Management, go for a long discussion and generate few alternatives. After comparing the effectiveness of all the alternatives one is chosen and implemented. It goes something like this.

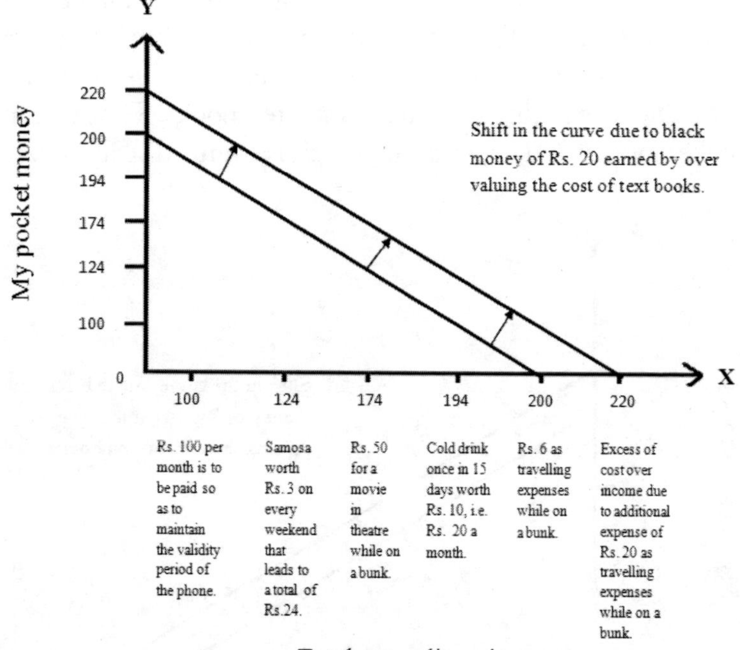

It's recess time and I am standing outside Rohit's class waiting for him.

"Rehaan, I forgot to bring my lab coat. Could you please help me out." Rohit asked.

"Ok, let me see. Today Sneha and group had their Practicals before the recess. Let me ask her."

I walked to the Medical section; Sneha is sitting with Shefali, Shivani and Kamana.

"Hey Sneha hi! I need your lab coat."

"Why, for whom....." Sneha asked. I was about to reply, but Kamana without saying anything gave her lab coat with a smile. For the next fifteen minutes before Rohit's Chemistry practical class I was roaming here and there wearing Kamana's lab coat and crossing limits of excitement.

Something strange is happening. There is a sudden change in Kamana's attitude; her Hello-Hi-Bye thing over phone, this incidence, now whenever we meet she gives me a cute smile.

"Hey, where is Rehaan? I didn't see him since morning. Is he absent? Otherwise the guy cannot survive without seeing Kamana's face." Sneha starts laughing.

"What date is today?" Kamana asks.

"16th February."

"Today is his birthday."

"How come you know?" Sneha and Shefali stare at Kamana. Kamana just smiles.

Next day I am standing in the corridor waiting for Sneha.

"Hey you know only Kamana remembered your birthday." Sneha smiles at me.

"Guess what? We were discussing about you, and Kamana said that she really likes your eyes a lot." Sneha smiles again and continues "Rehaan do me a favour; please give this gift to Anand." She hands over a small thing packed in a shinning paper and flower shaped ribbon on it.

I did not say anything. She is a clever girl and think others retarded as if they don't understand what is happening around.

Life is moving on looking at the smilling face of Kamana 2-3 times a day. With time competition also increases as two boys of Kamana's class also start liking her— one is Arun and other Kishen. Kishen even proposed to Kamana for friendship twice. Arun maintained a low profile. But there's an advantage that Kamana's name is always taken with my name. As my love for her is the *buzz* of the year. Even my class teacher knows that I like a girl whose name start with alphabet 'K'. I am the only one who interacts with Kamana's friend circle in school.

Kamana does not like me following her so I stopped that. I started visiting temple on every Monday. Actually the temple I visit is just in the neighbourhood of Sneha. In the evening Kamana goes to Sneha's house, so that way I got an official excuse to be there and also my visit to the temple made a good impression on Kamana. Lastly I am really a devotee of Lord Shiva. I pray for only one thing; you all know that. I also started fasting on every Monday to have Kamana as my life partner.

I am sitting with Rohit outside his house. After some time his friend Sohail joins us. Sohail was in our school till class 10th and used to play cricket with us. He failed in 10th class and joined another school.

Sohail a guy with a medium height, fair complexion, long hair, fond of changing styles of his beard and moustaches, looks more like a lover boy than a cricketer. His performance in the game many times suggested him to look out for fielding in girly areas than fielding on the cricket pitch. He is a non serious student of cricket. Rohit many a times boosted about love life of Sohail.

"Hey do you know Kamana?" Sohail asks.

"Why are you asking?" I questioned him.

"Actually many a times I saw her. Whenever she passes me, she gives me a smile."

"So you like Kamana?"

"Not like that. I am curious to know about her. That's it."

I told him about her. That I like Kamana and my feelings for her.

"Dude, at present I am the closest one to her, I guess. What I feel is that she does not like this love stuff. So you are wasting your time." I smiled at Sohail.

After discussing few other things, he leaves.

"Trust me he can do it. Sohail is a master in this love business. His past girlfriend record proves this fact. Your Kamana is in danger." Rohit jumps on his chair. I think nobody knows Kamana better than me. She will not even give Sohail one damn look.

Seven students of my class including me decided to change from 'Physical Education' subject to 'Fine Arts'. We have a total of five subjects amongst which one needs to be chosen from subjects like Music, Fine Arts and Physical Education.

The classes for these subjects are scheduled in such a way that all the sections have a common class for these subjects. Kamana is in Fine Arts, that's why I am the leader of the group. I on behalf of the whole group asked the Fine Arts teacher about our proposal, while Kamana's class was going on. The Fine Arts teacher agreed and asked us to get a permission letter from the Principal.

I am standing near canteen waiting for Rohit to come with burgers. I turned back and Kamana is standing in front of me.

"Hi Rehaan, I was looking for you." Kamana smiles at me.

Man this is it, Kamana is all mine. She has realised how much I love her. This is my girl and this is my day. I love you Kamana.

"Hi, what happened?"

I know what happened—Kamana has realised my depth of love for her. Common Kamana you can hug me, but please don't cry, I can't see tears in your eyes.

"I want to tell you......" Kamana stops and looks into my eyes. My dream is about to come true. She continues "I want that you should not take Fine Arts."

"What?" I am surprised. Suddenly I get an email from my poor fate, it goes like this 'Asshole, ha ha ha ha, you and your day dreaming sucks.' I replied it by raising my middle finger to my fate. After a while I realised Kamana is talking to me so I signed off from my bad luck email account and started listening to Kamana.

"I mean Rehaan it's too late, dear. After a month we will be having our final exams for class 11th and then Board classes next year. Fine Arts as a subject is not so easy." I forget everything in Kamana's presence—thanks to my subconscious mind I just said 'OK' after some time.

Meantime—Rohit came with the burger.

"That's it; I just want to say this. Take care. See you soon." Kamana smiles at me and leaves.

I kept on waving my hand till Rohit places a burger on it.

"I think she has started liking you." Rohit says.

"I guess so; I knew that one day my love for her will compel her heart to beat only for me. By the way, how is Nandini?"

Rohit just smiled. The moment the poor chap started revealing his 'snail-speed love story', the bell rang.

In the evening my cousin brother calls me to pick him up from Delhi bypass. That is also the time of Kamana's Biology tuition class. Her tuition class is on my way home so we crossed each other at around 5:10. She gave me a strange look.

After about an hour I again went to drop my cousin to his house. On the way back Kamana is also going back to her home. She stops her scooter in front of me.

"You will not correct yourself, right? You cannot leave your 'Road-Side Romeo Behaviour' of chasing girls. I started talking to you, so you thought you can convince me for you. Have you seen your face in the mirror, you joker. Yes, that's what you are—a joker. Now get lost and never try to talk to me." Kamana shouts at me. She took me in a wrong way—It was just a coincidence that we met twice that day.

"But I..." I tried to say something but she left saying 'get lost'.

I tried talking to her many times after that, but she never listened to me. I also noticed change in the behaviour of Sneha. My emerging graph of love story got a sudden down movement due to misunderstanding.

With a 'no scope' love story of Aadarsh & Aarti and a falling graph of my own friendship with Kamana, life is just moving on. But, there are buds like Manas and Rohit, who have started blooming in the spring season of love.

12

Redefining *Fattuness*, Rohit's 6 Consecutive Attempts and Not a Bad Start

"Rehaan, wake up." Manas shakes me up in the afternoon.

"Hmm, what happened?" I ask half-asleep.

"Its urgent. Get up you idiot" Manas snatches my blanket.

I am yawning like hell and waiting for this 5 feet creature to speak up something worth 'urgent'.

"I am in love and this time I am serious. Her name is Sheena." Manas starts moving here and there.

I again fall asleep.

"Hey you, I am serious." Manas shakes me again.

"Yeah, OK I trust you. Now what do you want from me?" I opened my eyes half-heartedly.

"She is on my tuition class. Many a times she smiled at me. Sometimes, I thought my leg is playing with hers under the table, but unfortunately that was the table leg. Yesterday I gave her my pen for 5 minutes and today that pen is in the showcase of my drawing room. She is very sexy and I am in love with her."

Manas crosses the limits of excitement. This is the 4th time that he is in such a kind of love. Couple of months and his love story will again start taking the auditions of a new heroine.

"Whatever? What do you want now?" I asked putting a finger in my left ear.

"I will propose her after half an hour and you are coming with me. You just be with me, rest I will handle."

"All right" I replied. We leave for Manas's new tragic end. It will be unique, that's my promise.

"Shit man! Look there she is in pink dress." Manas points to a group.

"That monkey faced girl." I laughed.

"Shut up and do me a favour. Just make her come to the main park of Sector 1, rest I will manage." These are his pet lines that I have already heard many times before.

"Hey Sheena, recognise me? I was with you in Mathematics tuition way back in 9th class." Her other friends are stunned by this unwanted surprise entry.

"Rehaan, yup how are you? Didn't see you around for a long time. Where were you?" Sheena shakes hand with me.

"Just like that. Hey, by the way, you know Manas?"

"Yeah, he is in my tuition class. What happened?"

"He wants to discuss something important."

She starts looking at her friends.

"Ok, where is he?"

"Meet him in the main park, Sector 1 in 10 minutes."

Manas is flying high in the sky, I somehow managed to make him land on earth, as we have to be in the main park in 7 minutes—three minutes were already wasted in the procedure of making Manas's Space Shuttle land on Earth.

Manas is the first person I have ever seen, who is going to propose a girl wearing his nightgown and bathroom sleepers, uncombed hair and I bet if he had even brushed his teeth. He is carrying a rough register of his tuition class in his hand; according to him he wants her to love him for his simplicity. Simplicity I can understand but no girl wants a *Junglee* as her boyfriend. We are going on our 11 number bus (on foot). Any way we somehow reached the main park in time. She is already waiting and smiles at us.

"Ok bro, best of luck, go for her."

I didn't get any response from him. He is standing still without moving a single damn part of his body, as if some 'bookish cruel black magician lady' has made him a statue.

"Holy shit, I can't do it. Dude, do me one more favour. Please ask her if she would be my friend. Everything else I will handle."

Please somebody over here, tell me what this 'else' means if I propose to her on his behalf.

Manas is standing in his old statue style while displaying his rough register, as if doing advertisement of that brand.

"Hey Sheena, actually Manas wants to be a friend of yours." Manas doesn't even look up for once and kept his head down. Sheena starts laughing aloud.

"Hey tell me your reply. He just wants to be your friend."

"No." She continues her laughing and leaves.

"Shit, shit, bull shit!" Manas starts shouting, kicking and punching trees like a mad monkey with slogans of 'shit'.

Manas is somebody who has great knowledge of shit, kinds of shit and how one shit differs from the other kind. He is the one who can easily explain about the evolution of shit and I know if the situation remains the same, then in the near future Manas will definitely write a book on shit, which will be nothing but shit. If you are one of his friends, then sometimes you will also think yourself nothing but shit.

After struggling with final exams of 11th class, today the result is announced and displayed on the notice board. This time I scored my usual 65%. Rohit and Manas scored around 85%, Aadarsh passed with mere passing marks around 35 in each subject that too thanks to grace marking. Prashant also passed with average marks, Vicky failed in one subject.

Then I got the biggest surprise of the year, Kamana and Sneha failed in Physics. Buzz is going around that the so called intelligent 90% scoring beauty is no more interested in studies. She is happy in making boys crazy after her. All those who failed in one or two subjects have to give a re-appear exam before entering class 12th. Imagine Kamana and Sneha sitting with students who were not able to score even the passing marks.

Today we played cricket match with Jat College team. Fortunately our team lost the match by scoring just 7 runs and that too against a target of 63 runs. I came back home very dejected and frustrated. The moment I entered the house my phone started ringing.

"Mom, pick up the phone." I shouted.

"Nope, it's yours. Rohit has already called you 4 times."

I pick up the phone and it's Rohit.

"She is cute, she is beautiful, I love Nandini and I mean it. I am coming in half an hour to pick you up. I am going to propose her."

"Hmm......" I cut the phone and started changing my clothes.

Day 1

Rohit is always on time; today he came five minutes before. He is dressed up as if he is going for any marriage party.

"The way she talks, the way she walks, I really like it. Day and night I just do two things, one study hard and the other, to think about her. She talks to everyone, but me. I want to be with her and be a part of her life."

"Alright, don't worry. I am always with you, buddy. I know Nandini; I think I told you before that she calls me her brother. We met in 6th class."

"So what's the point?" Rohit asks

"This is the right time when her old brother comes back to her life to make her realise that he is the only one in this world who cares about her."

We went to Nandini's tuition class. After sometime Nandini comes out.

"Rohit, what are you waiting for? Go and talk to her." I said. Rohit is lost and so is his scooter key. When he came to his senses, he realised that he is here for something called proposing Nandini for friendship but she is already gone.

Day 2

Rohit is again at the right time. This time I drove his scooter. We are standing at the same place waiting for Nandini.

Nandini leaves her tuition after fifteen minutes. While she was passing us I kicked the scooter, but Rohit stoped me.

"No, she is with her friends. I can't talk to her. Let's go home. We will try tomorrow."

"Not we. You will try tomorrow alone." I replied.

Day 3

Rohit is wearing a shining red shirt and a pair of black jeans, dressed up ideally for proposing a girl.

"Trust me, today I will propose her, definitely." Rohit says in a deep voice.

I am driving his scooter suddenly I saw a Police Check-Post. Neither I have a driving license nor is the scooter carrying its papers. The police man raises hand in front of us, which means we have to stop here for checking. I slowed down the speed but when we reached there I suddenly accelerated, in an attempt to run away. One police man throws his bamboo stick which smashes at Rohit's back.

We are waiting for Nandini. Rohit is in two minds whether to abuse the policeman or me. He is constantly rubbing his back. After a while Nandini leaves her tuition. I start the scooter. Rohit stops me in pain.

"Ouch! its hurting. I can't talk to her like this. We will come tomorrow." Rohit says.

I pat his back. He starts jumping and shouting in pain, with few abuses of his own.

Day 4

If anybody is interested in time management's practical lessons, contact Mr. Rohit. This time his dressing sense is telling a different story. I am sure this would be his excuse today of not talking to Nandini.

Again, we are standing at the same place, without any achievement. Yeah, Rohit somehow develops some friendly relations with street dogs, so that if ever he starts chasing Nandini, then these dogs won't accompany him. One fat aunty also developed few misconceptions, that we are interested in her 25 year old daughter, who is a carbon copy of a vamp of some cheap English horror movie.

At last Nandini comes; I start the scooter and started following her.

"I will drive this scooter at her right side so you can talk to her." I started accelerating the scooter.

"Not now, it's not the right place." Rohit replies

Mr. Rohit's right place did not come until she reached her home.

"Damn, she reached home. Don't worry we will come tomorrow." Rohit said.

"Not we, you alone will come tomorrow."

Day 5

Today I went to my school for depositing fees for 12th class. After school Rohit and I came to his house. Rohit went to the washroom, and I was sitting alone in his room.

"What is happening with my son? I mean is there any girl in his life." His mother asks me.

"I don't think so aunty. He is serious only for one thing and that is his studies and his result is the proof."

"But his lifestyle is telling a different story. He daily dresses up in his party wear, is in front of the mirror for an hour and his rising expenditure on costly deodorants are pointing towards the same thing. Everyday he takes Rs. 50 for refuelling his scooter. Day and night he keeps on listening sad songs. Son, I am old enough to understand what's going on. You can tell me her name; I will not reveal this to him."

I am cursing Rohit; what the hell is he doing in the washroom for so long?

"Aunty trust me, there is nothing like that."

Thank God at last Rohit comes in.

"Let's go. Mom, please give me Rs. 50." Rohit says.

I was about to burst out laughing but controlled myself somehow.

Today Nandini is having her tuition from 1 p.m. to 2 p.m. i.e. earlier then the regular timings. Rohit bribes the gate keeper of Nandini's tuition class by giving him small treats for information about Nandini and her tuition timings.

"I am not going with you." I declared.

"Why, what happened?"

"It's of no use. Today also you will repeat the same lines 'We will try tomorrow'"

"No. Trust me. Today I will not disappoint you. I promise you, I will talk to her."

"Are you Sure?"

"Yes, with each and every word."

At last we start following Nandini again.

"Hey, ask her to stop somewhere." Rohit says.

I speed up the scooter along her side. After a while she notices us.

"Hey, Hi Rehaan"

"Hi, how are you?"

"I am good."

"Actually we want to talk to you. I wonder if you can join us in some restaurant."

"No, actually I have to reach home early today."

"OK, somewhere nearby......?"

"Yup" She stops her scooter around a corner. I also park the scooter along side.

Suddenly Rohit whispers. "I can't do that dude. Do something. I can't talk to her."

"*Saley fattu* (bloody looser)." I replied. Now the problem is what the fucking important business should I discuss with her.

"Actually...I want to say....yeah, do you know Kamana?" I asked her.

"Yes, she is my friend, but not a close one."

"I just want to tell you that, I like Kamana."

"So, this is your important thing?"

"You once called me your bro, so I think you should know whom I like."

She gave me a weird look.

"OK. I am getting late. We will talk later."

Nandini leaves.

After that I kick hard on Rohit's ass. He starts jumping out of pain.

Day 6

My phone is ringing. Even before picking it up, I already know the name of the caller.

"Dude you have two option—either fuck me or come with me—as today I will for sure propose Nandini for friendship."

"I will prefer the first option. Anyway it's of no use going with you, as you will fuck everything at the right time."

"For the sake of our friendship please trust me for the last time. I am damn serious about my stand; I can do anything for her." Rohit says in a patriotic tone.

"This is the last time I am coming. If you won't take out your shit this time then don't expect me tomorrow."

This time we preferred to talk to her in school. In recess period Rohit and I are looking for Nandini. She is in the basketball court standing with her friends.

"Kick my ass. Push me in the running river. Put my ass on hot iron or do anything you want, but I can't do this. Forget it, let's go." Rohit sounded very sad.

"Fuck you! Come with me."

"Hey! Hi Nandini. May I have a couple of minutes with you, if you don't mind."

"Hmm, what happened?"

"Meet my friend Rohit. He is in your class."

"Hi, sorry but I neither know you personally nor recognise your face." Nandini smiles at Rohit.

"Hi, actually I want to talk to you." Rohit says

"Yeah sure"

"Nandini please be my friend."

This is the worst propose I have ever seen in the history of proposes.

"We will talk about it tomorrow." Nandini smiles.

Next day Rohit and I are roaming around Nandini's locality. After an hour she leaves for her tuition. I hand over the scooter to Rohit and signal him to go alone. He followed her for few minutes to know her reply.

"No, we can't be friends. I hardly know you." She replies.

My brother really felt bad. He is a great son; a great friend, a great brother and a great person so he deserves happiness. He is my friend for whom I can even risk my life.

I started talking to Nandini regularly and slowly-slowly tried to become a part of her life. Many a times I discussed Rohit in my talks. Sometimes I tried to make her realise that there is nothing bad in making somebody her friend. I started coming close to her and somehow succeeded in changing her views about Rohit.

"No Rehaan. My parents send me to school to study not to indulge in such activities."

"He just wants to be a friend of yours. Come on Nandini, grow up. Why you girls are only modern by clothes."

"OK, we can be friends. Happy."

I told Rohit the good news when we were going to his house after school.

"I talked to her, now it's all your game to play. And yeah propose her officially on your own."

"I can't say even thanks to you as there is no formality between us. I never asked you to do this for me, but you did it on your own. I had given up, but it's you who brought a smile to me all over again. Don't worry, tomorrow is Christmas, I will propose her for sure."

"Hi Nandini, may I talk to you?" Rohit asks

"Not here. Let's go somewhere else."

Nandini and Rohit move to a lonely street.

"Hi, how is your preparation going on for board exams?"

"Just fine. Rehaan told me about you. You are quiet intelligent." Nandini smiles at him.

"Not that much. Just........ Nandini, I want to say something."

"Yeah."

"Would you like to be my friend?" Rohit raised his right hand.

"Sure, but just friends." Nandini shakes hands with Rohit.

Rohit comes to me jumping out of joy. For him it's the happiest moment of his life. After that Rohit developed a new retarded habit of his own kind. He stopped shaking hands with people with his right hand, but uses left hand instead. According to him he still feels the warmth of Nandini's touch and doesn't want to lose that feeling.

I don't know what I will become in future, but if one day I somehow become a Psychologist then one thing is for sure, Rohit and Manas will be the biggest challenge in studying behaviour patterns of human beings for me. These two are the most complex creatures I have ever seen and really sucks, even more than Aadarsh.

13

Rohit's Pain, Aadarsh's Right Time and the Three Sad Monkeys

"Sorry Rohit, we cannot be friends anymore." Nandini declares.

"What? Why? I mean what's wrong? Have I done something?" Rohit asks in panic.

"No it's not you, it's me. People talk rubbish about us and I don't like that. I told you before, I am not interested in this relationship stuff. I hate dirty politics going on about me. So it's better that you forget everything."

"What's my mistake?"

"I told you not to disclose about our friendship to anyone, and now the whole class is talking about us."

"I just talked with Varun, who is a good friend of mine. He promised that he will not tell this to anybody. What's my fault if Varun betrayed me? What's wrong to be a friend of somebody? We are just good friends."

"I don't know? I know only one thing that we are not friends any more." Nandini comes out of the classroom.

That day changed Rohit. The smiling face, which made others laugh on his crazy doings, was lost in silence. He just keeps on studying continuously without any sleep and listening to sad songs . He always keeps a page of Nandini's handwriting with him; spends hours looking at it. Sometimes he suddenly starts looking at his right hand, which was once held by Nandini. He never complained to anybody about his state of sorrow.

One day Rohit and I were walking in the University.

"What's wrong with you, buddy?"

He doesn't reply.

"No, just tell me, for how long will you behave like this."

Still no reply.

"Are your friends and parents nothing for you. The only one you care about is that fucking Nandini?"

The moment I said this, two drops of tears fell down.

"Rohit what happened brother?" I hold his hand.

Rohit starts crying. For the first time, I saw such a bold person crying. He had seen many bad days in his life, but never broke down like this. Today for just a girl he is crying. May be this is what people call 'pain of love'.

Rohit is wearing a light blue shirt with white checks on it. He sits on the footpath and starts wiping out his tears with the sleeves of his shirt. I really feel pity about my brother's condition.

"Don't cry my brother. I will fuck everybody for you, you just stop crying, please."

Then Rohit reveals his pain—called Nandini.

"I noticed her first when I was with my classmates standing at a samosa shop. She smiled at Surya, one of my classmate. For the first time I felt that why she doesn't smile at me. I used to see her every day. She gradually touched my heart deeper and deeper. Every day her smile made me more and more to fall in love with her. On 1st November Papa got promoted and my parents had to shift to Chandigarh, so I thought I won't have her anymore unless I told her how I feel for her.

I got my hair straight and bought a new cap for the big day. For the 1st attempt I tried for six days, but could not make it. Then thanks to you finally I proposed her, "We will talk about it tomorrow" She replied and smiled in an astonishing way.

Her smile raised my expectations for some positive response from her the next day. That night was strange—I was happy for expecting a 'Yes' from her and also natural insecurity was surrounding me due to uncertainty regarding the future. That was the last night of my life when I was happy from inside—no pain, no regret, nothing. I had no idea where I would land in quest of love in the near future.

Then comes the big day. She crossed me on her scooter wearing sun glasses, gave me a strange expression and I got her answer. She said 'No'. I felt pain (little pain) that I found too much to handle, ignorant of the fact that this is what the future has in store for me.

I used to say lots of wisdom words just to make my hope and spirit alive. What the hell can happen if I don't talk to her. I was shy talking to her. Even a simple smile from her was enough for making my week spectacular.

Then, you went to ask about her decision and she said "Are you really my brother?" I created problems for you without any reason. It was me who lacked guts and you kept on arguing with her from my side.

Around Christmas thanks to you she became my friend and we shook hands. That day I was extremely happy but she said "We are just friends." which sounded a little harsh to my heart. Now atleast I had something to smile, but that smiling heart was shattered 2-3 days later, when she broke with me.

Now I just keep on listening to sad songs. I kept beard and moustaches for 2-3 months because I don't find any pleasure in looking smart. I was caught by the Principal for keeping long beard and hair in my last pre-board exam and was made to give the exam in the library. All sad things went along my broken heart and I don't understand why me? As I am living with my relatives, I feel alone without my Mom. I really love Nandini. I am not able to divert my mind from thinking about her for a single second, even. Thoughts of not getting her are worst then the pain of dying. And every day I am living with that." Rohit said sobbing.

"Don't worry brother, I will do something."

"No, please. You are already upset with Kamana. I don't want to increase your problems."

"Kamana is a different issue. I never ask from you anything, but today I want something from you."

"What?"

"Never ever cry again, please. I know you love Nandini and your love is real. Still there are some people other then Nandini, for whom you are the best part of their life. For me and Aadarsh you are our reason to be happy. Don't let us down ever again like this."

"I don't know whether I will get Nandini or not but I have a deep faith in one thing that 'Honesty Pays.'" Rohit says and washes his face in a nearby water tank.

I have never seen a guy like Rohit. He is the person who lives for his friends. Everybody was against Aadarsh in the case of Aarti. Even I sometimes felt that Aarti is far beyond the reach of Aadarsh. Rohit is always on his side. It's not the question whether Aarti will ever say yes to Aadarsh but it's about standing with somebody. Rohit always says one thing that honesty pays, no matter how much or up to what extent, but it does pay. If you are honest for your love, one day you will for sure get it.

Rohit made me understand the true meaning of friendship. I remember, the day before my birthday, I was feeling very low thinking about Kamana.

"Rohit do something, take help of anybody, and do whatever you can, but please……. I can't live without Kamana." My voice was trembling, I was about to fall on the floor but managed myself somehow.

The next day Rohit takes Aadarsh with him and went to Kamana without telling me.

"Kamana I want to talk to you. It's something important. It will take just two minutes." Rohit said while overtaking Kamana's scooty.

Kamana gave him 'not interested reaction.'

Suddenly a pothole comes on their way. Aadarsh did not notice and water splashed on Kamana's face as their scooter passesd over it.

Kamana gave them an angry reaction and left without listening to them. Rohit approached her because he wanted to give a birthday surprise to me.

They came back and told me the whole story.

"I spoiled your birthday." Rohit said.

"No my brothers you made my birthday the most special day." I hug them both tightly. Where will I find such caring friends.

Aadarsh is neither doing anything about Aarti nor for his falling graph of scores in studies. Day after day, month after month and year after year are passing and we are desperately waiting for Aadarsh's right time. Thanks to the 14 February at last comes the right time of Aadarsh.

On 13th February, Aadarsh saw a movie and felt a desperate urge from inside to talk to Aarti. He was missing her like never before. That evening he went for shopping to the Spyker Showroom. He bought his favourite white coloured shirt and blue denim jeans from there—Man for the first time he fucks 2000 rupees on his shopping which he had saved for the last 7-8 months to buy a mobile phone.

On 14th February, I, Rohit and Aadarsh are roaming around our school waiting for Aarti. Suddenly darkness surrounds my eyes and for a flick of a second I see Aarti coming on her scooter wearing black sweater, black jeans and wearing goggles. I told this to Aadarsh and Rohit. To our great surprise she comes in ditto same black dress, as I had visualised a few minutes earlier. Aadarsh felt really happy about that, he thought it as a good omen.

"Today is your right time. If you don't talk to her now, you will never be able to do it."

"School days are about to be over and you never know in which corner of the world she will be. So go for it." I pumped him.

"I know bro, today is the right time for which I waited for years. All things in the universe are on my side. Omen is also good and signalling to the same."

Aadarsh started the scooter and went alone to talk to Aarti.

"Hi Aarti. May I have a couple of minutes with you."

Aarti parks her scooter in front of our school.

"Aarti, my name is Aadarsh, I think you know me. I want to say that I like you. I saw you in 10th class the first time and after that am thinking about you all the time. I see your face whenever I close my eyes. I can't live like that; I am not able to concentrate on my studies. Many a times, I tried to talk to you but was not able to. I am not saying that you should love me also, but I want to be a part of your life at least as a friend."

Aarti starts yawning artificially, indicating that she is not interested.

"OK. Finished with your pathetic crap. Have you ever seen your face in the mirror? You want to be a friend of mine, now listen you ugly stuff, my name is Aarti and I have got some standard. Now go and look for some girl of your level. Buzz off." Aarti says and leaves.

I and Rohit are praying for Aadarsh. Aadarsh arrived with a sad face. Seeing his condition we got Aarti's reply, but our interpretation is just a tip of the iceberg of what that five feet bitch said to my brother. Rohit kicks the scooter and I sit at his back. We wanted to teach Aarti a lesson but Aadarsh held our hands.

"It was me, not her. I was in love with her."

We three then went to a nearby park. Aadarsh takes out from his purse a slip on which he had written with pencil:

"I want to tell you something,
that I really like you from my heart.
I can't live without you.
Please try to understand my feelings.
Whenever I see you,

I am not able to concentrate on my studies.
So don't say 'no', please.
I think you also like me and like to talk to me
And I believe in that line."

Aadarsh for the first time revealed his pain called Aarti.

"I had written this after seeing her for the first time in tenth class. Thereafter I always keep this slip with me. It is my good luck charm. You were right, Rehaan, I will never get her. It's not that I tried escaping from the fact that she is better looking than me. I know what people think about me. But I always thought that true love is greater than mere good looks. I am just an ordinary person from a middle class family who likes a girl truly from his heart. I told her only those things which I felt for her. I know I was wrong in going after her but I feel like dying, if any day I don't see her. I don't know what will happen to me next, but I know one thing that I really love Aarti." Aadarsh tore the slip.

My love story is full of twists. Kamana never listened to my explanation about her misunderstandings; neither I stopped trying to explain her my point. She has now even started abusing me.

One day Rohit, I and Aadarsh were standing in front of Vadillal, eating ice-cream. Kamana, Sneha, Shivani and Shefali were sitting in a restaurant in front of the ice cream parlour. They were clearly visible from the glass wall of the restaurant.

After sometimes they start talking to a waiter in a way as if they were fighting for the bill.

"I think they are in some problem. Let me check." I said.

"Wait." Rohit handed over his purse to me, Aadarsh also gave Rs. 300 to me.

Kamana and her friends leave the restaurant in an angry gesture.

"Any problem Kamana? Do you need any money?" I asked Kamana in a concerned way.

"No, no problem. Instead you are a problem, so you please go." Kamana replied.

I came back to Aadarsh and Rohit.

"Look at this sister-fucker; he will give money to us? Look at his clothes; I wonder if he can even afford proper meals for two times, asshole."

Kamana abused me in front of her friends, but as I had already left so I was not able to hear what she said.

According to an old saying 'When one door is closed, God opens another'.

A few days after my birthday, Kamana is out with Sneha, Shivani and Shefali. I had bought a friendship band for Kamana out of my saved pocket money of three months.

"Hi Kamana."

"What do you want now?" Kamana asks me arrogantly.

"It's our last year; nobody knows which college we will be next year. So let us forget what happened before, and end all this with friendship." I forwarded the friendship band to her.

She took my friendship band. I raised my hand for a handshake.

"So, Kamana can we be friends now?"

"No, your cheap friendship band is not good. Not interested." Kamana gave it back to me.

Kamana and Shivani then left the place. Sneha is also not interested in talking to me. Suddenly a fuse bulb in my brain glew up. I went to Shefali.

"I bought this friendship band to make a new friend. Would you like to be my friend, Shefali?"

Shefali is surprised with my unexpected proposal. She smiles.

"OK, just friends, right."

Shefali takes my friendship band.

My friends suggested me Shefali as Kamana's substitute, but for me the meaning of love is Kamana. I don't know what will happen to my love story but for now my each and every breath comes out with the pain of not having Kamana.

I gave my mobile phone to Aadarsh as I feel no need of it, now.

With Rohit's 'Honesty Pays', Aadarsh's 'I Really Love Aarti' and my 'Meaning of Love Is Kamana', we are going through a similar sad phase of our life. Our days are passing in praying for any miracle for success in our love lives, but for now we are 'Three Sad Monkeys.'

14

Love Hurts, Craziest Thing and the Hidden Talent

Anand dumped Sneha just because her face turned ugly with pimples. Her breakup with Anand broke Sneha fully. She locked herself in her room weeping all day lying on the floor. She stopped talking to everybody, and many a times would start abusing without any reason. I tried to talk to her but she doesn't like my face even, because seeing my case with Kamana, she thinks me to be a sensitive brainless emotional fool.

Seeing her condition, Sneha's friends and batchmates advice her to contact a Psychiatrist for her current state. What I think is that she really loved Anand and needs some time to forget him.

To my surprise there is no reaction of Anand on Sneha's current state. He never talked to her even after numerous requests from Kamana. Rather Mr. Anand is now going around with a girl of my class named 'Sveena', the boobless girl or in our jargon 'Flat TV'.

But my concern is not Sneha or my upcoming board exams but Kamana. I started feeling like a looser. My school days are about to become history and regarding Kamana, I am feeling helpless. Her tuition classes are also about to finish. Aadarsh and Rohit inform me whenever they see her around, but by the time I reach there she was already gone.

I am sitting with Aadarsh and Rohit, and feeling very low.

"What happened dude? Why our hero is looking sad today?" Rohit asked.

"I am missing Kamana. I am dying to see her."

Rohit looked at Aadarsh, smiled and whispered the plan to me.

"This is our plan."

For the last three days, Rohit and I are waiting for Kamana near Sneha's house. I am on my scooter and Rohit is sitting behind me with something which Aadarsh calls camera. Will this 'First Camera of Human Race' really work, I doubt. We have no option, as this is the only thing called camera with us. Prashant and Aadarsh are on a different scooter. They will inform us about Kamana's movement and if there is any police on the way.

"Hello, Aadarsh here. Kamana is coming towards you." Aadarsh calls me on Vicky's phone, which I borrowed from him for today. I kicked the scooter and Rohit put camera in on mode. Both of us are ready.

"Rehaan, let me know when Kamana will be in shooting range." Rohit hides the camera under his shirt, so that they don't get any clue of our crazy intentions.

Kamana and Sneha are on one scooter and Shivani is on another. Kamana and Sneha looked at me and start laughing.

"Rohit go for it." Rohit instantly turned back while sitting on scooter and took their 1st photo. I put the scooter in first gear.

Their laughing faces suddenly stuck into never expected situation. Sneha hid her face—let her do that—who wants to take a photo of her pimples. Kamana is driving so the poor girl was not able to do anything. Rohit clicked two-three times.

"You scoundrels, bastards, rascals @#$%#@%&!!!!" blah-blah-blah! Shivani kept on shouting and Rohit intentionally took a photo of her angry face. My Kamana prefers to get along silently with her ongoing photo shoot. Sneha kept on hiding her face—girls and their misconceptions.

Suddenly my mobile phone rings. I pick up the phone.

"Hey, there is a Police Check-post a few metres ahead, so wind up your business and escape." said Adarsh.

I turned the handle of the scoter towards the next Sector and we vanish in the streets.

In the evening me, Rohit and Aadarsh are standing at Balaji Samosa Corner. Sneha and Shivani came there, as they knew that we stand here every day.

"Rehaan, how dare you do that with us?" Sneha shouted at me. "What do you think of yourself? You think you can do anything and we won't react."

"Enough." Rohit shouted so loud that even his common friends, street dogs, ran away from there.

"What do you think of yourself, you 'Queen of Pimples'? Rehaan is silent because he respects you. He is my brother. I will take Kamana's photos today, tomorrow and whenever I feel like. I can do anything for my brother's happiness. Get lost from here." They left without saying a single word.

We three burst out laughing. I had never seen such a unique expression on Rohit's face before.

After a few days Aadarsh and Rohit gave me a gift, which is nicely packed in red paper and pink ribbon tied over it. I opened it, and there were 5 photos of Kamana. The photos are so nicely taken that I declared Rohit to be the next big face in the photography world. It revealed his 'Hidden Talent'. In one photo Sneha is looking C#^t!@ with pimples and unmanaged curly hair and in other one Shivani is looking like a Dracula or I can say a fat Dracula.

I selected the best photo of Kamana, got it laminated and always keep it in my purse. Whenever I miss her, I just look at it till my eyes are satisfied. But they are never satisfied.

15

THE NEVER ENDING DAY, TRUTH REVEALED AND THAT DEADLY NIGHT

Fortunately our last board exam is of English, which is the only common subject among all streams. Kamana and Nandini are sitting in Rohit's room due to shuffling of roll numbers and sitting plan.

I don't know when I would be able to see Kamana again, so I decided to talk to her and wish her goodbye. After the exam Aadarsh also arrived at our Exam Centre on his scooter. Aadarsh, Rohit and I are sitting outside the Centre discussing exam and waiting for Nandini and Kamana.

"Nandini, can we talk today? I am leaving this city, and I have to give you some of your things." Rohit asked Nandini.

"OK, let me see. I will call Rehaan and inform." Nandini's unique way of saying 'not interested'.

"Rehaan doesn't have a mobile, now. This is Aadarsh's mobile number. I will be with him." Rohit gave Aadarsh's mobile number to her.

I also talked to her for sometime, although I was not interested. It's not that she is not a good girl, but the moment I think about Rohit I feel bad.

"Hey look over there. Aarti is standing, under that Oak tree." I point her out.

"Yeah, she is looking cute, 'my Noni.'" Aadarsh said in a tone which lost its enthusiasm on 14th February.

Kamana also comes out of the examination centre with her friends. I had bought a box of chocolates and a yellow rose for her before the exam, which I had kept in Rohit's scooter.

I saw Kamana, Sneha, Shivani and Shefali and start following them. For the first time I am feeling lack of guts to talk to her.

After ten minutes, Kamana stops her scooter waved her hand as if she is asking me to come.

"What do you want now? Why don't you get lost and join your friends." Kamana shouted in anger.

"Kamana this is the last time. I just want to say good bye to you." I took out the chocolates and rose.

"Leave me alone you cheap roadside Romeo and take away this bullshit, which you carry in your hand. Get lost." Kamana shouted again.

I kept the chocolate box and yellow rose back in the scooter and turned in the opposite direction. I heard Kamana on my way back. "Sneha, he is the biggest idiot and emotional fool I have ever seen in my life. I will never say yes to such an asshole."

They both started laughing loudly.

After a while I called Aadarsh on his mobile. Rohit and Aadarsh came in 20 minutes. Rohit is carrying his two big bags of clothes and books. He is waiting for Nandini's call. Fortunately after about half an hour Nandini called on Aadarsh's cell phone.

Rohit took his scooter and went for meeting her.

"Hi Nandini."

"So you are going today. This is our last meeting, so best of luck for your future."

Rohit had feelings which he wanted to share with Nandini, but her line 'this is our last meeting' changed his decision.

"I have some things with me, which belongs to you." Rohit took out Nandini's passport size photo (Damn! Only I know how I got her photo for him) and a page of her writing from her register.

"You consider this our last meeting. Still anytime in your life, if you find yourself in some problem, please remember I am there for you. Take care." Rohit shakes hand with her.

Rohit comes back.

"Let's go." He said.

I sit on the backseat of his scooter.

"So what did she say?" I asked.

"Nothing, just." Suddenly a drop of tear stuck my face coming from Rohit's territory.

"Rohit are you crying?"

"No buddy, I am just sad. Sad for the way things are going around me." Rohit told me Nandini's 'Alvida' (bye forever) story.

"She said and you believed her. Dude this is life and it fucks the way it wants. Nobody can predict their tomorrow." I said. Meanwhile another missile of tear, from neighbour country 'Rohit' landed on my 'district nose'.

"It's not about Nandini. You and Aadarsh are my real treasure. I will feel very alone in Chandigarh."

"You are not going to America; Chandigarh is just 5 hours drive from Rohtak."

After sometime we reached the bus stand.

The bus for Chandigarh was ready for departure. Aadarsh bought the ticket and I helped Rohit in putting his luggage into the bus. It's time for Rohit to leave; We three hugged each other.

"We are fucking Tripod and we will remain best friends, always." I said.

"You are lucky bro. You are going to Chandigarh, which I heard is full of '*Totte*' (a term used for very beautiful girls); find some for us also." Aadarsh said.

"For me there is only one *Totta*, and that's Nandini, I am happy with just her sweet memories." Rohit steped into the bus.

After leaving Rohit's scooter at his uncle's house, me and Adarsh head towards my house.

"Hey I don't feel like going home, drop me at the lake side."

I wanted to be alone for some time. I went to the same platform on which I proposed Kamana in my dream of 'Mr. Pandey and all'. I sit on the floor, took out her photo and am thinking about the moments I shared with her—I remember her style of saying 'get lost' to me—a smile comes to my face. But today her words really hurt me. It started drizzling. Suddenly a girl's hand touched my shoulders.

"It's of no use, Rehaan. Kamana don't deserve you." Shefali said.

I am completely surprised by Shefali's never expected presence over here.

"Aadarsh told me that you are sitting here alone and I know the reason. You know Rehaan, I felt really bad when Kamana reacted so badly with you, today." Shefali sat next to me. One thing I hate the most—people making me an instrument of sympathy.

"It's not Kamana's fault, Shefali. It's me who loved her and wants her in my life." Repeating Aadarsh's lines, using the wonderful talent of mine i.e. making a copyright on others dialogues.

"If somebody likes you that doesn't mean you will treat him like bullshit." Shefali said in an angered tone and looked at me waiting for my response.

"But, still......" I am about to defend Kamana's stand but Shefali cut me in between.

"I felt bad because I know you are a good boy. I call you my friend and I mean it. Do you think that you really know Kamana?" Shefali questioned me.

"So, clear my doubts." I said in frustration.

"Kamana is now Sohail's girlfriend."

Listening that I felt like dying.

"What you know about Kamana is just nothing. Sohail and Kamana are meeting each other for quiet some time. He proposed her for love around January and she said yes." Shefali said.

I didn't know how to react and what to say? I just sit back in the worst surprise I ever had.

"Let me introduce you to the real Kamana. I never saw such a selfish, arrogant and proud girl. She loves to make fun of boys, especially you; she insults you in front of the whole class. Once she was writing the names of the boys who were after her and giving ranks to them. Do you know the rank she gave you?"

Then Shefali told me about the abusive language Kamana used for me in front of the restaurant (opposite the Vadilal ice-cream parlour).

"You know once she told Sneha 'I don't consider Rehaan even a human being.' She calls you 'a Sample' and 'a Joker'.

She considers herself superior to you in every walk of life. She used to say 'Let this asshole fall in love with me at least my *Ashique* score is increasing'. She says 'Rehaan is such a retarded emotional fool, I feel happy when I scold him.' She also commented on your financial position, 'Have you ever seen his clothes, poor guy; my servant wears better than him. Sometimes I feel like gifting him a deodorant or something. He uses some cheep hair oil and come to tuition on bicycle, right? But he always thinks himself to be a hero, trying to impress me, bloody beggar. He is so thin that sometimes I wonder if he is even eating two times food.' Kamana then laughed at you. She always hated you, and considers you inferior than herself. She also makes fun of your dream that you saw in 10th class."

"Do you want any proof? She is going to meet Sohail after sunset at about 6:00 P.M." She gave me the address.

Rainfall is getting heavier and heavier. It's the end of cold season, so I am shivering a little bit. I wanted to go to that place where Sohail and Kamana are meeting. I took an auto-rickshaw for going there.

I reached that place at around 5:55 p.m. It's a lonely place. I hide myself behind few dense bushes. It's around 6:05 and the sky is getting darker and darker with thundering clouds. I don't think they will come now, so I stood up and decided to go home. I walked a little distance, when I saw Kamana's scooter and a car parked near a group of trees. When I went closer I saw Kamana and Sohail.

Sohail is holding her and they are talking close to each other with naughty smiles in between. Sohail held Kamana's back, kissed her cheek and took his hand inside her T-shirt. He put his lips on Kamana's lips and they started smooching passionately. They hugged each other tightly while kissing for 4-5 minutes.

After some time they left from there.

I went to the same place where they were standing and sat there. I felt my heart and brain become numb, rainfall also started heavily and the time almost declared the arrival of night. I am sitting alone all wet; my shivering is increasing with passing time. Once in your life a time comes when you feel inferior to everybody in the world. All your dreams start crashing in front of your eyes. Life laughs at you and you have to start from zero all over again. You feel so down that given a chance you think that death is a wiser option.

Kamana's words are still rotating around my head and laughing upon me calling me 'a Joker', 'a Sample', 'Poor Beggar', 'not a human being even' etc. I looked at my cheap shirt. Are clothes the only thing which people care about? I touched my oily hair—A person's value is judged by whether he uses hair oil or gel. I am from a middle class family, my father worked hard even after his retirement so that he can provide me the best of education. So that in future I may have all the luxury which he was not able to get. Is love not for a middle class boy? Is living for other's happiness wrong? I never make fun of anybody on any criteria because I love God and respect his creation—the human beings. Is it bad to be good in this world? I don't have a muscular kind of body. Is having a slim body such a bad thing that you will be rejected for that?

Rohit once told me that Sohail is a Playboy, who changes girlfriend with every changing season. He is from a rich family, owns a personal car, costly mobile phone and spend lavishly. He knows how to approach and seduce girls. Is money and approach the only thing which matters? Is there no value for honesty, a true heart, and loving somebody more than anything in the world?

I stood up and started walking in heavy rainfall. My heart is feeling as if somebody has cursed me a life full of sad, horrible and the worst nightmare. The road on which I am walking, seems to be endless—there is not a single living being around. My legs are trembling out of cold and fear. It seems like the road and trees are coming to eat me up, this night is going to swallow me in a moment. I am walking in the 'Rain of Death'.

Whatever may be the fate of my life, I will never loose hope. I am not a coward like others who hurt themselves because somebody whom they loved the most broke their heart. I reached home around 11 p.m. My mother is crying, worried that something has happened to me. I made a fictitious story and went to my room. My head is bursting and I prayed continuously that this never lasting night would end. Somehow the sleep knocked my doors.

I am lying on a not so comfortable bed in a Dilapidated or ramshackle room. Cigarette smoke is all around and nothing is visible. My left hand is resting on one side of the bed with a burning cigarette and smoke rings surrounding me all over. I am constantly looking at not so clearly visible stationary aged fan, which seems like moving at its maximum. A girl is lying with me under a blanket with her face hidden under my arm. She is grabbing my vest with her hand, in which she is wearing a cute thin golden bangle. My right hand is moving back and forth on her back for making her feel comfortable. I crushed the half burned cigarette on the table nearby. I then kiss her cheeks again.

16

Chandigarh Tale, Proving My Worth and the Rise of the Evil Joker

Once upon a time there lived a boy named 'Rohit' or we can call him 'Rohit, the fool'. Rohit a very intelligent boy, but a total nerd. With a simple oily side-partition hairstyle, 0.5 numbered specs, that tells the story of the evolution of specs and incisors clearly visible 'medically termed as overbite'. He fell in love with a girl named Nandini. Nandini didn't understand his love and chose her career instead. Rohit, after his schooling left Rohtak and went to Chandigarh with tears in his eyes and hope in his mind.

'Rohit, the geek', studied hard for the Engineering Entrance Exam. One day Rohit went to McDonald and bought a burger. He then called his driver to pick him up.

The moment Rohit was about to leave, a stunningly beautiful girl holds his hand from behind. That girl was so sexy, that given a choice, I would have left thousands of Nandini for her, but as it's not my story, so let Rohit, the nerd continue with the scene.

"Hi honey, I am noticing you for quiet some time. You are very smart and I like you. What is your name, darling?" The gorgeous asked the nerd.

'Rohit, the fool', for whom even thinking about any girl other than Nandini is the biggest sin, stuck into fear, and tried to go out.

"Can we be friends?" The 'Angel of Beauty', asked the 'King of the Nerds'.

"OK. At least tell me your name." She insisted, still holding his hand.

Thank God Rohit's father shouted his name in anger. As it was the closing time for Rohit's father's office, so the driver had first picked his father before coming to Mc Donald. 'Rohit the nerd', ran like a baby towards his father, as if the 'Queen of Beauty' will snatch away his lollipop.

"So your name is Rohit. I will wait for you here, at same time tomorrow." The gorgeous said.

His father scolded him for never happening thing, i.e. 'Rohit's Affair with a Beautiful Girl.' The girl with her friends started following Rohit's car. She was driving Honda Accord, which means the girl is a high class beauty. Rohit's old Maruti car, on the other hand was further strengthening his identity of a nerd. The girls took few rounds around Rohit's house. On the other hand Rohit prayed to God to forgive him for the sin, as a girl other than Nandini has touched his hand.

A beautiful girl and that too from a rich family, approaching you for a date with her. If this thing happens to anybody except Rohit the fool, then the other guy will jump from the building or go mad out of excitement. Rohit didn't go to meet her the next day, because for him Nandini is the most beautiful girl in this whole universe.

"I am honest for Nandini and my honesty for her will pay me one day." 'Rohit the fool'. :)

Today is May 25th. Aadarsh and I are sitting in front of a computer looking for our results on CBSE website. Rohit and Manas scored around 85%. I scored 64% marks. Vicky and Prashant stick to 60%. But Aadarsh failed in Physics.

Aarti scored 84%, Nandini 74 % and Kamana just in 60's. Among Kamana and her friends, Shefali scored highest i.e. 75%.

I had filled up many entrance exam forms i.e. 5 year LLB course, 5 year MBA course, Hotel Management and BBA. I wanted to prepare for them but wasn't able to concentrate on studies.

That 'Never Ending Night' changed me completely.

I used to be an extrovert before that night, now I am kind of introvert. I used to have a smiling face, and liked talking and entertaining others, but now I am not even able to hear my own voice. I noticed that I have started writing 'r' in a way Kamana writes, like this ɤ.

Kamana is not my only concern. There is someone in this world whom I consider my brother, Rohit. So, thinking about Kamana, Rohit and my other friends, I fell asleep.

Rohit, Aadarsh and I are sitting below a tree. There is some music of *Shehnai* coming from Nandini's house. It seems like a wedding is going on. But her house also seems empty as if there is nobody inside.

"I really love Nandini." Rohit said and started crying.

Its Nandini's wedding day.

"Good bye brothers." Rohit said and vanished in a flick of a second.

Aadarsh and I are crying, that was Rohit's soul talking to us as Rohit is no more in this world.

'Rohit' I shouted. My heart is beating very fast. This dream is more scary than all the others I had seen before.

One day I was sitting at my study table with an open book in front of me, but lost somewhere else. My mother came, sat besides me and put her hand on my shoulders.

"I know you are worried about your career. Today I am going to tell you the story of a great man and his great sacrifice."

"This person was born in a small village in a farmer's house. His family depended on their small agricultural land for their food and livelihood. He had four brothers, two elder and two younger, three sisters two elder and one younger than him. He was just 14 years old when his father died. He used to go to school, which was 7 kilometres from his village, on foot. He stood first in 10th class, with a score of 197 marks out of 200 in mathematics. He was the brightest student of his school. He wanted to become an Engineer. At the same time his elder brother took admission in an Engineering College. His family declared that they can afford fees for only one of the two brothers. He sacrificed his studies for his elder brother. He joined Indian Air Force, but his curiosity for studies never died. During his stint in Indian Air Force, he completed his graduation in first class marks and studied law from Mumbai Law College. He retired from Indian Air Force as Master Warrant Officer and started practising Law after that. He worked hard for days and nights so that his son would never have to sacrifice his studies because of money shortage. I married that man and he is your father and I am proud of him."

My mother's eyes were moist .

That night, for the first time, I cried. I am a looser. I failed in love. I could not help my friends in their love stories. I disappointed my parents with my poor academic performance.

That was the day I decided to do something—something that will bring smile on my parents sad faces. My father never scolded me for my low marks, as he had a strong belief that one day his son will do something big.

My entrance tests are after a month; I started studying seriously for days and nights. I didn't care about what I was eating. I left everything; I had only one thing in mind that I have to make my father feel proud of me.

Number of candidates appearing for exams was never a big deal for me. Crowd is a crowd. 'Sheeps are many in numbers, but there is only one wolf .' I used to say this to everybody but I myself didn't have any idea about what I wanted to convey. I cracked almost every entrance test I appeared for. I took admission in 5 year MBA course in Institute of Management Studies And Research (IMSAR), M. D. University, Rohtak, where I got 23rd rank. As it's in my hometown so I preferred to be with my parents. Also this Institute has a good reputation among other B-schools and Indian Industries.

Manas cleared the preliminary exam of IIT, but failed in the second subjective papers. He got a rank 8,435 and Rohit 9,240 in AIEEE. They both got calls from many top Regional Colleges of Haryana and other states. Both of them also got a call from National Institute of Technology, Kururkshetra. There Manas got Electrical and Rohit Civil Engineering. But as Rohit wanted to be an IT engineer so he took admission in Regional Engineering College, Faridabad. Prashant and Vicky failed to crack any entrance exam so they took admission in the Government College in B.Com course. Aadarsh dropped that year as he had to reappear for Physics in August.

Kamana and Sneha topped from the last in PMT Entrance Exam. Sneha took admission in BA in English course and that too from an ordinary girl's college. Kamana somehow cleared NIFT Entrance Exam and took admission in Fashion Design. Shefali took admission in Bio-Technology in a private college.

Shivani dropped one year for preparations, but the truth is that she didn't get admission anywhere.

Nandini is also among the toppers from the last ranks in AIEEE. The girl whose parents sent her for study only, also failed to get any seat in MBBS or BDS in any college. She took admission in a newly started Ramlal College of Engineering, where it's the first batch.

I proved my point that marks scored in boards are not the right measure for intelligence. People around me appreciated my admission out of happiness, some out of jealousy and others with reasons they know better. But this doesn't make any impact on me. I didn't throw Kamana's photos neither I will do that, because her photos keep on reminding me about that deadly night. Her photos make me realise that what the fuck I had done till now. Her words keep me charged up. Her photos are giving me reason for doing something big to show her one day what Rehaan is? I was a good person and I got the worst reward for that. What should I do then?

That Never Ending Night

I am living in darkness; where the days are darker than nights. I have sleepless and restless nights with the nightmares coming from that never ending night.

I wake up in the middle of night as if I am digging up my own grave. I am walking on an endless straight road with darkness darker than nights, without any clue where I am going. I saw myself trying to escape from that night but I find myself again in that never ending night.

Sometimes I saw Kamana going away from me and I am trying to stop her but I find myself running at the same place. I have dreams of setting of the sun and finding myself crying on Lake Side in that never ending night.

I find myself running on the road asking for help to rescue me from that never ending night.

Days are passing, the whole world is moving, but I am still standing there and waiting for Kamana to come, in that never ending night.

I loved Kamana deep from my heart but I didn't know how to make her love me.

The next morning I woke up and am standing in front of the mirror for washing my face. I am not able to recognise my own face. Something is wrong. I washed it two-three times but still I don't recognise my own face. This is not the face of the old Rehaan. Who is he? Something is strange today, something is changed. This new face killed the genuine person, or you can say the Real Rehaan. The old joker is dead; this is the new joker 'The Evil Joker'. He is emotionless, feelingless and with his deadliest arrows of sarcasm, he laughs at others and show them their real place. Love is something, which he knows nothing about or can never be able to understand ever. He knows who he is and what he is capable of becoming and he knows what he has to do.

"Hi, my name is Rehaan and trust me you all will always remember this name" I gave a sarcastic smile to myself in the mirror. "I am the joker, 'The Evil Joker.'"

17

Those Golden Days, Searching for a Lab Monkey and My 1st Official Ugly Girlfriend

'I will never make any of my college girls, my girlfriend.' This is my pledge. There are many reasons behind this; one simple one is that if you make one girl of your college your girlfriend, you will be a copyright property of her only and that way you are out rejecting the hundreds of other opportunities in the form of other girls in your college.

My father gifted me a Hero Honda CBZ motorcycle and a new coloured Nokia mobile phone. I arrived early to my Institute, and parked my motorcycle. A Ford Ikon stops besides my motorcycle and a person having short height, charming face, and wearing specs came out of the car. His head is showing a complete cycle of balding and his dressing sense is declaring him as some professor kind of stuff. He looked at me for a second and left the parking lot.

As it was my first day, I had difficulty in finding my classroom. Being a good looking junior, I prefered not to ask any senior about my classroom. Thank God my 'Department of Brain' suggested me to check the notice board.

"May I come in, Sir?" I asked

"You are 5 minutes late. This is your first class that's why I am allowing you." He is the same guy I saw in the parking lot. I took a seat in the front row.

"I am Dr. Daleep Singh. I am here to teach you Psychology and the Principles of Management."

"So why you chose MBA course?" he asked and students started giving weird answers.

"You tell me." He pointed towards me.

"I chose this course to get an answer to one question. How one person alone is able to manage thousands of workers in factories and offices?"

"After many years, I have heard something different. Good, sit down."

"There are many reasons for choosing MBA by you people. Many of you took this course because you have passed entrance exam, some girls chose as it will assist them in their marriage. Some came here just for the perks given to MBAs by business corporates, and others took admission because their parents think it's the right option for them. Now that you are here, I am not concerned with your reasons. Let us start with what I am here for i.e. Psychology."

'Sex and Aggression'. He writes on the black board.

"Sigmund Freud said that these are the two animal instincts present in human beings, and are the root cause of every problem in our society. Now, how far you are able to manage these two, that is management."

After the class is over and Dr. Singh left, few ugly faces come in.

"Juniors, we are your immediate seniors. You are supposed to follow few Rules made by us." An ugly fat-ass female shouted.

"Rule number one 'Seniors are always right'. Rule number two 'If you have any problem with any senior, follow rule number 1.'" One medium height uncle looking nerd shouted.

"My name is Surinder, I am your super-senior." He introduced himself.

They started taking our introductions.

I notice that one of our super-senior, a not so fair complexioned girl, is passing a smile to me.

"Don't look at her; she is a bitchy kind of a girl." One of my classmates said.

"Hi, may I know how come you know that?"

"One of the seniors told me in the morning. I have got a list of this kind of girls."

He showed me a paper with around nine names of seniors.

I laughed.

"What's your name brother?"

"Harsh, I am from Chandigarh." We shake hands.

"Hey you, why are you talking? What's your name?" Surinder asked me.

"My name is Rehaan."

"Your tone is showing arrogance. Lower down your pitch, junior. Respect me or else you will be nowhere in this college. I am the one who manages everything here." Surinder blew his own trumpet.

In the evening I am listening to songs and reading newspaper, suddenly my phone rang.

"Hi Rehaan, this is my new mobile number." Shefali said.

"Hey, how are you?"

"Awesome, how was your first day in college?"

"Not bad. Some Professors and Lecturers are really good, especially Dr. Daleep Singh. Some ugly bald seniors raised objections on my long hair, Idiots. Some seniors are good also, but who cares."

"What about girls, hero? Its college now."

"Oops, I know only one girly thing and that's you." I laughed.

"Flirting? Good going, but try this on someone else." Shefali also laughed.

"I will honey, till then I am happy with my part-time girlfriend." I tried to crack a poor joke in an astonishing way.

"Ok, my part-time hero. I have to unpack my suitcases. I got the hostel here and my classes will be starting from tomorrow. So I will talk to you later."

It's just the beginning and many boys of my class and seniors started approaching girls of my class as 'a salesmen of their own heart', as their product. These salesmen are going for door-to-door selling. Their customers 'the girls of my class' started trying different products and judging them for their quality, quantity and utility. I saw the same girl with a different boy on different dates in university cafeteria. This phenomena depends upon.

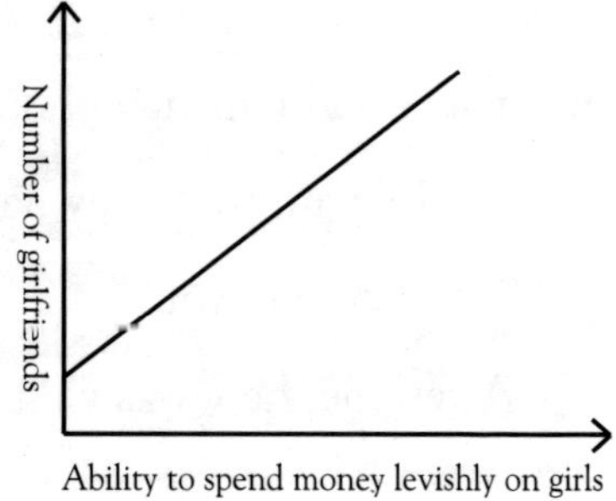

The number of girlfriends of a particular person increases with his increasing ability to spend money lavishly but goodness still exists in this world. There are a few girls who don't run after money so even if anybody like me is having recession period in his pocket money, then trust me these girls are the best target customers and I have got a list of a few in my hand.

"Why girls carry books as if they are hugging them and boys with loose hands swinging in air?" Professor Daleep Singh asked to a topper of entrance exam.

"I think because girls buy brand new books and boys go for second hand or lend them from some senior friends. So as books are a costly affair for girls and not to boys, that's why...."

"Sometimes I wonder what's wrong with this generation. Sit down"

"It's because it is psychologically proved that girls are by nature more caring than boys." Professor stated.

I tell you the real difference. If a boy proposes a girl and she said yes then they say "She is of a loose character, she will say yes to everyone." And if the girl said no then they say "She is thinking herself to be a Miss Universe or what?"

Regarding girls; if boys don't look at them, they say "Bloody dog, why is he not looking at me?" and if boys look at them then they say "Look, bloody dog is staring at me."

I am sitting alone in the university cafeteria eating omelette and sipping a coke. After a while Nandini came with Varun, who is Rohit's good friend and his old classmate.

"Hi, how are you?" She asked.

"Hi, nice to see you here"

We talked about college life. Varun joined his friends but Nandini prefered to be with me.

"So, how is your college? And what about Kamana?"

"College is awesome. By the way, who is this Kamana?"

She started laughing.

"OK forget about her. How is Rohit?"

"Why don't you ask him? By the way, what are you wearing; this is college gorgeous, try something better & colourful."

She became speechless.

"I am having my class now, so will see you later. Please, concentrate on your studies for which your parents send you to college."

"Wait Rehaan! What's your problem? Why are you behaving so rude to me. I call you my bro and I really mean it." Nandini said in a high pitch.

"I am not at all rude to you, still you feel bad. Now think what is the condition of innocent Rohit, with whom you broke friendship just because he committed honestly that he likes you and just because few bastards of your class talk rubbish about you both. That is what is called rude, Madam. What's going on between you and Varun? Not a bad couple." I taunted her.

"What do you mean by that? We are just friends. Varun is a good friend of mine. Keep your dirty thinking to yourself."

"If I am talking rubbish about you and Varun, then why don't you go and break with him. If you did this to Rohit then why not to Varun? Rohit never asked you to be his girlfriend. I agree that if you love somebody that doesn't mean the other person should also love you. What's wrong in making someone your friend? If your friendship brings a smile to any sad face, that is the most divine prayer. Rohit wants to be just a friend of yours, but you don't consider him worth your friendship, even. This is what is rude. On which ego trip are you on, Madam? Wake up, you are the same Mamma's girl, who was to do wonders. Rohit got 10% more marks than you and he is in one of the best colleges of Haryana, unlike you, who has joined the first batch of a new college."

I stood up, but she held my hand.

"Can I have Rohit's mobile number?"

In the evening I was out walking in the park, when my phone rang.

"Dude, Rohit this side I got a call from Nandini, today."

"Congratulations! Just talk to her and try to impress her. Make her feel that you are the only one for whom she was waiting for. At least change your old ways." I suggested.

"I can't bro. As then she will love the fake Rohit, not the real old nerd who loved her."

"That thing happens in movies only. Here girls say something, mean something and do something else. Just hope for the best. Please keep in touch."

I met Harsh, a new good friend in college. Harsh is tall, dark and handsome with curly hair. He is one and a half year elder to me. He did his schooling from St. Joseph High School in non-Medical but took admission in MBA. He got his own justification for that. He is a good person at least for now. Being from a convent school, there is no question about his English. He would correct my grammatical mistakes and taught me communication skills.

"I love you Shefali." I pulled Shefali towards me. Her heartbeat is very fast.

"I love you Rehaan. I can't live without you."

"You are my darling, sweetheart." I said and we start smooching like hell. I throw her on the bed and fell on her. We are kissing as if we are going to eat each other. I am licking her all over as if she is a melting ice-cream. After a fabulous foreplay cum circus, we did something which people call 'Pre-marital Sex'.

I saw that there are tears in Shefali's eyes as she is waving towards me and going away from me with her friend.

"Damn." I woke up suddenly. What a dream that was? Why was she going away? What happened to our intimate scene? Who was the other girl with her? Whatever....... it was just a dream. I think I should stop watching porn movies on my computer before going to sleep at night.

I went to the bathroom for dressing up for a get-together of my class.

It's not-a-bad-hotel for a get-together with not-so-bad-food and not-so-bad-girls dancing on the floor to the tunes of a DJ. I am sitting on a not-so-bad-chair and thinking about not-so-bad-dream. Shefali is just a friend and I don't think that she has anything in her mind like that. I am in the middle of recalling mine and Shefali's past conversations, when I saw some hostel girls pointing me out in a naughty way inviting me to dance with them. I don't know what has happened to these girls? Today they are looking hotties with short T-shirts, mini skirts and Capri jeans. I bet they must have spent an amount equal to one-fourth of their total budget on their complete makeover.

I think I had done some good deed in the past that these hotties are calling me for a dance. Truly speaking I am a curse to the dancing world. If ever I get to see my video of dancing, I am sure, I will pass orders of shoot-at-sight for myself. For now let me taste the hostel flavour.

I don't know where my hands were going or where my legs are scrolling, where my neck is moving and what the fuck is my back doing, still the poor girls were managing with me. This is what is called 'disaster management'. I am the only boy in the centre with three girls dancing around me. One of them is dancing so close, that if I get a push from anyside my lips would have flavour of her lips. With every single move of her belly I became very hot and it raised the need of a fire brigade.

But the good time is always short-lived. Some girls around the cold drink counter recovered a bottle of whisky which was kept under the table.

"Oh my God, we had a glass of coke sometime ago. That means we consumed whisky." Saying that the three hostelers started trembling like drunkards.

Girls are girls! They were dancing in a normal way, but the moment they came to know that somebody had mixed alcohol in their cold drinks, they now need attention and sympathy. They started competing in over-reacting championship. Some of them started scoring points through their not so unique outstanding talent of crying, while others started behaving in an awkward manner as if they have consumed the whole bottle. I don't think that one small plastic glass of cold drink mixed with a little bit of whisky could make someone crazy. After sometimes a team of so called experts (our seniors) headed by Mr. Surinder came to investigate the situation.

"You have reached your limits boys; I will look into the matter on my own. You don't know what kind of a person I am." Surinder boosted as if he is the Chief Investigating Officer.

"We know what you are, c#^t!@." Someone from the back commented. Some of my classmates rounded him up and forced him and other seniors to leave. Some of the girls with other boys of my class took the girls to their hostel rooms. The party must go on, after sometime other girls of my class also joined me in dancing.

With some flavour of flirting with girls, I declared my day as awesome.

One day in the evening I was eating my breakfast. Yes, actually I was getting late for the morning class, so I left home without breakfast. My father and mother were out of town for a religious ceremony in the family and they will be coming late night. So here I am eating my breakfast in the evening. I almost finished it when my landline phone started annoying me.

"Hello, who's this?"

"Your Nightmare."

"Vicky, how are you? Long time not talked to you."

"I am fine; today is my birthday and I am inviting you for a party. I will pick you up from your house after half-an-hour." He cuts the phone.

Now this is what always happens to me. I had just completed my 'so called breakfast' and was not hungry at all and just then I get an invitation for a treat.

I am going with Aadarsh, Vicky and other new college friends of Vicky on their motorcycles. Many of Vicky's friends are older than me and some of them are smoking cigarettes also. We were going to an old friend's house to pick him. On the way I saw Surinder who was standing outside his house in white T-shirt, shorts and slippers. He stopped me.

"Hello, junior."

"Hello, Sir. How are you?"

"I am fine as always. Why are you roaming here?"

"I guess it's a public road, sir. By the way I am here to visit a friend."

"Who is your friend? Where does he live? What for are you going to him?"

"That's none of your business." I replied in an arrogant way.

"What did you say? You know I am your senior and my name is Surinder."

"Then fuck your seniority."

In the meantime Vicky and his gang also reached.

"What happened?" Vicky asked.

"Nothing. This chap is my senior and entertaining me with his 'circus of seniority'." I laughed.

One of Vicky's friend parked his bike and come close to Surinder.

"Listen you asshole, this your so-called junior is my younger brother. Mind your own fucking business, else....." He smiled and threw cigarette smoke at Surinder's face. Surinder got really scared.

After picking up our old school friend, we went to the restaurent.

We are sitting in a costly restaurant. I noticed that Aadarsh is looking quite upset these days. May be first Aarti and then reappear in Physics might be the reason. I am really worried about him. Many a times I tried motivating him to forget the past and work for the present. Whereas I myself was also upset. Upset with my breakfast. There's one big question. How the hell am I going to eat? I am not at all hungry, but still want to eat, as this is the chance when I can eat whatever I want and that too free of cost. So I just ate and ate and ate.

"So, how many girlfriends do you have?" One of Vicky's friends asked me.

"None" I replied. Everybody there started staring at me, as if I have committed a rape.

"Fuck you! Don't make a fucking fun of us, dude. A fucking chocolate hero like you, not having even a single girlfriend. Today is not 1st April." Another one taunted me.

In college you are authorised to say 'fuck' twice in each of your line. Guys here read novels to cramp slangs and use them on their friends. For girls, these people use the age-old two lines, 'Fuck you' and 'Sexy Slut'.

Friends are categorized into various categories like college friends, school friends, friends with whom you discuss studies and philosophy, some other friends with whom you just exchange DVDs and CDs of new movies, songs and even porn movies.

Gone are the golden days when people ask you about your marks, how your studies are going? How many subjects do you have? The moment you get into college you will encounter certain new questions, 'How many girlfriends do you have?' 'Don't you have even one girlfriend?', 'Are you still single?', 'Are you sure you are still a virgin? No girl in your life, are you gay?'

The concept of love is shifted to the concept of lust now. If you are single, you are an underdog. Having good looks is not sufficient. Time has come when porn movies are not enough for rise in your career graph in the world of 'Studs'.

We have gone through just the theory part; time has come to have some practical exposure to clear with the concept of so called love. Being in a college a new department was inaugurated in my body 'The Department of Sex' and this department overshadowed all my other departments. The worst part is that to start Practicals I need a lab monkey i.e. a girlfriend, so that I can make experiments on her and write a thesis by exploring the complex hidden areas of the relationship. I want to research in evergreen field of 'Love-cum-Lust'.

Something is wrong with beautiful girls. When I approached them in school they said 'We are still in school and it is not the right time for love.' When I joined college I found the same girl committed to another guy. Somebody please tell me where I lost the track of beautiful girls and what the fuck is their problem.

I remember once my school teacher said to us "If my son has a girlfriend in school then there is a problem. At the same time if he does not have any girlfriend in college then there is a bigger problem."

Fuck! I need a girlfriend.

In the night stars are glittering and my parents are having a sound sleep. Whereas I am sacrificing my sleep in the toilet (I call it my thinking room), interrogating myself by asking questions that why I ate my breakfast in the evening? Why I ate so much at the party when I was not hungry and just promising myself that I am not going to repeat this in the future. Also applying few concepts of Physics like Force = mass x acceleration. While observing chemical reactions taking place in my stomach, I thought about where

I will find my lab monkey i.e. my first girlfriend. My mobile phone beeped in my pocket, I opened the message

'I no u luv Kamana n u wud nvr b abl to frget her, bt stil i wana say tht i luv u. I don no wht u fel bout me bt my luv is unconditional, tc, Shefali.'

Crap it takes about 10 minutes to understand what she had written. I got an erection reading the message and started my best exercise to tame my Monster, which took another ten minutes.Fuck you Kamana! I finally got a girlfriend.

It's Sunday and I am sitting with Shefali in her car in the parking lot. It's the best place for proposing a girl, especially when you intentionally want to propose with some naughty stuff.

"Kamana means nothing to me now. I can't call her my past even, as she was never in my life. It's you who I care for. You are the true meaning of friendship. I don't have words to describe your place in my heart. It's just that my day is incomplete without talking to you. So how can I imagine living my whole life without you? You are my meaning of love. I love you, Shefali!" I hold her hand.

I don't know what the fuck I am barking, but who cares when the job is done.

"I love you too, Rehaan." Shefali said and grabbed my hand tightly. I pulled her close to me. I am feeling her heart-beat getting faster and faster with decreasing distance between us. I was about to taste the girly flavour but my fate had something else in its pocket.

"What are you doing here?" A watchman knocked the tinted windows of the car.

"Open the door and get out of the car, right now." He shouted.

Shefali out of fear pushed the accelerator. The watchman ran after the car for a few minutes, but the poor chap was not an athlete so despite of his best efforts his large belly declared strike after some time.

"He is no more after us and we are in a moving car, so just relax." I kept my hand on her hand, as the car touched 120km/hr. Girls and their driving. I always prefer walking then to sit with a girl driving. She tried to negotiate a round-about and that too in a speed.

Boom!!!

Girl+Driving+Speed+Propose=Crash-Landing !!!

She lost control of the car and made modern art on front and back doors of the car.

Thank God! Our 'Body Parts' were spared from the dents and scratches.

I never expected this kind of propose, but my life never disappoints me.

18

Breakup, the New Girl and the Worst Luck

Another benefit of not making a girlfriend from your college is that you can make 'n' number of girlfriends outside the college but still enjoy the status of being 'Single' among college girls. Although I was committed to Shefali but for my college girls, I am still single and ready to mingle.

I am the first person and the only one in my friend circle who has a girlfriend, that way I am sitting on a VIP seat (seats for only Very Important Persons) among my friends.

It's winter season with cold waves at its maximum. Thank God I already have a heater named Shefali. Something strange is happening these days. I am loosing curiosity in talking to her. It was not like this before the proposal but the moment she became my girlfriend she was like my other belongings i.e. mobile phone, motorcycle etc, which are taken for granted.

Before I proposed her, I somehow liked her face, her way of talking, her smile etc. etc. The moment she said yes, she seemed to be the biggest curse on my eardrums. I started noticing her fatness, her messed up hairstyle, not so trimmed eyebrows, no makeup sense and just average face or in my words, my first official ugly girlfriend.

I am sitting on my computer; I got a forwarded email from Manas it goes like this.

'When you see the beauty somewhere, when you fall in love with someone, the next impulse that comes to you is to posses it, have it and when you have it, it loses all its significance.'

My days are a total mess. Half of my day is passed in sleeping, one fourth in talking to Shefali on phone and the rest in eating food, attending classes and meeting with other friends.

Your girlfriend can call you anytime, anywhere and anyhow. You have to listen to her emotional drama. If you don't do that then you have to spend atleast an hour to explain the reason and to console her that she is the only one for whom you are living in this world. Girls are so impatient that they want to know everything about your private life.

I called Shefali.

"Hello dear, How are you?"

"Hello my love! How is my baby?" For my Shefali I am 18 years old 6 feet 1 inch baby.

"Fine honey!"

"Hey, guess what? There are two more girls from our school in my college. They were fighting today." Shefali said. Now someone please tell me, what's wrong if two girls are fighting.

"So, what's the big deal?"

"They were fighting for you." Shefali starts laughing and continued "Actually both of them used to like you in school. The moment I told them that you are my boyfriend, you should have seen their faces." Shefali kept on laughing for ten minutes; somebody please tell her that my phone balance is getting screwed, so say something, jerk.

Now this is something strange that I am never able to understand. When I was single, where were these girls and the moment I become committed, I am the most wanted ass in the girl's world.

"Heart-Head-Hand, these are three Hs which are responsible for doing any work efficiently. First, you should have curiosity to do the work from your heart, then your brain will decide how to do it and lastly your hands will do the work, accordingly. In the absence of any 'H' you are not able to do anything with your full efficiency." Professor Daleep Singh stated in the class.

'Musibat'(Shefali) is flashing on my screen. I message her that I am in my class. She messaged me back.

'I m cumin hom t'day. Let me see if i got tim to met u. Misin u, lv ya, tc.'

When we were not in a relationship she had only one thing i.e., lots of time and now she checks if she has time. For one day only I liked her from my heart so my brain decided to propose her and my hands did the pre-decided task. But now time-after-time I am losing all my 'Hs' one by one.

Shefali parked her car near my bike and came out. We started with formal hellos and love you.

"You know, Rehaan, I respect my parents more than anyone in this world." Shefali said.

This is our 3rd face-to-face conversation and the 47th time she is explaining the importance of her parents in her life. It really sucks, but who cares. She has got a copyright over me and I have to listen. After a while my naughty bulb starts glowing in my brain, seeing that both of us are standing at a lonely place.

"Hey you are looking gorgeous today." I tried to change the topic. Trust me she was looking bad compared to our previous meetings.

"Just for today I am looking gorgeous! How mean." She pats on my shoulders. Girls, why do they take everything in negative sense? As the aura has been already set, so I kissed her hand. I pushed her gently to the wall and hugged her. I held her face, moved my fingers over her not-so-beautiful-but-soft-lips. My lips were about to declare the first French Kiss of my life but words from a third party came in between.

"What you are doing here? Go from here or I will call the police." A lady shouted.

"I didn't see your father's name written anywhere here? So buzz off and don't disturb us." I shouted back.

"OK then. I am calling the police."

"Come Rehaan let's go from here. We will meet tomorrow honey." Shefali said, and my poor lips were left with few '!@$%$&%$^#' remarks.

That way my so called 'First French Kiss and the Coward Girlfriend' story had an interval.

Next day as usual Shefali had some urgent piece of work so came late.

"Hey Shefali. We will get married to each other one day. It is so exciting." I said.

Who wants to marry her, I will prefer to die a bachelor, instead, but girls love to talk about their marriage.

"Long time for that" Shefali gave a 'Let's Discuss Something Else' answer.

"OK. How is your family?" Love this honey; this is what you want to discuss—your boo-boo diaper, your Mamma-Papa.

"They are all fine; my elder brother got a five-figure job in an MNC."

Who cares about your brother? Moreover, I am interested in knowing about my first French Kiss Inauguration party or if I can think about foreplay with you, at least in my dream.

"Yeah congratulations for your brother."

Yeah congratulations for your virginity, restore it for your ugly husband.

'Cardinal utility'. Mrs. Mukherjee, our Economics lecturer wrote on the black board.

"Here utility means satisfaction. Let me explain you with an example. Suppose you are hungry, then the utility which you get from the first *chapatti* will be maximum and this utility declines with more and more *chapatti* you eat. After a while the utility will become zero and then negative i.e. if you overeat then you will lose your appetite. Cardinal term is being used because here utility is derived in numeric numbers like 1, 2, 3 etc"

With increasing phone bills and declining satisfaction with not so happening date, one day seems like a decade. Shefali frustrates me all the time by asking where I am and why I am there. Her 'My Best Mom-Dad in the World' story also screws me like anything. She was quiet humble before becoming my girlfriend but now she thinks herself a celebrity.

Moreover, sometimes when I am with Aadarsh and others, especially when Rohit came to Rohtak for just a day to be with us, Shefali kept on arguing with me over small issues. The moment I was able to clear things, I find Rohit packing his stuff for going back. That way I remain mentally absent to my friends even after being present with them.

I also noticed that I have started loosing interest in her day by day. As per cardinal utility, it goes on diminishing and now I am sacrificing with her negative utility.

This is the 56th time I asked myself if I really love Shefali. And this is the 67th time, I am replying the same answer 'It's time to leave my lab monkey to her natural habitat'.

Shefali is in a heated discussion with me over the phone. This is the right time to show my monkey the way back to her jungle.

"Shefali I don't find any reason for fighting like this over phone. If you don't know what to do, let me help you out. Let's celebrate our breakup." I smiled.

"What did you say?" Shefali got surprised.

"You heard me right, honey. I am breaking up with you." I laughed and put the phone down.

Fuck, the moment I broke up with her, my curiosity in her revived again.

Afterwards I received many messages from her 'Sorry if I hurt you', 'I have changed myself', 'I really love you', 'Please come back', 'Talk to me for the last time, please', 'This is my last message', 'What you think of yourself' blah-blah.

At last I am single again. I love this feeling.

After the breakup a new problem arose. How to perform traditional rituals of breakup, starting with gaining sympathy from friends by proving myself innocent and convincing them to the myth that it's because of Shefali I am suffering.

"Dude what's your problem? Why you broke off with Shefali?" Rohit asked. Aadarsh is also waiting for my response. We are over teleconferencing.

"It's not me but Shefali, bro. She was screwing me every day so I had no choice but to screw her back, forever." Yeah I succeeded in proving my not so innocent side.

Nandini and Harsh are happy with my decision, as according to them I deserve a better chick. Prashant and Vicky didn't bother as usual. But Manas, trust me, was screwed more than Shefali, even.

"Are you mad? Are you nuts? What the fuck man, she really loves you. How can you do this to her?" Manas shouted.

"Simple. Get me another girl and I will show you how I did that. I have already told you it's because Shefali didn't have time for me. So I did a favour to her. Now she can concentrate on her important work only."

"Look at you buddy. You were so nice with girls before and what have you become now. Why did you hurt her?"

"My honour" I replied.

"You don't know how much it hurts. I know because I really loved Jyoti." Manas said sadly.

"Now who the fuck is Jyoti?"

"She is in my class in the Institute. She was my good friend or you can say best friend. One day she was getting emotional. I told her that there are so many people in this world. I want to be someone who is different from the crowd. I discussed about our syllabus. Afterwards she started seeing another boy."

"Dude, when a girl is emotional, she wants her man to console her, to wipe out her tears and to make her smile—not to declare your fucking career philosophy. If you discuss studies when a girl is alone, then I am happy for poor Jyoti."

My problem is different. I miss Shefali not because I loved her but she had become a part of my routine life, as we daily used to talk to each other over phone. So my problem is not Shefali but those 6 hours, which I used to spend daily in talking to her before break up. For some days after that, my friends came to me as if they are here for mourn prayers. My unshaved beard and listening to sad songs further strengthened my imaginary innocence.

"Hello, is it Rehaan?" A feminine voice asked me over phone and I am lost.

"Yup, may I know who is it?"

"I am Priya, Shefali's roommate." I know what the fuck she was about to say, 'Rehaan, Shefali really loves you', 'Shefali this, Shefali that'.

"How can I help you?"

"Rehaan please speak with Shefali. She really loves you." Ditto as I guessed.

"OK, I will do that. By the way it's hard to find a true friend like you. Shefali is lucky in that matter. Keep it up, buddy." I started my flirting business.

"You know when you were committed to her, she used to write your name on every page of her registers. Nice na?"

"Yup, there were some issues which led to this situation. It's neither Shefali's fault nor mine. I just thought it is better to break up relations which made us fight with each other. But I really respect Shefali." Fuck Shefali, I respect you honey; I want you, whosoever you are.

"You seem to be a nice guy."

"And you seem to be a lovely girl, as per your sexy voice."

"Thanks."

"By the way, a nice guy deserve friendship of a nice girl like you."

"Sure buddy, we are friends from now."

Mission accomplished. Make one girl your friend and enter into her friend circle. It's a supplement of 'My Theory of Networks Among Girls.' That way you can approach other girls for yourself or for some of your retarded friends.

Shefali is at home for weekend. She was talking to me on phone, suddenly she broke into tears.

"Rehaan I am sorry. Why are you doing this to me? I never cried for anybody in my life. But for you, I don't know why, I weep daily whenever I am alone."

"I want to meet you right now in front of the Central Library." I said.

I anyhow convinced her that both of us are unhappy because of the breakup and its better that we be friends again. May be one day we could again be into a love relationship.

Afterwards I and Priya often talked to each other. Priya is daughter of NRI, her father is a businessman in Dubai. After few calls in a week Priya started calling me many times in a day. I used to get one call from Shefali and four calls from Priya everyday, but good days never live long.

One evening I got a call from Priya.

"Rehaan I don't know what to do?"

"What happened?"

"Shefali feels bad that I talk to you. She is kind of jealous of our friendship. Many a times she shouted at me 'to stay away from you'. I will never hurt Shefali, at the same time I don't want to loose you." Priya said.

"Ok, don't worry. I am coming to Noida this Saturday; I will meet you both there."

On Friday, I called Rohit and asked him to bunk his classes and come with me to Noida.

Next day we reached Noida. Shefali arrived with an ugly fat boy having not so curly hair.

"Hi, meet my close friend, Suyansh." She introduced me to him. I was more interested in my sexy voice and high expectation stuff Priya.

"Where is Priya?"

"You said you are coming here to meet me. If you want to meet Priya you are free to go and meet her." Shefali said in disappointment.

"Please don't start all over again; she is just a friend like you. I came here to meet both of you."

But in real I am here to see my baby, Priya. Man she should be stunningly beautiful.

"She will join us later."

We four entered the mall. Shefali brought Suyansh to make me feel jealous, instead I felt sympathy towards poor Shefali.

Shefali and Suyansh are at their best in making me and Rohit bored.

After some time a group of girls approached us.

"There she is, your most awaited Priya." She pointed towards the ugliest girl of the group. She is Priya! I travelled such a long distance just for this Miss Ugly.

After that the job of making me and Rohit bored was also shared by all her friends, especially Priya. The so called 'sexy voice' is my worst nightmare. I got a lesson; never judge a girl on phone. Crap, it hurts.

"You know Priya, I thought about it many times. I don't want to become a reason for creating differences between you and Shefali. Shefali is lucky to have a friend like you."

I love this fake emotional drama of mine. I am my own fan. In reality, I would prefer to jump from a building then to make you my girlfriend. Let me run from here.

Rohit as usual placed his hand of sympathy on my shoulders, cursing my bad luck. You call it bad luck. I call it the worst that can happen with any guy.

19

1st Battle of the Nerds, 31 against 1 and Nandini's Hating Aspects

It's about 8:30 in the morning and I am sitting in Accounts class and snoring. Harsh shakes me up as a light is blinking on my silent phone.

It displayed 19 missed calls of Rohit and one message from him.

'Pic up dis phn demit. I m cumin to rtk. It's sumthin urgent. Its abt Nandini i wil tel u rest aftr rechin. I wil be thr by 10:00, bunk all ur clases.'

"His name is Naveen, he is in Nandini's class and he is troubling Nandini." Rohit said in a worried way.

"How do you know that?"

"I have many of my old tuition batchmates in Nandini's Engineering College. One of them told me about Naveen who is a bad guy."

"Nandini often talks to me but she never said anything like this." I exclaimed.

"May be because she knows that Naveen is a dangerous guy, and he might hurt you if you try to interfere."

"So, what now?"

"Let us talk to him over this issue." Aadarsh came into the scene.

"So, why are we wasting time here? Lets go." I said.

Harsh and Parminder (another classmate of mine, who is a part-time model) also came with us. Aadarsh had already seen Naveen so he spotted him on his way to the hostel.

"Your name is Naveen?" I asked

"Yes, any problem with that."

"No. We are here to create a problem for you." Aadarsh replied.

"It's not good for you to trouble Nandini. Get your hands off her." I said.

Naveen smiled in a sarcastic way and started dialling numbers on his mobile phone.

"Do you have any idea with whom you are messing up? You all are putting yourself in great trouble." He smiled again.

"Don't you worry? We will take care of that later. Now shall we discuss Nandini?" Rohit asked.

We all are here standing with Naveen but Harsh is sitting alone away from us.

"Do you know that I am brother of Baljeet, who has done 10 murders." Naveen boosted about his brother and his non-exsisting celebrity status.

"Do you know that I am brother of Rohit? I don't have any experience of murder and will open my murder account starting with you."

I laughed at my poor joke.

"Fuck that Rohit." Naveen shouted.

I pulled out the front lock of bike for hitting at his head.

Parminder is about to punch Naveen on his face but Rohit stopped us saying "We are here just to talk, not to pick up a fight."

"Look bro, Nandini is a nice & innocent girl, so stop bothering her. We are here not to fight, but just to talk and convince you that it's not good to trouble any girl" Rohit said.

Naveen didn't say anything and left on his motorcycle.

We went to a nearby park. All are thinking that Naveen's matter is sorted out but it was just the beginning of the countdown. After about half an hour my phone started ringing.

"You sister fucker! Where are you? You meet me and I will tell you who is Naveen. You will be killed today surely, asshole. Come to the college. I am waiting for you there." Naveen shouted and cut the phone.

"What to do now?" Aadarsh asked me.

"What, what? It's a declared fight now. Now it is nothing called one-on-one fight. We need people to make our battalion. This is the right time to test your friends and others who once said to call them in your bad times." I stated in panic.

Aadarsh phoned his friends who were generally indulging in fighting and all. They refused to come by making silly excuses. Same was the case with Rohit's friends. Vicky was not in Rohtak so it's useless to call him. Rohit also called Varun but he straightaway said no, although he was a good friend of Nandini and Rohit. Only Prashant and Manas came to fight for us. So we were a total of 7 guys.

"Rehaan, I have to leave for Chandigarh. My father just called me." Harsh said.

"But bro I need you."

"That I understand, but I have to go." Harsh made a number of other silly excuses. I really felt bad. I considered

Harsh to be a friend like Aadarsh and Rohit but he left me when I needed him the most. On the other hand Parminder, who is not so good friend of mine is still standing on my side to fight for us. Harsh is gone, now we are just six left. One of my classmate informed me that there are 13-14 people with Naveen.

"What should we do now?" Rohit asked.

I could see the fear in Aadarsh and Rohit's eyes. It's obvious as none of us had ever been into such a big fight. I can't say about Parminder, because he seemed to be experienced. There was no fear in Prashant and Manas's eyes, I don't know why? Manas is a national gold medallist in Karate, but he alone can't handle more than 2 or 3 boys, I guess. Honestly speaking the clouds of fear started emerging in my heart also.

"There is only one way out and that's Hunny."

Hunny and Manas were on same tuition classes way back in 12th class. Manas had introduced me to him. He was interested only in two things in his life, fighting and only fighting. As a person he is the biggest brain sucker, I have ever seen. His poor jokes sucks more than mine. But if you are in Rohtak and expecting any fight in future, you must have what locals call 'Back'.

"That's it, you don't worry? I am with you now, buddy." Hunny said and stopped his bike in front of an office. One dark muscular man came out of the office. He shakes hands with us and made a couple of phonecalls.

I called Naveen to ask where he is. Naveen who was waiting in front of his college gate kept on abusing me on phone. I, Aadarsh and Rohit went to Engineering College first, followed by Prashant, Manas and Parminder. Seeing six of us, Naveen and his group of around thirteen boys started moving towards us aggressively with iron rods, chains, swords and knives. The moment they were about to reach near us, around twenty five men on 15 motorcycles came. All of them were about 5feet 10inches or more in height, bodybuilders. Seeing them, there was nobody standing behind Naveen, all his so called companions took different corners to hide their asses.

"Go and hit that 'Sister fucker' Naveen." Hunny said to Rohit.

"I just wanted to talk to him for Nandini. I don't want to fight." Rohit stated.

"This is not right, Hunny. He has just seen what we are. That is enough. There is no use of beating him now."

I wanted to beat Naveen, but this 31 against 1 is something more then unfair.

"Cowards" Hunny shouted at me, Rohit and Aadarsh.

Hunny jumped on Naveen, slapped him and punched him on his face. Some others also started beating Naveen and nobody came to his rescue. After a few minutes lecturers and security personal came and Naveen ran inside the college. We all ran away from there.

We are all relaxing in the office-cum-coaching centre of the gangster, Hunny's friend. In the afternoon the gangster got a call.

"That fellow is Baljeet's brother. Baljeet is now coming with his men. We have to call all our people and sharpen our weapons. This could be the big fight. This time either Baljeet or I will survive." The gangster declared.

Fifty men, some with knife and sword, few with daggers and two or three with guns assembled at the office.

"May be that fellow Naveen would be killed today. So get ready to take the blame." The gangster told me and I was stuck in fear. I didn't know what to do. What will happen now? What about my parents if I get jailed in a murder case?

The gangster and Baljeet talked for about ten minutes; after some negotiations the issue was now compromised by both the gangs. I thanked the gangster for his help and left with Aadarsh, Rohit, Prashant, Manas, Parminder and Hunny.

I dropped Parminder to his room and after sometime Hunny, Prashant and Manas also left.

"Thanks buddy. Thanks for everything."

"Not a big deal for me. You all take care." Hunny replied.

Friendship is betting the sacrifice of your life for the cause of a mere year old friend. Hunny's stand taught me this.

Rohit, Aadarsh and I are sitting in Sector 1 main park drinking a coke and eating chips as we three are hungry. My mobile phone rang up again.

"Hey, its Varun here. Naveen went to the Principal and took Nandini's name and made her responsible for everything that happened today."

I told this to Rohit.

"I think we must go to Nandini's college as she is in a problem.

The conflict is finally resolved but the problem is still on. I, Aadarsh and Rohit went to the Principal of Nandini's college.

"Sir it's not Nandini. It's we three who are responsible for today's mess."

I somehow convinced him that there is no issue related to Nandini. We were about to leave the college, suddenly Nandini and her elder sister Mona came.

"I hate you Rohit. I hate you more than anybody in this world. You can never be my friend." Nandini shouted in anger.

"And you Rehaan, this is the last time I am talking to you. You are no longer my brother. I don't want to see your face again." Nandini said to me. "You ruined my image in front of everyone. You just get lost from here."

Nandini left with her sister Mona.

Rohit didn't say anything; he just took the bus and went back to his college hostel. Aadarsh also left for his house. In the evening Hunny met me.

Hunny asked me, why did we go to Nandini's college again. I told him the whole story.

"So dude we are not cowards, but I believe in one-on-one fight not in 31 against 1 fight."

I thanked Hunny once again because he had really helped us.

20

Lost in Smoke, Changing Time and N for Nelisha

I am running faster beyond my limits, continuously asking myself, why me? Why only me, always? But that black dog is not giving up. May be the owner of the dog has taken special care for its diet. The problem is not with this particular four legged poor chap running after me, but every dog in this world is born with a dream in their small eyes to bite my ass one day. May be I was a dog in my previous life and as if I had teased sisters, wife and girlfriends of these dogs.

I somehow jumped over a wall taller than me; unfortunately the wall is broken from right side and the intelligent dog easily came from that. Wow! even dogs are more intelligent than me. I somehow climbed a tree near the wall. My heart is beating fast. The dog kept on barking under the tree. I am sitting up on the tree and kept on abusing the dog '!@#$% ^ &' as if the dog is understanding me. The branch of the tree is unfortunately cracking down-and-down with every passing second. After a while the dog started jumping to catch my leg, but I am still far away from his reach. Suddenly my mobile vibrated in my pocket.

'I m misin u bro. I m realy felin lonly here. May be ths is the worst phase of my lif. Pl cum here, Rohit.'

How can I tell him that my present condition is even worst than him.

Next day I bunked college.

"I will come late from college, as I have to do some urgent work for my presentations." I told my parents while going to the college.

I took a bus to Faridabad in the morning and reached there by 10 a.m. The door of Rohit's room is open. I silently step into the room without making any noise, so as to give Rohit a surprise. Instead there was a surprise waiting for me. Rohit is lying on the bed with his eyes closed, a tear just trickling out of his right eye. He is holding a cigarette in his left hand. There is smoke all around the room and a sad song is being played on computer. When I came close to him I saw that he has written 'I am sorry Nandini' on his hand and there is also a fresh burnt spot of cigarette on his right hand. His face is lost in long rough beard.

"Rohit, I am here, bro."

He jumped up in surprise and hugs me.

"Thanks bro." He didn't say anything after that. Cigarette butts were thrown all over. There are more empty beer bottles around than books. The room is a complete mess with clothes and other things spread all over, like any 'boy's hostel room'.

"I never wanted that fight, it just happened. I just went to talk to Naveen, and make him understand that what he is doing is wrong. I never intended to create trouble for Nandini." Rohit takes a sip from his beer.

I am just shocked seeing his condition.

"All the time I see her saying 'I hate you'. I am just feeling guilty and the pain of this guilt is unbearable for me." Rohit took another sip of beer.

"Rohit, time has come when you should......"

Before I completed my sentence I saw that, Rohit is nowhere. Where is he? Few unpleasant noises are coming out of the bathroom. I opened the door and saw that Rohit is vomiting.

"May be last night I exceeded my limits." Rohit laughed.

"I was saying that time has come when you should move-on."

"Professor Rana is looking for you. He has something to discuss regarding the coming practicals." One of his roommates said while entering with two more friends.

"Hello, I am Rehaan." I introduced myself.

"Well hi, my name is Arun. Rohit often talks about you and Aadarsh."

"What is he up to—cigarettes and alcohol? He is not the same Rohit I knew in school." I asked Arun.

"He was against smoking, when he joined the college; he was so friendly and jolly that everybody in this hostel prefered to be in this room than their own. Two of our friends were habitual of drinking and smoking but he always resisted. From the day he came back from Rohtak last week, he is a different person. That night he started drinking and was so frustrated that he also smoked for the first time. Last evening he was talking about Nandini when suddenly he crushed the burning cigarette on his hand."

Arun told me before leaving for lunch.

"If cigarette and alcohol is the solution, then after Kamana's chapter, I would be a chain smoker today and you will find me drunk and lying unconscious on the roadside. As I always say it's not only the girl that matters in life but there are other relations also. Think about your father. He would be shocked seeing you in this condition. And what about me, your friend. You think that I will feel good seeing a cigarette in your hand"

"I know all that. But trust me buddy, I can't bear that pain, that invisible pain called Nandini, which is incurable." Rohit said.

Next day I re-opened 'Nandini-Rohit-Love Case' file.

"Nandini at least talk to me. OK. It's totally my mistake." Best way to convince a girl is to take everything on you.

"I don't want to talk to you." Nandini said and went.

Next day I again approached her.

"I have already told you to stay away from me. For me you are a nobody."

Again I approached her the third day.

"OK fine, this is what I was in your life. Just a small storm weakened our so called friendship." I approached her with full preparation. I continued with high level emotional drama and guess what? I hit the bulls eye. She started crying, which means the job is done.

"You know Rehaan, every thing is messed up now. Students laugh over my character, talk ridiculous on my back; lecturers of my college also don't consider me a good girl. It's impossible for me to survive. I did nothing still I am the sufferer. I will never forgive Rohit."

"You listen to me first and then you are free to decide whatever you want to do."

"Please leave me alone for some time." Nandini stood up.

Leaving a girl alone means you have lost her.

"I can't let you do that because you are a part of my life. You are somebody who has taught me the meaning of friendship. Letting you go is like drinking water from an empty glass."

Blah-blah! I kept on making high scores in passing old set of nonsence dialogues. Never underestimating the power of my emotional drama.

At last I convinced her that it was all due to some misunderstanding and that Rohit cares about her. Thanks to me and online networking sites, Rohit and Nandini started talking again.

I scored 72% marks as average of two semesters of 1st year, the first time I have seen something like '7' at ten's place of my percentage. I also scored highest internal marks in the class. I think my 'Impression Management on Lecturers and Professors' worked. Rohit, who never even thought below 85%, for the first time got mere 60%. Prashant and Vicky also scored something between 55-60%, Manas as usual more than earlier scored 10 out of 10 and hence I gave him the name 'the 10 pointer geek'.

I am waiting for Aadarsh. He has some good news after a year at last. He is now a different person altogether. He is on his newly bought Bullet motorcycle, with new Motorola mobile phone and long hair tide with a band and smoking a cigarette.

"Hey bro I got admission in B-Pharmacy. My department is just behind your Institute in this University only."

"Congratulations for that, but why have you started smoking?"

"Just like that." He smiled. Buzz is in the market that Mr. Aadarsh also bought a new laptop and now for days he keeps on screwing girls on online communities.

Hunny got admission in the Ramlal Engineering College of Naveen and Nandini. Nandini started talking to me normally like before. She also talks to Rohit, but just for formality. Varun took the place of a close friend of her, instead. That's also a relief to me. Because in school being a friend of Rohit, Varun also wanted that Nandini should say yes to Rohit, and once he said to me that 'Rehaan you should try your best to help Rohit.'

My days are all about busy routine life with assignments and presentations in second year. Today is Aadarsh's birthday, so I dressed up well. I am wearing a white shirt with folded sleeves, a pair of blue denim jeans, black Aviator sunglasses and messed up hair.

I left college early as this is the 23rd time Aadarsh abused me on phone, because I was attending my classes.

On my way to the birthday party I saw an extremely beautiful girl. Another girl standing with her came on my way, I applied brakes to my motorcycle.

"Hi Rehaan, remember me?" That girl asked me.

"Wait, shit! Ruchi, are you really Ruchi?" I jumped in surprise.

Ruchi was with me in 11th and 12th class in school. At that time she was just a normal girl or in my words an unwanted 'Nerd'. She was quiet fat, with messed up hair in an orthodox pony tail and a big plastic frame specs. Although she hadn't changed much—just straight hair, no specs and overburdened eyes with *kajal* and an over-dose of makeup.

"You have completely changed; I mean you are looking stunningly beautiful." I lied to her whereas deep inside the 'Members of My Brain Department' were laughing loudly. 'The most renowned tittle of 'Miss Ugly' for this year goes to...... Miss Ruchi........ Wooo....... Hurray'.

"Thanks." She smiled. My belle girl, standing next to Ruchi kept on looking at me. I intentionally avoided her as if I am unaware of her presence.

"How are you, buddy?" Aashish asked me. He is with Ruchi and my belle. Aashish was also our classmate in 11th and 12th.

The moment I was about to answer him, my phone rang up again and its Mr. Aadarsh shouting at me.

"Hey I will talk to you some other day; I have some urgent piece of work. So I have to go."

For the last time I looked at that beauty.

Next day in the morning I am going to my classes and Aashish met me on the way.

"Hey, you won't believe this."

Aashish started smiling.

"What happened, dude?"

"You remember that girl who was with me and Ruchi?" Ashish asked.

What a stupid question. Even if I forget who I am, then also I will remember her.

"Yeah, what happened?" I made an innocent face.

"She was asking about you. She was impressed by your voice. Her name is Nelisha and she wants to talk to you"

I am about to die out of sudden unbearable shock of excitement.

21

Booze Party, Last Man Standing and the Chain Smoker

"I think Aashish already told you everything. We all asked Nelisha to talk to you, but she is afraid of her big brother, who is a gangster. She is having many family problems going on right now." Ruchi said and I got the answer what Ruchi wanted to say round and round.

"It's Okay buddy. I can understand. Tell her to take care of herself." I added some unnecessary emotional drama.

Many a times I saw Nandini holding Varun's hand and sharing coffee with him. Still I think Nandini is not that kind of girl who believes in love and relationships. I guess it's just a friendly gesture.

There is an Inter-College Competition organised by CITM College in Faridabad. CITM is affiliated to our University that way all other colleges including Prashant and Vicky's College, Nandini, Varun and Hunny's College, Aadarsh's College and Rohit's Engineering College were also invited.

Whereever I go my bad luck follows me. I forgot my Identity Card at home so now my ass is not welcome inside the college.

Thanks to Rohit who discovered a way in from the back door. Rohit and I had to cross a rocky jungle to be in the college. The worst part of that was climbing the 10 feet wall, don't ask me how we did that.

At last I am also sitting among audiences to laugh at others performance specially at Hunny's group dance and Nandini's street play. Trust me both their acts really sucks as they themselves do. Vicky, Prashant, Harsh, Aadarsh, Hunny, Varun, Nandini, Rohit and I are present there. Except Hunny, Harsh, Nandini and Varun others including me prefer to take our usual chairs of criticizing each and every performance, being not so happy audience.

Right from the beginning, Nandini is roaming around with Varun as if she is some kind of his wifey material. I pumped Rohit to go and talk to Nandini while taking care of others, so that they won't interfere with their bums.

Rohit came back at the end of the event with an expression of disappointment. Nandini and Varun left for Rohtak in their college bus. We all friends decided to have a drinks party at Rohit's room. Being a cold drink sucker, Harsh also prefered to go to Rohtak with other seniors in the university bus.

I, Aadarsh, Prashant, Vicky, Hunny, Rohit are sitting in Rohit's room. Manas later joined us in the evening after travelling long distance from his Institute to be here. After a while two other roommates of Rohit also came. We bought two bottles of whiskey and four beer bottles with some peanuts, Haldiram namkeen, soda, ice etc.

Party started with cheering up the first peg of whisky. We heard couple of declarations from few misconception studs.

"You bought this brand of whiskey? It never affects me an inch, even if I drink the whole bottle." Prashant boosted.

"Well you are just a kid in drinking world. Today you all are honoured to have the company of a top gun in drinking world." Hunny started blowing his own trumpet, while Vicky is in misconception as if Hunny is talking about him, poor chap it's just the first peg.

"It's just two bottles, once I had taken twelve standard pegs of Vodka." 'Manas the geek' declared after his first peg. May be one peg is sufficient for him to make an impact.

Aadarsh on the other hand was passing a sarcastic smile as if he would be the shining star of the night, going to break all records of drinking today.

We all are on the completion of the third peg and a bottle of beer as some so called experts preferred cocktail. Suddenly Rohit felt as if the bathroom is calling him, the dude started trembling with a feeling of nausea. He throws out whatever he had taken and calls it an end of his innings.

Vicky after drinking beer, started talking without any full stops and commas, suddenly the dude declared that he is going to sleep. He heads towards another room but instead made a modern art of 'Beer Cum Eating Stuff' on the wall. I and one of Rohit's roommates carried Vicky like luggage to the other room. In the room also Vicky went for the second round of vomit, this time on the floor. Seeing him Rohit's roommate also runs to the bathroom. So I left them both in the room and returned back to the party room.

Manas is struggling with his 2nd peg, where as others reached to their fourth.

Well, when we started, all were laughing with some spice of sarcastic humour. At the end of the 2nd peg there was only unnecessary laughter. In the mid of 3rd peg many of my so called friends started cracking poor jokes. Hunny being a Phd in poor jokes irritated all of us. On the start of fourth peg the sudden laughter of everybody turned to 'Their Tales of Frustrated One-Sided Love Stories'. At the end of fourth peg there was pin-drop-silence.

Manas, 'the 12 peg-Vodka geek' slept after his 2nd peg. We covered blanket on him. Let the geek enjoy his 'Story of 12 peg-Vodka' in his dreams.

Mr. Prashant on the completion of his fourth peg started asking for another to a wall near him. Poor chap after a long time realised to whom he has to ask for the next peg.

Tushar the roommate of Rohit is sitting with his first bottle of beer.

I am not feeling much high as others, but still I call it an end of my innings after the 5th peg, as I should be in my senses to take care of others.

"I will go on my own, I am OK. As I said before, this brand doesn't make any impact on me." After the 6th peg Prashant got nature's call. He had hardly walked three steps, the next moment he was talking to our sleepers and shoes. We carry this bulky ass to the other room. Prashant the hunk vomitted everything on the bed sheet and made Hunny's shirt designer one by throwing again on his shirt. Rohit brought few lemons & water for Prashant and we carried him to the park in front of the hostel. Prashant is lying on the grass in only knickers. All of us also came to the garden enjoying the fresh air.

After 5th peg Aadarsh started sharing his tragedies of life with a poor street dog thinking him to be Rohit. Aadarsh's story is so tragic that it brought tears to that dog, even. On the other hand Hunny the top gun of drinking is discussing some serious issues of drinking world with an oak tree. After a long struggle the poor street dog got independence from Aadarsh. We sent Aadarsh to the room for sleep. There was some whisky left in the bottle; Hunny in excitement took that whisky neat inside his 'World of Digestive System'. He started discussing his struggling life of how from an innocent chap he became a street fighter. I bet if I and Rohit showed any sympathy to a single word of 'His Worst Story Of The Century'.

Mr. Hunny's struggling story got new listeners in the face of plants and bushes with frequent doses of vomit by him. After his vomiting record, we took him to the same room where Aadarsh was lying. Rohit and I then shifted Prashant between Hunny and Aadarsh.

We are sitting on a bench in the park. I noticed that Rohit is feeling very low. He took out one cigarette, lighted it and started speaking slowly.

"Today when Nandini and you all came over here to Faridabad for that competition, I was excited but the experience was rather terrifying. I saw her in the morning and ignored her. When you pumped me to talk to her, I went. She was with Varun and was not feeling well. She asked him 'Please check if I am suffering from fever'. To my surprise, she folded her shirt's sleeves up and Varun touched her above the elbow—I almost died seeing that. Tears were just fighting to come out. Seeing her with someone else, I just can't express in words, how bad I felt. Later in the evening I saw them going together holding hands.

"Today I died 3 times. Two I have already told you and 3rd was when around 7 in the evening she was watching dance performance in the crowd. After 10 minutes she put her head on Varun's shoulder. I felt tears coming out from my eyes but I continued looking at her, as I knew that she has already gone too far with Varun.

"Then Varun took me aside and asked whether I still like Nandini. I said no, so he asked 'Can he take her?' I was not surprised, rather it proved that I have already lost her. Later I called Nandini and asked if she wanted to be my friend again? She did not reply and went back with Varun."

Rohit said and crushed the butt of his fifth cigarette.

Next day, I went to meet Nandini, to plead Rohit's case.

"Hi Nandini"

Nandini is standing with Varun, who wanted to leave but Nandini asked him to stay back.

"Hi, Rehaan." Nandini said.

"Actually I want to ask you something. Are you and Varun in a serious relationship?"

"What do you and Rohit want to prove? You are screwing me for quiet some time. You want to know what is between me and Varun? Yes, we are in a relationship. Happy now."

Nandini left by holding Varun's hand.

I still didn't believe her as I know that she is just pretending in front of Varun.

22

Not So Perfect Dates, Family and Kamana's Friendship

Life is boring and moving like a snail. I am enjoying my lunch time at my Institute's library searching for adequate data regarding my upcoming presentation. I am standing next to a book rack; suddenly I am the attention of everybody in the library, as weird ringtone of my mobile starts annoying others. I step outside the library and pick up the phone.

"Hello."

"Hi Rehaan. Sneha here, remember?"

"Yup, hi." I sound harsh.

"Do you know Nelisha?"

"Not exactly."

"Nelisha is my classmate. You know from the day she saw you, she is asking about you from everyone. She really likes you a lot. So Ruchi and I decided to make you both friends."

No, this can't be true. Nelisha the belle likes me? Please I will become mad. Somebody please throw me into prison as I am dangerous to society.

In the afternoon I got another call.

"Hello, Nelisha this side." Her voice is even sweeter than her looks.

"Hi Nelisha"

"I don't know what to......"

"Even I don't have any idea. Still it's a pleasure to receive a call from you."

"You really are good looking."

"Yeah, I know" I laughed. "This good looking fellow wants to know more about you. So may I have the honour to be a friend of yours."

"Sure we are friends, but friend is pronounced as frens." Nelisha corrected my pronunciation. I don't mind that. Who would not want that a stunning hottie corrects you.

"So shall we meet some day?"

"Why some day? Why not tomorrow?" She said.

Next day I went with Harsh to meet her. I am wearing from top to bottom all new cloths, which I bought for the wedding of my cousin brother. Also wearing a trendy blue denim cap, which is torn up from all sides, presenting a fashion statement. Nelisha came with Ruchi and another friend named Tanvi. It seems as if some VIP is coming with bodyguards.

"Hi Nelisha."

"Hey Rehaan." She shook hands with me.

"Nelisha I proposed you over phone but, that's not my style. So, gorgeous would you like to be my friend?"

She smiled and gave a naughty touch to my cheeks.

"You know Nelisha my friends are few and special. I want to make you my best friend." I said by adding some more irrelevant philosophy.

"For me you have already taken that place, my dear." Nelisha held my hand.

This declared emergency in 'My Department of Sex'. I wonder if she noticed some unethical movements in my pants.

Ruchi is talking on phone to her boyfriend. Harsh was speechless, still unable to believe that such a stunning beauty is talking to me.

My state is even worst than him. Many a times I asked Harsh to pinch me, if it's a dream. For me it's something impossible. How come that belle is talking to me? Why me only? Please everybody here check if this text is written in Times New Roman or if I am writing a dream. But for malfunctioning of 'My Heart Department' it's real.

That day was the start of my best ever days of life. Nelisha and I started meeting regularly in parks, restaurants, university and other not so popular places. She would always come with two-three of her friends. Beacuse if her big brother finds her with me, she will say that I am her friend's friend.

Harsh discovered new areas of friendship in Ruchi. Ruchi was also looking forward to that, but we know that she is already committed to a Delhi guy named Abhinav. Once Sneha also came with Nelisha, but I didn't give her any importance. After that day Sneha never came—may be she got the message that she is an unwanted crap.

Nelisha sometimes showed me her childhood photographs. Whenever I said anything naughty to her, she would pull my cheeks with her soft hands. One day she was wearing a thin trendy anklet—which was looking damn sexy on her milky skin.

"What does Nelisha thinks about me? I mean she likes me or what?" I asked Ruchi on phone.

"Yeah! she likes you. She talks about you all the time. She likes your eyes the most. If anybody speaks anything bad about you, she gets angry. All the time she looks forward to meet you. It's because of you only that she keeps smiling all the time."

"Ruchi, I need a favour from you."

"What's that?"

"I want to propose her. You please bring her to Hariom Restaurant on Thursday. Don't tell her about me as I will give her a surprise."

On Wednesday, I got a call from Ruchi.

"I asked Nelisha, that if Rehaan proposes you what will you say? She replied that you are really a very good friend. First you become something in your life then definitely it would be you only with whom she wants to marry. I didn't get any clue of her yes or no."

"I can't step back now. You just bring her to Hariom Restaurent, rest I will handle."

Nelisha was surprised to see me there. I was wearing a red shirt and trendy blue jeans. My face and hairstyle were proof of my heavy expenditure in the parlour. Nelisha didn't have any clue about this surprise date, so she was dressed in an ordinary way. But her dressing sense was so amazing that in casual clothes also she seemed like dressed for her ring ceremony..

"Nelisha, my life changed for better after I met you. I like the way you dress; I like the way you wear that pretty anklet just for me; I like the way you show me your childhood memories; I like the way you pull my cheeks every time I say something naughty; I like the way you treat me as a special person in your life. I want to say that I really love you."

"I like the way you express yourself, Rehaan. I will let you know my answer at the right time."

If I let her go this time, I am damn sure that her fucking right time will never come. So I have to give a 100% to my emotional drama performance.

"Look into my eyes and just say from your heart. Don't you love me, Nelisha?"

She looked at me continuously for 3 minutes and said.

"I love you too, Rehaan."

"I need you Nelisha; will you hold my hand, forever?" I forwarded my hand.

"Always my sweetheart, always" Nelisha held my hand.

One day Harsh is back to Chandigarh on holidays. Nelisha called me to meet. As usual she came with Ruchi and Tanvi. Tanvi's mother had called her home so Ruchi decided to drop her. For the first time ever in the history of 'My Not So Private Love Story' there came a twist. Nelisha and me were alone! I had written a poem for her. Which I give her.

I was walking on the road under the sun asking why?
Why am I living?
Why am I supposed to wake up every day?
Then one day you came in my life. I knew why.
It's just because you love me.
I love you, Nelisha.

"Rehaan I love you, I can't live without you."

"I think the poem is sort of stupid stuff." My innocence is at it's maximum.

"You are stupid, not the poem; this poem is everything to me." She kept her hand over mine.

"I don't understand why, but I think you are unhappy about something. Hey Nelisha, at least you can share with me."

"It's my family, Rehaan. My elder brother always creates problems."

"Don't worry I am with you, honey. Whenever you are in any problem you will always find my hand clutched into yours."

Nelisha's emotional tides are at their peak and the right time to taste her lips. Other couples were also busy in their own stuff. The moment I brought myself a little close to her shining lips, Ruchi came back and declared that it's time to go home. So, even being with the most beautiful girlfriend, I am begging for just one single French Kiss or just a kiss, at least.

One thing is for sure, this belle is optimum stuff for showing off in society. Boys are jealous of me and start calling me a stud for having such a sexy girlfriend.

Aashish proposed Ruchi. His father is on gazetted post of state government and that way he belongs to a rich and powerful family. Seeing the opportunity, Ruchi dumped Abhinav and said yes to Aashish. I once met Abhinav, he is a genuine guy though not so good looking. Abhinav asked me to help him out; I raised my voice against Ruchi's decision. That way differences are being generated between me and Ruchi. Clever Harsh takes a diplomatic stance and in return took my position in the life of Ruchi. I have some values that I will never sacrifice no matter how much I have to pay. Nelisha is also against me for taking the side of Abhinav, saying who am I to interfere in their story. But I interfered because Abhinav asked for help as all others were on Ruchi's side.

"Rehaan I am alone at home and missing you a lot. I want to meet you right now. Tell me where should I come?" Nelisha asked me over phone.

This is the chance for ding-dong and not only ding-dong, but ding-dong with a belle.

"I am coming to your house."

"No, not here"

"Hey, trust me. Don't you have faith in me?"

"I do, but darling...."

"No more arguments honey. I am coming in about half an hour."

I reached her house in just twenty five minutes. Shit, I forgot to bring condoms; I went back to a medical store, it took another fifteen minutes; I parked the bike away from her house. Nelisha was waiting for me, wearing a white short skirt and an orange T-shirt. She invited me in and gave me a glass of water. I held her hand and said.

"I love you, darling."

"I love you too."

I throw her on bed and fell on her. I was about to put my lips on her juicy lips, but suddenly someone started knocking the door.

"Nelisha, open the door." Nelisha's big brother Manoj shouted.

"Oh no, it's Manoj. What should we do now? If he see you here, he will kill both of us."

My heart beat is louder than any full volumed 2800 watt music system.

"Open the door, otherwise I will break it." Manoj started striking harder.

I climbed the window, jumped out, and started running in just an underwear. Seeing my performance I deserve to get a chance in the Olympics. Manoj is running after me with a gun in his hand.

This way my story of 'Please Just One French Kiss, Please' got a deadly end.

Thank God my mobile started ringing. Else if not in real life then at least I would have experienced the pain of a bullet in my dream. Weird dream but 'My Department of Sex' gave its optimum performance.

"Hi Rehaan, where are you?" Nelisha asked me.

"I was sleeping and thinking about you."

"I am really missing you a lot and want to meet you right now. Tell me where should I come."

"Are you alone at home?"

"No idiot, I am outside. Why did you ask?"

"No, just." Now, how can I tell her that I was just about to fuck her in my dream.

"Tell me where shall we meet?"

"OK. Let's meet at Standard Restaurant where we always meet. I will be there in half an hour."

I reached the restaurant in twenty five minutes. Shit! I forgot to bring chocolates for her. I went back to the market and bought two chocolates from there, which took another fifteen minutes. Nelisha was waiting for me outside the restaurant. She took me inside by holding my hand. After some time service boy brought two glasses of water. I held her hand and unintentionally said.

"I love you, darling."

"I love you too." She replied.

Suddenly her brother Manoj came in and saw us sitting together. He asked Nelisha to leave and gave me an angry look. I just kept looking at him, searching if he had any gun with him. For the first time my bad luck had some good news for me that he took her away from there saying nothing to me.

After that Nelisha never called me. Many a times I asked Ruchi about her, but she also didn't reply me positively.

One day my mobile started ringing flashing Ruchi's number.

"Rehaan, I am waiting for you at the university gate. It's something urgent."

I went to the university.

"Nelisha is not expecting any further lessons with you." Ruchi said and I started scratching my head to find out if 'My Department of Brains' could provide me the meaning of a single word she said.

"What's that by the way?"

"I mean that she doesn't want to continue her relationship with you"

Oh! I see. These girls always make things difficult. What's the big deal if she wants to break-up. What's that further lessons? Blah-blah! But I acted as if I am the one who got hurt. Call it a drama of innocence.

"But why? I really love her." I lied. I am ready to stand on a sharp pointed arrow, if even once I ever loved her.

"Rehaan, Manoj told everything to her parents. Her mother has high blood pressure. She fell ill hearing about you and Nelisha. Everybody in the family scolded her, blaming her for such things, you cannot even imagine. Manoj warned her that if he sees her again with you, he will shoot you. Trust me that gangster can do that. She is really afraid."

> *There are few similarities between a car and your girlfriend. The day before you are about to buy a car, you can sacrifice anything to buy it. You are so excited that all night you dream about driving your car. Similar is the case, the day before you are committed to a girl. The moment you buy a car it starts losing its charm, similar is the case with your girlfriend. After sometime you become habitual of your car for which once you were ready to sacrifice anything, same is the case with your girlfriend. If your car meets with an accident it's all over and then you go for a new car. Similarly, now I have to go for a new girlfriend. Accidents hurt you no matter how minor, same is the case with Nelisha, but trust me I have got the best insurance policy.*

Breakup no problem, the problem is I lost the belle whom I used to show off to others. Many a times I tried to talk to her. I also miss her but slowly became habitual of her absence. One day I succeeded in arranging a date with her, or in Nelisha's word 'Our Last Get Together.'

I gave my best ever performance in emotional drama. I was speaking and it seems like I am crying out of pain of losing her. I am expert in this. She gave me many irrelevant reasons in return for my emotional drama. She started crying. She literally cried like anything. After some time, she went from the restaurant with Ruchi and left me with three empty cups of coffee, one half eaten pizza, Mr. Harsh and a restaurant bill of Rs. 400. Fuck! I forgot my purse at home. Aadarsh, where are you dude?

It's the end of my second year at the Institute. I am maintaining my 70s as an average. Aadarsh failed in six subjects out of nine, but in any case in B. Pharmacy you are promoted to the next year. Aadarsh will have to re-appear in November, that way he made his yearly papers a semester system. Manas as usual remained the 10 pointer geek. Prashant and Vicky struggled in fifties, my ex-girlfriend Nelisha and Ruchi are having a score around 60 %. For my biggest surprise Rohit failed in one subject.

"You are looking upset for quiet some time. What happened?" I asked Harsh.

"No, it's just......"

"Come on bro, you can share with me."

"I like Nandini."

"What? Nandini, OK. By the way I was already suspecting you on that account. Don't you know that Rohit likes her."

"Yeah I know, but I can't stop myself."

Nandini and her sister blamed me for this; wondering why only my friends get into such things—first Rohit and now Harsh. Harsh also asked Rohit if he has any problem. At least a person should be honest to his friends. Many a times Harsh tried talking to Nandini or chat with her, but the poor guy is nowhere in her life.

News is that Aashish has dumped Ruchi for another girl. Now that's what is justice.

Ruchi and Nelisha both migrated to a college in Gurgaon.

Its Aadarsh's birthday and Rohit came here to celebrate. Vicky, Harsh, Prashant, Manas and Hunny are also present. We are standing in front of "Dimpy Food Corner."

"Hey I am going to Gurgaon tomorrow to meet Ruchi. If you are interested I will ask her to bring Nelisha along." Harsh asked me.

"No, not interested."

"How will I go alone?"

"Don't worry, I am going back to Faridabad tomorrow, I can come with you to Gurgaon and from there go to Faridabad later." Rohit said.

"Yeah that's fine."

"Hey! Look! Kamana with Shefali and other girls." Rohit shouted.

I looked at Rohit's pointed direction.

Kamana, Shefali, Sneha and Shivani were going somewhere on their scooters; I felt as if I am living in those old school days. I saw them together after a long time. Kamana is looking at me, but I am not interested.

After about half an hour Kamana with Shefali on her scooter crossed us. She did that once again and moved her hand as if she is calling me. I think it's just my illusion. When for the third time Kamana did the same, I took my motorcycle and went after her.

"I guess you want to talk to me or something." I said stopping my motorcycle besides Kamana's scooter.

"Yeah! How are you?" Kamana asked me.

"Awesome."

"Rehaan, Let's go to some restaurant."

"Yeah sure." We went to the Standard Restaurent, where I used to meet Nelisha.

Unfortunately it was closed so we three sat on the chairs outside.

"How are you, Rehaan?" Shefali asked.

"I am fine, especially after my break-up with Nelisha." I laughed.

"Break-ups really screw you. I remember when I broke up with Sohail, I threw my phone out of frustration." Kamana said.

Hmm! Sohail broke up with Kamana!

I cracked a few jokes—allright poor jokes to be more specific.

"You have changed a lot." Kamana said.

"Not much. Just that people have started calling me a stud." I passed a sarcastic smile.

"Rehaan, we are getting late. Dad must be about to call me." Shefali interfered.

"OK." I said and we three started moving towards the parking.

"By the way, I am a better person because of you, Kamana. Thanks. I respect you a lot."

Respect you, sorry darling I mean fuck you.

"Yup I know Rehaan. I heard about your academic performance. I am really proud of you." Kamana puts her hand on my back.

"So here I am again. May I have the honour to be your friend?" I forward my hand to Kamana.

"My pleasure honey." Kamana shook hands.

I notice fireworks in Shefali's ass.

I gave Kamana and Shefali chocolates. Kamana really got excited getting chocolate from me.

"Hey Rehaan! Give me your mobile number."

I told her my number and she gave me a missed call.

"This is my number." Kamana smiled showing her not so cute dimple.

I again shook hands with Kamana and Shefali and went back to my friends.

Thanks to Rohit today we decided to make a night out. According to him, it will introduce another chapter of adventure to our lives. Sometimes I wonder why Rohit doesn't go for those idiotic reality shows, at least they suck less than Aadarsh. Rohit and Aadarsh went to bring few bottles of beer and something to eat. I am sitting alone at the top of the stadium waiting for them. Suddenly my phone started ringing, and Kamana's name is flashing.

"What makes a gorgeous like you turning your steering wheel to my side?"

"Just like that." Kamana replied. She kept on talking to me about her life after school and the same girly stories.

"Hey as we are friends now, so no formalities, OK? By the way, I am like a glue to all my friends, so even when you stop talking to me, I will still remain stuck to you." I laughed.

"Same here" Kamana said with a smile.

"Then, it's a deal. Whenever I call, you will pick up your phone."

"OK baba, now you are my 'Man'. Anything for you, buddy"

"I will call you tomorrow."

"I will wait for that."

When I turned around I saw Aadarsh and Rohit standing behind me, quietly listening to our conversation.

23

END OF THE FLASHBACK, THE BET AND ROHIT'S FIRST UGLY GIRLFRIEND

I looked around; Mr. Aadarsh is snoring loudly, making two empty bottles of beer his pillow. Mr Rohit is searching for a new corner for vomiting the second time. He is the biggest insult, the drunkard world could ever have.

It's 4.30 a.m. and throughout the night I was telling them my story.

"What's the moral of the story?" Rohit asked after completing his 'Mission Vomiting'.

"Moral of the story is that there is no 'Best Approach' for all girls, still it is the 'Right Approach' which matters. Different situations call for different approach and it's the right way with which you can have even the most beautiful girl." I said.

"Nope! let me tell you—The moral of the story is that even after having three girlfriends, Mr. Rehaan is still a Virgin." Aadarsh shouted half asleep.

"It's not like that, you asshole. I never really loved any of my girlfriends and neither do I love Kamana, who has now started seeing her Mr. Perfect in me. So that way I don't go for Kamana also. I will lose my virginity to someone I fall in real love."

"That means you will remain a Virgin, all your life." Rohit laughed at his unique kind of intellectual side and again started searching for a new corner.

"Exactly" Aadarsh appreciated Rohit's statement.

"You just don't open your mouth. Whatever Rohit says, by default you are on that stand only. Why don't you both become 'a Couple', as I think both of you will never find a girl in your life."

"OK, that's the bet then. Let us see who will lose his virginity first. If you ever find your so called 'Real Love', first, or Aadarsh and me find 'A Girl'."

"Deal bro." I forwarded my hand, Rohit puts his hand on mine and Aadarsh followed. But one more hand also falls on ours.

"I heard there is some bet going on here." Vicky said.

He just came to the stadium for a morning walk and saw us sitting there.

"The bet goes like this. There will be a total of 100 marks. 5 marks for hugging a girl, 5 for kissing her, 10 for a French Kiss, 30 for the foreplay and 50 for losing your virginity, that too, to a virgin girl. The one who loses his virginity first or scores a total of 100 will be the 'Real Stud'." Rohit said.

"Done." We all agreed.

Rohit left for Gurgaon with Harsh to meet Ruchi and her friends. I am lying on my bed and thinking about everyone. Rohit and Aadarsh have completely changed. Aadarsh, Rohit and Vicky are chain smokers. Hunny smokes occasionally and Manas also in a month or two takes two or three cigarettes. I am the only one in the group who doesn't smoke. Same is the story with alcohol. Only I and Manas are occasional and social drinkers, but the rest of them drink regularly. Thinking about my friends, I fell asleep.

> I am lying on a not so comfortable bed in a Dilapidated or ramshackle room. Cigarette smoke is all around and nothing is visible. My left hand is resting on one side of the bed with a burning cigarette and smoke rings surrounding me all over. I am constantly looking at not so clearly visible stationary aged fan, which seems like moving at its maximum. A girl is lying with me under a blanket with her face hidden under my arm. She is grabbing my vest with her hand, in which she is wearing a cute thin golden bangle. My right hand is moving back and forth on her back for making her feel comfortable. I crushed the half burned cigarette on the table nearby. I then kiss her cheeks again.

What the fuck! Again the same old dream. Man something is wrong here.

I never expected Rohit to ever fail in any subject. My parents always gave example of him whenever the topic of studies was discussed. The most hard-working, studious, innocent, and honest person now has a packet of cigarette in his pocket instead of pen, and making a bet like this. Truth is always stranger than fiction.

The next day early in the morning Rohit called me.

"Hey, guess what? Ruchi gave me her mobile number yesterday." Rohit shouted in excitement.

"Ha ha ha, there is nothing to jump. Ruchi gives her number to every second person she meets."

"But still buddy, as the ball is in my court let me hit it."

"Go for it then."

"I need your help; girls are still a mystery for me."

"Just relax and be nice to her; never disclose your fucking intentions. Listen and console her no matter what. Always remember it's just the right approach and you can fuck any p***y."

Many a times Kamana would call me. To my surprise I came to know that now a days Ruchi is the best friend of Kamana.

Whenever I talk to Kamana, I still try to impress her, may be deep inside my unconscious mind the same old school boy Rehaan is living in a small hut. Whatever be the scene, my friendship story is going smoothly. Kamana told me that although she broke off with Sohail but even now they talk and meet sometimes.

Now a days, I got a new job—The job of a 'Love Consultant'. Seeing the overwhelming response of my friends-cum-fans, I am thinking of opening a consultancy business i.e. 'Rehaan Love Consultancy Pvt. Ltd.'

Note: We have no branches.

Case No.1-Manas

"Dude I will die if I don't get Pooja." Manas jumped in excitement.

"So what way can I help you Mister?"

"I met her on my college trip; she came there with her friends. She is doing BDS. The moment I saw her, I realised the true meaning of love. I was crazy in looking for love in all the girls who came in my life before."

"I think you were just after those girls and to the best of my knowledge no one came in your life."

"No. That's not so. I mean yes...... that is true, but... whatever.......... fuck....... I want Pooja."

"OK. This time do what I tell you."

"I have already told her the story of my life and what I feel about her."

"What was her reply?"

"She said she is not ready for a relationship, so for now we can be just good friends."

"I already knew this will happen. Never, never ever tell the girl 'everything'. Let the mystery continue. Don't worry there is still a scope of 'My Guilt Theory'."

"Now what the fuck is this 'My Guilt Theory'?"

"That's not the question and neither is it of your concern. You just call her right now and let her feel that her words made you really hurt ."

I tried to cope up with Manas's ever sinking loveship, but the dude always wants to remain the Captain. Many a times I tried to take over the captaincy but the moment he gets some success he would start applying his own '10 Pointer Brain Department' and hence the ship sinks, always.

Case No.2-Rohit

"So how is your story of 'Ruchi, the Monster' going on?" I asked Rohit over phone.

"We are good friends and life is going just great. She is really a very nice girl."

"There is nothing in the name of 'nice girl' exists in her. Time has come when you should take your friendship to greater heights."

"I too want to commit, but don't know how?"

"Propose her. Fix a date with her and let me know."

Case No.3-Vicky

I never expected that Vicky would ever try for a girl like Ishita, who is on his tuition classes. If you look at Vicky's face and Ishita's beauty, then I don't mind if you declare that Vicky would be the last option for Ishita on this earth. Whatever, the dude wants this girl anyway.

"There is only one way out to 'Your Not-So-Possible Love Story'. Show her that you are 'A Pot of Gold'. As you already know that she is the kind of girl who changes her boyfriends as if she is changing a pair of sandals."

"But how?" Vicky asked.

"Just try to look relaxed. Wear expensive clothes, take a different car on different days to your tution, be sober and please change your fucking hairstyle."

Case No.4-Aadarsh

Log on any time 24x7 you will find Mr. Aadarsh online searching for a girl. He is all the time copying photos of girls from online communities. After going round and round he found Tania who is doing B.D.S. from Jaipur and that too just as a friend. Don't get excited, their friendship is mere an accident that occurs once in a billion. I will take his case in the next chapter.

Case No.5-Prashant

One more stud who is cracking nuts on online communities searching for his Miss Right is Mr. Prashant. He anyhow cracked the code for a Delhi girl's account and got a chance for interacting with her. But the stud faced other problems, being extraordinary in breaking 'The Legs of English', he needs 'An Angel in Disguise' like me. Prachi, the poor girl got impressed with Prashant, when actually it's me who all the time chats with her in the name of Prashant. I hate this kind of social service. A month later Prashant declared himself committed.

One day Prashant took me to Delhi to meet Prachi. Two girls were coming towards us. Prashant pointed out one calling her Prachi. The girl is beautiful, fair complexioned, nice features and her dressing sense complimenting her further. The earth revolved around me in a flick of second when I realised that the girl whom I just described is Neha, Prachi's friend. Prachi was total opposite—my sympathy with Prashant. That day for the first time I went to a disco in Greater Kailash, Delhi. There the boyfriend of Neha was already waiting for her. I am the only one 'Unfortunate Stag' and the worst dancer present in the disco. But thanks to the bottle of beer I had something to smile.

I wonder what pleasure my friends get in smoking. Sometimes it came to my mind to try it out once. But I hold myself back. Whenever I see cigarette smoke around I get a strange feeling. Sometimes I feel that the cigarette smoke is calling me towards it but I always resist my temptation. So, till now I am not an active smoker, but thanks to my best friends, at least a passive smoker.

Kamana's holidays are over and she is going back to her college. Sometimes it feels good talking to somebody whom

I once loved the most. Kamana and Nelisha both suggested Ruchi to go for Rohit, considering him a genuine guy. Who will tell them that there is nothing 'genuine' in Mr. Rohit's profile now.

So lets now come back to Mr. Rohit's tale of, 'My Love for Dracula'.

"Harsh and I are going to meet Ruchi tomorrow. I think Nelisha will also come with her." Rohit said over phone.

"I will also be coming with you, but with a girl."

"I guess Nelisha would be the last person who wants to see your face. By the way, who is this girl?"

"Shefali. She was asking for a hangout with me. The scene will be great when I introduce two ex-girlfriends of mine to each other. And guess what? You are going to propose Ruchi tomorrow."

"No way bro, I can't do that."

"There is nothing called 'No Way' in 'My Books of Ethics'."

The next day Harsh refused to go to Gurgaon as he doesn't like Ruchi anymore. Once he told me that the only use of Ruchi is that his room is full of gifts given by her. I tried my best to convince him but he said, 'Only a desperate 'Sex Insect' like Rohit, can accompany that 'Ruchi, the Dracula' in public places'.

Rohit and me are waiting at ISBT, Kashmere Gate for Shefali. Rohit started his 'I Can't Propose Her' business once again.

"I can't propose a girl, I mean I don't know how to propose effectively." Rohit said while scratching his head.

I gave him a few tips and gifted him readymade proposes for Ruchi in a gift wrap with ribbon above it. Somehow I motivated him to propose to an obvious 'Yes Girl'.

Shefali stepped out of a Honda City, as one of her friends dropped her. We three are now heading towards Gurgaon. Shefali was expecting that I will take her in a car but the poor girl had DTC bus in her fate.

"You know my father never let me step out of home without a car. And here I am first time travelling by DTC, that too standing in 'not so adjusting' crowd." Shefali taunted me.

"Many things happen for the first time babes. Just enjoy it." I replied.

Rohit and I passed our time by making fun of each other. This is the best possible way of passing time when you are accompanied by a boring girl.

Ruchi was stuck in surprise, thrice. First, when she saw me. Second, when she came to know that Harsh hasn't come with us. Nelisha was also unpleasantly surprised to see me and that too with another girl—Somebody please dial 101. Nelisha after sometime joined her other friends. I signalled Rohit to propose Ruchi as I took Shefali with me to the ground floor, leaving them alone.

Then came the third surprise for Ruchi.

"I think I like you......, I mean....... I guess........ I love you." Rohit spoke in broken lines.

"So you are going to propose me this way." Ruchi said surprisingly.

"This is the best of my talent in proposing a girl. Let me put it like this, Ruchi you are my moon, my star......"

"My planet, my galaxy, my sun, right? Are you proposing a girl or some crack Astronomer?" Ruchi said sarcastically.

"OK, OK, OK. Ruchi I love you and that's it. Fuck, I can't innovate any more."

"You disappoint me, still I love you." Ruchi puts her hand on Rohit's hand.

"Ruchi, you make me feel special, dear."

"You know Rohit, today is the most special day of my life."

I wonder if they left anything ordinary as everything was special around them.

'I can't tolerate 'Shefali the bore' anymore.' I declared to myself and made a not-so-surprising entry to the ongoing celebration of Rohit and Ruchi.

It's time to go back home.

On the way back, Rohit told me about his worst propose.

"Yes, Ruchi said 'yes' to me. I am the most special person in her life." Rohit jumped in excitement.

"Yes, you are the fourth most special person in her life." I laughed.

"While coming here, you both were making fun of Ruchi's looks and now you made her your girlfriend." Shefali taunted Rohit. We started laughing loudly.

Rohit left for Faridabad and Shefali came along with me to Rohtak. While sitting in the bus she fell asleep on my shoulders. Girls look cute while sleeping, especially when they sleep on your shoulders, holding your hands.

That way our hero Rohit got his first girlfriend or in my not so acceptable language 'Rohit's First Ugly Girlfriend'.

I don't know what more I have to see because of that bet.

24

The Worst Idea, the First Foreplay and the Message

Prashant completely changed after he commited to Prachi, who dominated him like anything. Prachi is one year older than Prashant. Seeing her, only one line comes to my mind for Prashant '*Jab dil aya gadhi pe to pari ka kya kasoor*' (When your heart fall for a Jackass then what's the fault of an Angel). She manipulated him against everybody and made him run away with her. Prashant's mother had died many years ago, that way his father was left alone in the house—the old man had nothing but tears in his eyes. Fuck you Prachi and Prashant. They came back home one month later, after getting married in a temple. I really felt sorry for his father.

I consider myself the most insignificant asshole, although I have an inborn talent to make others love-stories successful. We are sitting in Aadarsh's house. Rohit had came to Rohtak to meet us and just finished his call to Ruchi. Aadarsh was upset as he had asked for phone number of Tania which she refused.

"Hey, Tania is online. What should I do now?" Aadarsh asked Rohit.

"Asking me? You want to lose your so called online friendship? Don't ask me, ask the stud" Rohit replied to Aadarsh pointing at me.

"The answer is simple. Time for applying 'My Guilt Theory'. For that you have to handover your laptop to me." I said. He gave me a few tips about the way he chats with her, so she will not be able to notice that it's someone else who is chatting in the name of Aadarsh. After a formal Hi-Hello, I started 'My Guilt Theory'.

Aadarsh*: i wanna say sumthin*

Tania*: ya tell, wat happen*

Aadarsh*: i always thot u a gud frn of mine and i mean that but i hide sumthin, i wanna confess sumthin.*

Tania*: wat?*

Aadarsh*: i hav sum guilt feeling*

Aadarsh*: u remember i asked u for your ph. no. weeks ago*

Tania*: yeah i remembr and i said tht i wil giv wen rit time cum.*

Aadarsh*: dat time i felt bad, bt i dint let u no that cause i don wanna spoil ur mood*

Aadarsh*: u no Tania that day i thought u don think me worth ur frnship*

Aadarsh*: u shuld hv notice that i often sound strange while chating with u last days*

Tania: *yeah me too wanna discuss wid u bout that, bt then thot may be thts just my misconception*

Aadarsh: *actually i felt guilt tht i m not worth knowing ur mobile no. or if i m just bothering u unnecessary daily over here*

Tania: *thats not so yaar, u r realy a sweet frn of mine. Actually that time i was about to change ma number so tht way theres no use of giving u that no.*

Aadarsh: *n pl don take my words to heart, its just buddy that u r realy good frn of mine n i respect u tht way i don wanna hide nything from u so i confessed this*

Tania: *u no today r frnship become stronger thn before, be with me like this always n ya hers my no. 0989*******

Aadarsh: *I just wanna say that no matter whatever the situation may be bt i will never let u down. U r ma best frn, be with me always.*

Tania: *U too now become a special part of ma life n i wil never let u go.*

I continued my emotional drama for some more time till Tania declared that today is the most special day of her life and Aadarsh being the best part of it.

Call my life boring or in my words a porn movie without any porn stars. Love is in the air all around. But being in the final year of graduation, I have just one thing in my mind, *i.e.* I want to crack the 'CAT exams'. Kamana would always boost up my morale by saying 'I know you can do it Rehaan. I am with you, dear.' But my mock test scores are making an up and down graph always. CAT is near and I had not talked to Kamana for quite some time. Few days before the CAT I received her message.

'Hey budy sory I wasn't able to call u, ur CAT exam is near. Do ur best. I knw u cn do it. Do it for me, I wil pray for u dear, tc sweets.'

I am sitting in the examination hall. There are 40 students and a strange looking invigilator. Well DI was not a big deal for me, I will get maximum score in this section. Then I took care of Verbal Ability (English Section), and in the last faced my most fierce enemy 'Quant'. For me every question in Quant seems to be the same. I came to a conclusion that the right choice or option for every question would be 'none of these'.

My exam centre is in Gurgaon so Rohit had come with me. The fact is that he came for Ruchi and to gain some score for the bet. Rohit met Ruchi at Sahara Mall. Mr. Rohit is struggling with only a sweat shirt because of his so called style statement, if somebody removes it, the dude is perfect for a photo shoot for showing the condition of persons below poverty line.

The first thing Ruchi did was hug him i.e. 5 marks. As my paper is of three hours so Rohit decided to go for 'a not so interesting movie', as he intends to do something more interesting with her in the cinema hall. A song is going on in the movie where hero and heroine are running towards each other in slow motion accompanied by Ruchi's yawning.

"Hey Ruchi I love you."

"I love you too darling." Rohit kissed Ruchi's not so rosy cheeks. That means another 5.

Hero and heroine are still running and singing, but Mr. Rohit took his lips to Ruchi's lip balm factory. It's hard to say whether Rohit is kissing Ruchi's lips or eating her lip balm. Anyway the poor chap scored another 10 points. Rohit's hands are engaged in rock climbing in Ruchi's hilly areas, I think the dude is thinking about making a half-century today, but got run out when an old school mate recognised the most sincere, most studious student of the school doing some unsocial things.. Ruchi saw the rest of the movie sitting straight in her seat and away from Rohit's exploring hands. That way Mr. Rohit remained stuck on a mere score of 20.

After the CAT exam I was waiting for Rohit to come. To pass my time I groomed up my aeronautical skills by making paper aeroplanes of CAT question paper. At last Rohit, the dude came with a 'Shit Man' expression on his face.

Mr. Rohit now a days is making frequent visits to Ruchi's 'Department of Brain' and 'Department of Heart' to convince her to open the gates of her 'Department of Sex'. Or in simple words, to have sex with her or in ethical words to be physical with her. But clever Ruchi kept all her 'Departments' closed for Rohit by making some silly excuses.

"I am fed up now." Rohit said in frustration.

"Hmm...... There is only one way out then." I replied

"What?"

"Breakup! Why are you screwing your ATM card unnecessarily on a 'Cost Without Benefit Product'?"

"How should I do that?"

"This is the breakup style which is now in latest fashion." I told him a set of dialogues.

Rohit thought for a while and dialled Ruchi's number.

"Hey honey, how are you darling?"

"You are with me, so obviously I am the happiest person on earth." Ruchi replied.

"Ruchi please smile"

"Smile, but why?"

"Come on Ruchi smile for me."

"Alright." Ruchi smiles.

"My sweetheart sounds nice with a smile. Ruchi I want to say something."

"About what?"

"I am so cute, right?"

"Yeah you are."

"You don't want to spoil my cuteness, right?"

"Of course not, my sweetheart."

"So, that is why I am dumping you."

"What?" Ruchi shouted in shock.

"Yeah, darling you are so boring. I mean you really suck. So try your 'touch me not' philosophy somewhere else." Rohit said and cut the phone.

Rohit is on a mere score of twenty. The worst victim of Rohit's break up is me, because after that Kamana also stopped talking to me or responding to my messages. I tried Kamana's phone many a times but she didn't pick up. Who can understand a woman; Fuck you Kamana; who needs a fatty aunty.

Rohit's Dard Bhari Theory

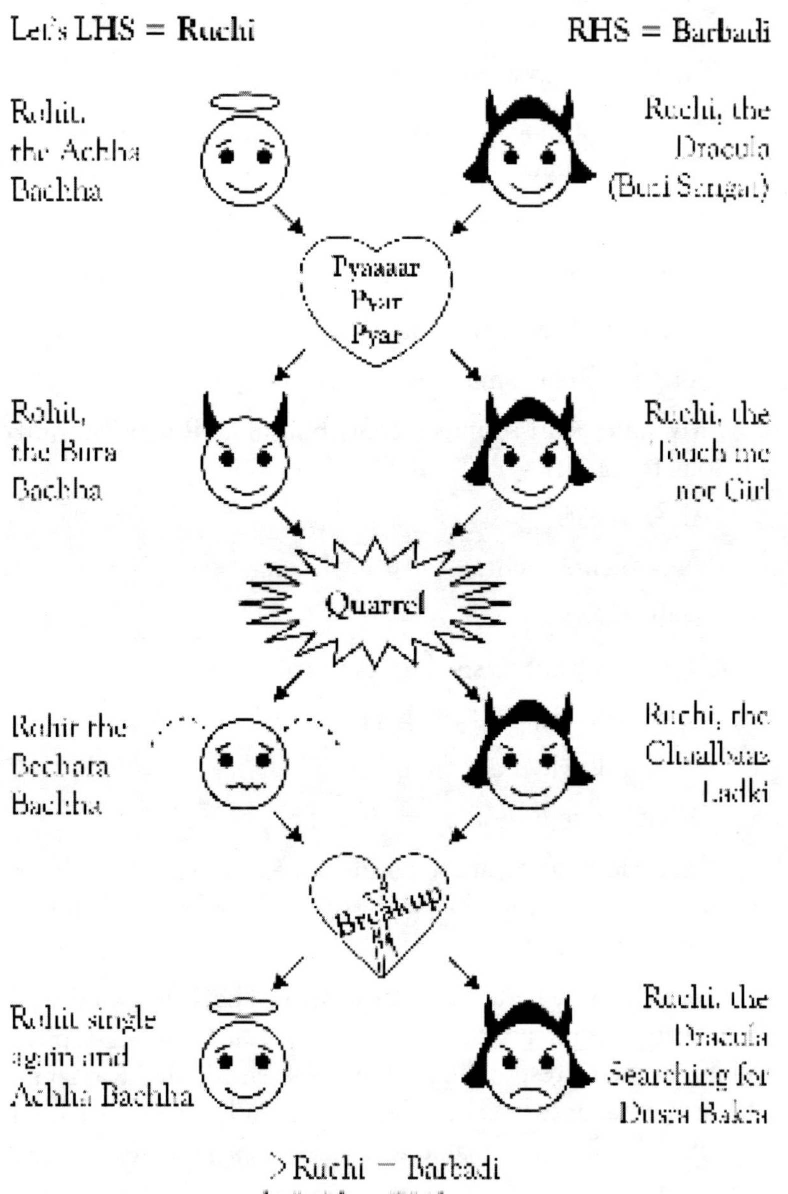

$\because$ Ruchi = Barbadi
$\therefore$ LHS = RHS
Hence Proved

Placement season is on in engineering college. Rohit got a job in a MNC. Manas on the other hand got placed in three i.e. IOCL, DRDO and NTPC, that too with good packages.

We are celebrating Rohit and Manas's placement. I also got a score of my CAT exam.

"What's the score?" Rohit asked.

"It's 80.2 percentile, I scored badly in Quant section, but in rest of the two, I cleared the cut off. Whatever, 80 is also not a bad score, I guess."

"So what next?" Manas asked.

"I will write a novel."

"Ha ha. Jokes apart, seriously, what next?" Manas asked again after laughing out a bit .

"Yup, I am serious. I am going to write a novel." I smiled.

"And what about your MBA?" Rohit asked.

"I will continue from IMSAR, but my first priority will be writing the novel."

"Write a novel? What the fuck will you write?" Aadarsh questioned.

"I will write our story."

"This is the worst idea I have ever heard." Aadarsh criticised and continued with his bottle of beer.

I reduced my social interactions and concentrated on my so called worst idea. Writing a story is not a big deal, but writing it in an interesting way is something like fucking ten times the same girl in one day. Others are planning to win the bet and I am burning the lamp oil by thinking and writing a best seller in the name of my novel.

"Don't behave like a bird which sits on one branch of the tree and shits all day. Be a man, propose her." I said to Aadarsh.

My dialogues really sucks but works too.

"What if she says no?" Aadarsh asked me.

"That is not what matters. You just propose her. Even if she says no, don't give up. Just try to convince her."

After a couple of tries, at last Mr. Aadarsh made the goal and proposed Tania. Tania initially said no but again thanks to 'My Guilt Theory' the dude succeeded. This way Mr. Aadarsh got something in the name of a girlfriend, although 'A Touch Me Not Stuff'. There is a sudden change in routine life of Aadarsh now. He is busy all the time on phone with his girlfriend, discussing every fuck of their life. I think that they have also started asking for permission from each other for going to the toilet. But I wonder if Aadarsh ever told her the truth about himself. What Tania knows about Aadarsh is not the real Aadarsh. As I mentioned earlier, Tania is something called touch me not stuff, but Aadarsh is still looking for an opportunity in her, for the bet.

"Tania, define our relationship." Aadarsh said.

"Are you allright darling?" Tania asked

"No seriously, just define what I mean to you?"

"You know Aadarsh, I love you. You mean everything to me. You are my man who makes me happy all the time. For you I can do anything, darling."

"Don't say that Tania—anything means everything. That's a broad term." Sometimes I feel, if Aadarsh had used these terminologies in his studies, he would be something worth today.

"What do you mean exactly?" Tania asked.

"I feel that time has come when we should take our relationship one step ahead."

"You are talking about sex?"

"Not exactly, somewhere near about."

"Aadarsh I never expected this from you. Do you have any idea what this means to a girl? I have some values." The usual heavy dialogues of a 'Touch Me Not Middle Class Girl'.

> *Always remember never use the word S, E, and X, it sounds harsh. Instead call it love-making which means the same but is more sophisticated.*

Aadarsh being a bright student of mine, somehow coaxed her for a foreplay.

Describing 'not so astonishing features' of Tania is something worth discussing, if we consider her with Aadarsh. Even after being best friend of Aadarsh, I think that Aadarsh and Tania are the oddest couple I have ever seen. Tania is of medium height, normal figure and with pathetic sense of humour, she is the best way to screw a torture like Aadarsh. She is three times fairer than Aadarsh and that makes me to say 'hats off dude'. At least he is doing something worth for the bet, not like me screwing his days in writing the crap you are reading now.

Aadarsh and Tania took a not-so-happening room in a not-so-happening hotel which is situated at a not-so-happening place. After a few non-directional dialogues, Aadarsh hugged Tania and kissed on her bulky-cheeks. There are four or five attacks on Tania's face until she applied a tissue paper to wipe away the unwanted saliva.

A four minute continuous French kiss is enough to declare urgency of oxygen by their 'Department of Lungs and Environment'. After a couple of further tongue-rollings, a time came when they both moved ahead for making two bodies one soul. Aadarsh's train is moving fast over Tania's tracks, going around few specific stations again and again.

Everything is fine until Aadarsh puts off his T-shirt. There are times when you have to reconsider about your decisions; it's the same time for Tania. With a wide range of dense forest, Tania bet everything on the existence of wild life on Aadarsh's body. Thanks that Aadarsh had taken a bath; Tania is visiting the forest in monsoon season. Aadarsh is enjoying the moves of Tania's belly, declaring the foreplay reaching its heights. But local Police are in a mood of playing their favourite game 'Knock Knock Guess Who is There'?

There are times when you think why you throw your clothes here and there when you were excited. The door was about to be broken, the two inside are trying to escape from the window. Tania shouted and broke the record of being panicky. Aadarsh is cursing that it would have been great if he had pursued his career in 'Crisis Management' instead of B. Pharmacy.

I guess nobody likes to have lunch in the police station. It took us about two hours to reach that police station. Aadarsh is exceptionally shining being just in his branded underwear (that too bought from Janpath) among other criminals. His face and body marks are telling the story of 'I Am Innocent Please Let Me Go' with police. Police let them go after signing a bond that they will never do it again. Police dropped Tania to her hostel but also complained to her warden.

We are sitting at a tea stall near the bus stand waiting for a bus to Rohtak. Rohit gave a one rupee coin to a beggar, out of frustration the beggar returned him Rupee 2 coin. That way Rohit didn't miss the opportunity of getting insulted from the beggar community even, my sympathy for him. What's better than morning newspaper with tea and that too when Aadarsh's photo is published as a celebrity for the article 'Police Regulating

Call Girl Business'. Aadarsh made rounds of the press office worried if this newspaper is also distributed in Haryana.

For me I got the matter for my story. What else a struggling author like me needs.

"Dude you scored 50 out of 100 and crossed Rohit's score. You are the current *buzz* in my novel." I laughed.

"Fuck that bet and fuck your novel." Aadarsh shouted in anger and steped into the bus.

Nandini's elder sister is doing M. Tech from Mangalore University. She is having holidays now a days and wished to meet me. I am on my way to some place with Manas but I prefer to meet them first. We four were sitting in a restaurant, while eating pizza Manas showed his over smartness, trying hard to impress Nandini and her sister, even after knowing that he is the worst geek ever born.

On the way back Manas is sitting at the back of my motorcycle with head down. I knew what he is about to say.

"Nandini is really a nice girl." Manas whispered in a deep voice and trust me I got the idea for the story of Manas in the next chapter.

Not every morning brings such a news as this. I am half asleep when I notice my phone blinking, declaring an unread message in the inbox. I opened that message.

'I am no more a virgin, I scored 150 n she is Ishita. TC, Vicky.'

25

Nandini's Downfall, Manas's Love Dilema and Unrecognizable Kamana

Mr. Vicky can't score 150 as the bet in itself leads to a highest total of 100. I investigated the whole matter. The moment I saw Ishita, I recognised her. She is a friend of one of my college classmate, who had introduced me to her. She was interested in knowing about CAT preparation. I taught her DI and English and also how to prepare. So that way, I somehow verified about her relationship with Vicky. According to her Vicky is just a friend.

Ishita's friend in my class told me about Ishita's past. From the schooldays she used to have many boyfriends and one should not be surprised if she had already lost her virginity way back in school.

On my confronting him, the poor chap accepted that he had lied to us, on the other hand Ishita had actually used him. Vicky just reached to a hug, a kiss and a forced French kiss. That means the asshole is having a score of just 20 i.e. level with Rohit.

"I can't believe this." Aadarsh jumped in surprise.

"Its true, dude. Aarti is getting married to Dushyant, a businessman from Delhi. It's love-cum-arranged marriage. They like each other and the marriage is fixed by Aarti's mother. It's a money game boss."

"But Rehaan, Aarti is only 20 years old. How come her mother marry her now, when her elder brother is still single."

"Money buddy, it's all because of money. Dushyant is from a rich business family of Delhi. He will help her brother's business also. Aarti is a product being traded for mutual benefit of two families. She is happy as she has got an ATM machine in the face of Dushyant."

"Materialistic world." Aadarsh said sarcastically and lit his cigarette.

I am writing about the background of my novel and the incidence about Rohit's downfall. Suddenly my phone started ringing, It is Nandini.

"Rehaan, I want to meet you." She is not sounding good.

"Now?"

"Right now, please Rehaan."

"Let's meet in front of the Central Library; I will be there in fifteen minutes."

Nandini arrived by car five minutes late. She comes to me and sits quietly.

"What happened, Nandini?"

"I am sorry Rehaan."

She breaks into tears.

What happened to her? Nandini was crying and instead of stopping her I am looking around that nobody sees me with a crying girl. People are always ready to beat a scoundrel like me for making a girl cry. Trust me, to the best of my knowledge, I have done nothing to her. Why is she crying? Please stop it otherwise my parents will have to incur unnecessary expenditure on buying garlands to put around my smiling photo on the wall with burning incense sticks below it.

I placed the crying girl into her car and drove away from the library.

"Now stop crying and speak up." I said while searching for something called music system. At last I find it, but fuck, where are the Audio CDs.

"It's Varun. He is mentally distubring me. Remember when you asked me about Varun. At that time he was the closest friend of mine. I told you that yes we are in a relationship. Actually there was nothing between us and I just said so that Rohit can move on. After that Varun started convincing me to become his girlfriend. He always used to say that 'You are my best friend and whatever we share is love. Actually you are in love with me, but think it as just friendship. So be my girlfriend.' For days he kept on playing the same music. I also thought that maybe he is right, so I said yes. The next day he called me to his house. I was sitting with him when he said to click a photo of both of us, so that in future when we get married we will keep it as our good remembrance. We clicked two photos: one simple and in other he clicked while kissing me on my cheeks. He then kissed twice on my lips. I got up and ran away from there, as I doubted his intentions. I didn't talk to him after that and broke up with him."

"That's it?" I gave a fake smile as if nothing has happened. She started crying again.

"Now listen to me. This is not a jungle where he can do whatever he wants. Secondly, kissing on cheeks is not a big thing. It's just that you somehow trusted a wrong person. We are human beings and doing mistakes is in our nature. Don't worry I am with you, always." I said

"But he is disturbing me by sending messages and picture on my mobile and email."

"Listen sweetheart it is like 'flicking of eyes' to beat him alone. The point is that I want you to teach him a lesson. This way you can kill your fear of him."

"We are having a conference of all students of the Engineering Colleges which are affiliated to M.D. University. It will be day after tomorrow in Gurgaon. Varun would also be there." She told me.

"Great, then show him his level. But don't go alone. As Rohit's college is also affiliated to M.D. University, I will ask him to be with you."

"Rehaan, I am feeling really bad. Rohit is a genuine person. I behaved badly with him for which I can't forgive myself." She said and started crying again.

"Wait, I will also come as I have to accompany Manas. He is visiting head office of some organization to submit a project report. I will catch you and Rohit in the evening. Just don't worry and yell up everything on Varun's face. Show him his standard."

I told the whole story to Rohit. This is the time to prove whatever he promised to himself for Nandini. The next day Nandini sits with Rohit in the conference.

After the conference Varun comes to Nandini as expected.

"I want to talk to you, Nandini."

"Yeah, bark."

"I want you back anyways and will make sure that you come back to me."

"Have you ever looked at yourself, you asshole? You won't even get me in your dreams, you ugly dog."

"You know what? You are yourself responsible for everything."

"Fuck off! You are not worth even my foot; now take away your scum face out of here."

"You know you are of a spoiled character. I will see you." Varun shouted.

"Wait, this is your reply." Nandini slapped really hard at Varun's face and showed him her middle finger.

"Get lost from here otherwise you will be responsible for your broken ass." Rohit said in aggression.

Varun got scared and went away whispering to himself.

Nandini left with her cousin brother, who came to pick her up. Rohit, Manas and I went to a showroom in the shopping mall to buy a pair of jeans, suddenly Rohit shouted.

"Look, Kamana! It's Kamana."

I saw to my right side. Kamana was coming with Sohail and continuously staring at me. Rohit is shouting and shaking me in excitement as if he has seen any Alien.

"So what, dude. What should I do then? Relax! There is nothing to jump." I said and entered the showroom.

I had seen Kamana before Rohit notified me about her presence, but I didn't recognise her. For the first time there was no movement in 'My Department of Heart'. Kamana is looking like a mature lady and was more bulky than before. I have four magical alphabets for her U, G, L and Y. But it's not about her looks, as it was never before.

"Hey how could it be possible? You just saw Kamana, and no reaction from your side. It is really strange." Rohit is surprised.

"It's just that I really didn't recognise her. How could an unrecognizable stuff make an impact on you." I passed a smile. Its strange to me also that how I didn't recognise Kamana.

On our way back in the bus 'Manas, the Geek' opened his book of love tragedies to introduce another chapter to his yet another 'Unique Love Delima'.

"Does Rohit still like Nandini?" Manas asked me.

"I think so."

"I want to tell you one thing. I feel bad about it but I can't resist myself. I want to say that........" Manas was about to move further but I interfered.

"That you have also started liking Nandini. You are serious for her. Blah-blah." I laughed.

"How do you know? I never told this to anybody."

"My name is Rehaan, that's why." I smiled.

"Do you think it's wrong on my part?"

"It's not a matter of surprise, dude. By nature opposite sex attract each other. Nandini is really a sex bomb and you are not the first one dreaming about her."

"Not that way. I often chat with her over internet. She is really a nice girl and I am happy to be her friend."

The most social person is now the most unsocial being, as all the day I keep on screwing my mind and laptop in writing something that even I don't understand. Inspite of writing a novel I flirt over internet with girls to be up to the mark in the dynamic world of girls and their ever changing philosophy.

For the first time, I noticed some serious changes in Manas' attitude. He used to come on every weekend and most of the time be with me roaming here and there. Now a days, most of the time he keeps quite. And if he has to say anything, he talks about Nandini only. This way he screws me with his bore qualities whether he speakes or not. But I know that deep inside he really likes Nandini. For the first time I too agree that at last Manas can say that he really likes some girl. Nandini told me how 'Manas, the geek', tries to impress her but instead bores her the most. What else you expect from a '10 pointer geek' who got three job offers and that too with handsome packages.

Who cares, I have got something more important to do i.e. writing my novel. It's evening time and I am writing Chapter 6 (Expectations, Results and the Blame Games) and writing this

There was no limit to my happiness as I scored first division. I am crossing the school gate, suddenly Kamana comes in my way. My heart started demanding more fuel with increase in the product input.

"Hi, Kamana" I said instantly.

"Hi Rehaan" She replies with a smile.

"How was your result?"

"Hmm, I got 91% marks. What about you?" She asks.

"I am just going to check it out." There are times in your life when you realise if you changed your priorities in the past to studies. I never wanted to reveal my 'average boy' image as my first impression.

"OK, best of luck!"

"Yup same to you. No, I mean thank you." Man, I didn't know what I am talking and what I should say. Her presence ruined my thinking capabilities.

"OK, bye." She smiles at me and leaves for her home. I am on the Seventh Sky.

Suddenly my phone rang.

"Hello" Shefali said.

"Hi."

"Hi Rehaan, where are you?"

"I am at my home. What happened?" I said in a not interested tone.

"Actually I wonder if we could meet."

"I don't think so. I am not in the mood."

"Actually Kamana is with me and she really wants to meet you. She was talking about you all the day. She will feel good if you take out some time."

"So what. I don't have any time right now. I have some more important work."

"Actually Kamana wants to meet........" Shefali is saying but I interrupted.

"I will try some other day. Till then take care. Bye." I cut the phone.

Life is so strange. I was just writing about those days when I would die to meet Kamana for once and today she herself wants to meet me. Today she is a nobody for me. Now that's how your priorities change with time.

26

Aarti's Marriage, Honesty Pays and Emptiness in Love

Aadarsh is quite enthusiastic about Aarti's marriage. If dad had given me the car at least our pockets would get screwed a little bit less, as compared to now going by a car-on-rent. It's me, Rohit, Aadarsh and Vicky with a driver. Rohit is giving a weird look for choosing Honda Civic, that means a bigger dent on our pocket money. I somehow convinced my mother over phone to allow me a night out as someone really special is getting married. Today is Aarti's marriage.

It's obvious, Aadarsh always resist at the last moment. We are standing at the gate of the farmhouse where the wedding is taking place. For the first time we four emptied one and a half bottle of whiskey and that too in just thirty minutes. After little hesitation we make Aadarsh the first to step into the farmhouse.

The crowd is awesome, with over-dressed aunties all around, thanks to the make up they too can now participate in Ms. India beauty contest. There are *Papus* on dancing floor, grooming up their dancing talent by doing hip-hop on classical music. Food is fantastic and free alcohol is something Vicky is living for.

Rohit is going around a busy washroom, I guess the last peg of whisky was not meant for him. I am tasting every thing from *chaat* to sweetdish, like a food inspector. Aadarsh is stuck in fear that Aarti's brother or mother might recognise him.

Barat arrived at the gate. We three axcept Rohit are eager to see the guy for whom Aarti left other *Aashiks*. Don't ask me how Dushyant was looking like? Come on the dude is here for his own wedding so obviously his face is a live example of recent developments in makeup and beauty products. I can bet one thing for sure, I know he is wearing a designer suit which cost five figures, but trust me I can get a similar dress in Chandni Chawk for around Rs. 350 and that too with a scope of further bargaining.

After some time comes the wedding girl for *Jaimala* Ceremony. They put garland over each other's neck. Then both sit like King and Queen of a not so big empire restricted to the walls of the farm house.

Time has come to implement our plan A. As per that plan Aadarsh has to go to Aarti, give her roses and wish her best of luck for her married life. After that we all will go to Faridabad. Aarti's mother and brother are standing besides Aarti and Dushyant. Their face expressions are indicating that they have no future plan to move from there. We know that if they see Aadarsh they will throw him out and in any case won't allow him to say a single word to Aarti. So we didn't have any other option but to go for plan B. Thank God Rohit at last came out of the washroom. I signalled him for plan B.

Vicky went out of the farm house.

"Oh shit" Rohit said and pushed me hard.

I abused Rohit loudly and punched him. Rohit kicked me and pulled my collar. I am holding his hair—asshole at least for today he could have used hair gel instead of odd smelly hair oil.

"Let me show you your reality, you scum dog." I said and punched Rohit again. He replied me in the same way.

Rohit and me became the source of entertainment. Almost all people present out there are seeing our fight by making a circle around us including Aarti's mother and brother. Aarti and Dushyant also stood up from their seats to see what is happening.

Aadarsh as per our Plan-B went to the stage.

"Hi Aarti, remember me."

"You! How did you get inside? I will call security." Aarti shouted but everybody was busy in the action pack fight of Rohit and me.

"Hey dude, you are lucky. Take care of my girl." Aadarsh handed over flowers to Dushyant instead of Aarti. "Happy married life to you."

Aadarsh signalled me with a unique voice meaning mission accomplished. Rohit and I stopped our fake fighting.

"Hey that was just a publicity stunt. Thanks for being such good viewers of our show. Love you girls." I said.

Before anybody could notice what is happening, we ran away from there.

Vicky was waiting with the car ready at the farmhouse gate; we three entered the moving car. Aarti's brother ran after us for some time but the poor fatty ass needs some more workout in gym.

We went to a friend's flat in Faridabad. Aadarsh started drinking again. After some time he went outside in the balcony. For the first time I saw tears in Aadarsh's eyes. He hugged me. I had once told him in 11th class that he will definitely see this day, which created the differences between us. At that time he thought that I am not with him. I am always with him, that's why I wanted to prepare him for this day.

Next day I came back to Rohtak. Rohit went to Chandigarh. Aadarsh went to Gurgaon with Vicky because he wanted to be away from Rohtak for some time.

I am sitting in the classroom attending a lecture on current ongoing financial crisis.

"This is the era of globalization and we are facing its side-effects in the face of worldwide recession. Indian Economy is also facing problems but not as much as other countries. Companies developed new practice of firing their employees or giving them pink slips, to cut their cost. According to me this will lead to even worst situation, to the emergence of vicious circle."

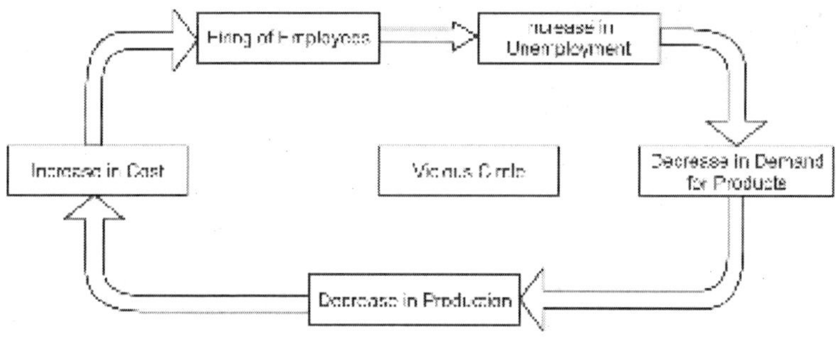

"Employees are not the liability but the asset of organizations. Good Army never makes good soldier, it is good soldiers, who make the best Army."

There is one sufferer on the name of recession in my group also, the renowned Mr. Rohit. His American MNC filed for bankruptcy, poor chap.

I had just raised my hand to ask a question, suddenly a message blinked on my phone.

'Dude I am no more a Virgin. I lost it to a prostitute last night. Aadarsh.'

Vicky and Aadarsh are no more Virgins. Last night both of them lost their virginity. But there is no impact on the bet. As to win and be recognised as a stud one has to loose his virginity to his virgin girlfriend.

At present I am least bothered about that bet. For me the only thing that matters is my novel. Now-a-days what is bothering me the most is the end of my novel which I am unable to find. I promised Manas and everybody that I won't write a fiction. Whatever is written, is the truth, a hardcore truth. Rohit got stumped on mere 20, same is the score of Vicky and Aadarsh is at only 50. Although Aadarsh and Vicky lost their virginity to a prostitute, but it was decided earlier that this won't be counted and they too accept it. Now what to do? What would be the end of my novel? Who will be the hero in the end? Wait a second, why you all readers are looking at me. If I emerge as a hero in the end, you all will say 'Asshole what's new in this crap of his? The same aged Hindi movie ending.' But who cares about you all? You have already spent money for buying this novel, so read whatever end I give you.

If I seriously think about that bet then I have only two options worth considering.

Option No. 1 Shefali.

Option No. 2 Consider option No. 1 again.

I opened my email account to mail Shefali. But saw an anonymous mail in my inbox. I opened it.

Hi Rehaan, how are you?

Nelisha

So should I explain what happened next? OK for nerds like Rohit and Manas here it is. The tale of 'Rehaan I loved you only' started with the above mail. Things have changed now. We talked casually but my emotional drama somehow brought her back. Nelisha was no more a friend of Ruchi. After her graduation, she is in Delhi now and thinking about joining MBA. One day I got her call. After 'Hi Hello-You are Buffalo' she said

"Tomorrow is my birthday so obviously you have to come. I will be with my younger brother and my friend Chetna. You can also bring any of your friend with you. I have a surprise for you." She cuts the phone after giving me time and venue. Thank God she used 'younger' before 'brother' otherwise I would end up with a surprise of Manoj firing bullets at me.

Its 6:00 a.m. yet I did not wish Nelisha, I am preparing myself for the big day. One of my classmates arranged a flat in Rohini, Delhi, for the day. I am wearing a pair of jeans that I bought yesterday, matching check blazer and a pink sweat shirt below. I put a packet of condoms (that contains three pieces) in the inside pocket of the blazer. With flat shoes, black double shaded goggles and a new sexy make over, I can say by looking in the mirror, that 'today is my day'.

After waiting at the bus stop for 20 minutes, a bus for Delhi arrived; Aadarsh waved his hand out of the window. I step into the bus.

"So, how am I looking?" Aadarsh asked me. An old villager lady sitting on the next seat moved her head towards Aadarsh.

"You know you are a stud." He bought a sweater worth Rs. 1500 yesterday for the birthday of somebody whom he doesn't even know.

"OK bro, no need to fire your sarcastic bullets on me." Aadarsh said. After a while he again opened the shutter of 'His Shop of Crap'.

"Why don't you fuck Nelisha? She is damn sexy." The old village lady made a face as if she is about to slap us.

My mind is making traps for her for the big surprise. I am planning to celebrate Nelisha's birthday in that flat in Rohini. Me and Nelisha and 'Ding Dong'. But I don't want to reveal anything to Aadarsh. I want to hit their asses with surprise but let me do the job first.

"Why don't you shut up? You already played your game with your fat ass Tania, right. Now mind your fucking business and wait for the result."

Thanks to roadways drivers, they always transport asses even before the time. This is the 2nd time I am washing my face in ISBT Metro Station washroom. My face wash is about to finish and I can bet that if I go for the third time, Aadarsh will start playing by kicking my ass.

"Want to use it." I forward the face wash to Aadarsh.

"It's of no use as it will not make any impact on my black skin." Aadarsh laughed.

"Try it first and see the results." I forced him to wash his face.

"Now look at yourself. You are looking fairer than before and mind it, your colour is not black."

I am trying to impress him because when I take Nelisha to the flat then Aadarsh will have to take care of Nelisha's friend and her younger brother.

We are waiting for Nelisha and her friend in a shopping mall.

"Where are you?" I asked Nelisha on phone.

"Rehaan just 5 more minutes, we will be there." Nelisha said.

If a girl says five minutes that means she just left her home and will take another 25 minutes or more. As per my calculation she comes exactly after half an hour. She is looking damn hot. I decided to tease her.

"Rehaan I reached the mall. Where are you?"

"Oh! I just left my home; I will be there in 2 hours." I cut the phone. She kept on calling me, but I did not pick her phone.

'Rehaan don do this baby M waitin 4 u nly pl. today's ma B'day, Nelisha.'

I suddenly came in front of her.

"Happy birthday, Nelisha." I wished and shook hands with her. The moment she held my hand I felt sudden unwanted movements in my pants, which is prohibited in public places.

'Relax this is not the right place. Have some patience' 'My Department of Brain' passed this message to my 'Department of Sex'.

"Meet Rehaan, my boyfriend on whom I trust blindly." Nelisha told Chetna. I wished a not interested hello to her friend.

"And this is my brother, Ambuj." Nelisha introduced her younger brother.

"Hello." Ambuj said.

"Hi."

"By the way meet one of my best friends, Aadarsh. Actually calling him brother is better." I introduced Aadarsh to them.

After a couple of Hi-hellos-not-interested formalities we adjusted ourselves in the Food Court. Nelisha asked me to choose any food point, being a free treat and taking the rising income of Nelisha's parents into concideration, I chose the costliest restaurant.

"I have got a surprise for you as I promised yesterday." Nelisha said.

Gone are the days when friends were expected to give a gift to the birthday girl or boy. In today's materialistic fast changing world, birthday girl herself is supposed to give surprises to others.

We are sitting in a manner as if sitting in a primary school classroom. We three boys sitting on one side of the table and the two girls on the other side and people say that Delhi girls are modern. Chetna against my expectations is not saying a single word, another side-effects of my looks.

"We will join you in a moment; we are going to the washroom." Chetna said.

"Rehaan take care of Ambuj." Nelisha said, which indirectly means Rehaan congratulations you are hired for the 'Baby Sitting' job. The moment the girls left for their headquarters Ambuj raised his eyes towards me in expectations as if his new 'Baby Sitter' will sing a jingle for him or give him a lollipop or candies or a bottle of milk. But sorry dude, I have three balloons in my pocket and they are for your sister not you.

"So you like video games?" I asked him, the favourite subject of a child.

"Yup, I have many computer games" Ambuj replied and started naming the games he has. I can bet if anyone from my side is listening to any of his gaming skills. My point was just to start his engine, now he will keep on speaking. Let me think about my love game that is to be played with Nelisha in that flat in Rohini.

"Do you know any website for cheat codes?" Aadarsh asked. God is so merciful, the poor chap Ambuj has at least one keen listener in the name of Aadarsh. Meanwhile I am making few adjustments in my master plan as per my forecasting for ongoing discussion in the washroom.

> ***Washrooms:*** *Right from the evolution of washrooms, this place is considered to be the headquarters of girls. Always notice that girls move in a group to the washrooms. What do you think they do there? Let me tell you—they do everything there other then for what the washroom is meant for. Now my girls are going to share their expert views on how we boys are looking like and what's their next strategy.*

"Nelisha your Rehaan is so sexy, I am flattered." Chetna said in excitement, while checking the fitting of her pathetic black T-shirt.

"It's of no use honey. He will never go for you types. Also don't try to mess with him as you do with everyone. His gun is always loaded with extreme sarcasm." Nelisha suggested Chetna, opened her small makeup box and rechecked her lipstick in the mirror.

"Whatever." Chetna replied and combed her hair again. "By the way, he looks sexier than in his photos."

"Let's go as boys will die without us." Nelisha said.

This is the 3rd time the service boy asked for order from me. Why always these people choose me. Service boys and I never had good relations ever.

"We will let you know in a couple of minutes."

"OK, Sir." He actually meant 'Make it fast you asshole or drink mineral water, pay for it and get lost.'

"So what's going on, boys?" Chetna asked, as girls joined us.

"Nothing much. Just discussing who is more beautiful: Chetna or Nelisha." I laughed.

We placed the order for food.

"So all of you are trained in making me bored or want to play something." I said.

"Like what?"

"Anything worth playing."

"I got an idea." Chetna picks up a bottle. She is about to rotate the bottle, signalling the start of the age-old game 'Truth and Dare'.

"Oh! Wait. This is the worst game I have ever played. It should be named as 'lie and betrayal', because nobody speaks an inch of truth." But who cares about my feelings. Nelisha insisted to play. There is something wrong with the bottle, every time it stopped at me, a master in telling lies.

For last ten minutes I was feeling constant vibrations coming from my right side. I was about to declare it an earthquake, but the next moment I realised it's Ambuj who is shivering.

"Hey dude, what happened?" I asked.

The two girls jumped in for the rescue of mere shivering of a boy.

"No it's just that I am feeling very cold here." Ambuj declared. This introduced new worries to Aadarsh's not so imperfect life, that would he get his burger with extra cheese in time or we have to leave this restaurant.

I am considered as a hero who rescued his girl's brother 'who is shivering out of cold' by giving him his blazer. This emotional scene would bring tears to even the worst devil, but please clear your misconception, as I am a villain and not a hero. In the end, it's me always who is expected to hold the flag of humanity.

There was no problem for me to give my blazer to Ambuj but my concern is the packet of condoms. What if the dude pursue a search mission and my unauthorized weapon gets into the notice of crime branch sitting over here. I somehow took out the condoms from the blazer and put them into my trouser pocket before giving my blazer to Ambuj.

"Rehaan, I think Ambuj is getting bored. Why don't two of you go for video games?" Nelisha asked.

Fuck her, I will prefer to throw a hundred rupee note into fire instead of spending it on boo-boo games and that too playing with an 'I need a lollipop kid'.

"I think we all go for the games." Chetna said.

I love you Chetna for rescuing my ass. The poor Aadarsh on the other hand is still looking if his burger with extra cheese will arrive today.

"OK." Nelisha, paid the bill and we all left the restaurant. Sympathy to Aadarsh's not so perfect 'imperfect fate', may be the extra cheese took so much of time, who cares.

Ambuj is still not feeling good, so we dropped him at the metro station, from where he will go to his home, alone.

Aadarsh and Chetna intentionally left me and Nelisha alone by putting phone on their ears bluffing as if they are talking to someone.

Nelisha and me are standing at a lonely place.

"Here's your surprise." Nelisha gives me a greeting card on which 'love you forever' is written.

"So shall we go now?" Nelisha asked me.

"Yeah, give me a hug." I said. I hugged her and kiss her cheeks.............

Ha ha ha......I can't hide it anymore. I was lying There was nothing I got on the name of an 'e-mail' from Nelisha. I don't even know where she is. *April fool banaya aji aapko gussa aya...la la la...Ullu banaya charkha chalaya.* I am still single and ready to mingle. Well regarding my Option No. 1. Shefali, she is a nice girl and one of my good friends. I can't play with her. So let's come to the real world again,

where I am not a stud but a struggling author searching for a struggling end.

Nandini is now a good friend of Rohit. She realised that it's very easy to find a friend but impossible to find a real one. She is fortunate to have Rohit as a real friend of her.

Manas on the other hand is lost in his own dream world. His chain of love started when he was in eighth class. According to him he fell in love with Richa when he was a kid, then came Somani his first school girlfriend for two days, next Monika at his Taekwondo Academy, then his neighbour Rima and Sheena in high school. Jyoti, Pooja and Sandhya in his NIT (National Institute of Technology, Kurukshetra). And now he is saying that Nandini is just a good friend, but in reality I think for the first time he really loves a girl from his heart. It's Manas's birthday and he is totally drunk with his hostel friends. After thinking for some time he comes out of his room and dialled a number.

"Hi Nandini, Manas here."

"Hi Manas, Happy birthday."

"Why didn't you call me at 12 in the night. In the morning also you just sent me an sms."

"Actually I was busy. Anyways, Happy birthday."

"No, you didn't have any important work. I know that I mean nothing to you."

"It's not so Manas, you are my friend. And yes never expect anything more then that."

"Nandini I know I am boring. I know I am pathetic. But still I want to make you my girlfriend. Would you like to be my girlfriend."

"Manas be in your limits. I think you are drunk."

"No Nandini, today I am in my senses. I can't hide my feelings anymore, I really love you Nandini."

"But I don't love you, Manas."

"Why is it so, because I am not good looking and humorous like Rehaan, or just because I am a nerd? What about a person's feelings? Does it not matter that a person is honest from heart?"

"It's not that Manas. You are just a friend to me nothing more. I don't love you. I can never do that because I love somebody else. I am committed to him."

"Who is he?"

"His name is Rohit. He is the only one." Saying this Nandini cut the phone.

Manas kept on sitting in the balcony and after some time looked towards the sky and said:

"Every girl I choose is the right girl for me, but I was never able to prove them that I am the right guy for her. When a child is born, he is pure, and free, the situations decides the direction of his life. Sorry Rohit, sorry Rehaan, I chose Nandini over you. Today I have realised the real me. Enough is enough, I know what I have to do in my life."

It's not Manas' fate which made him loose in the case of Nandini, but it's somebody's honesty which paid him. Rohit once said "*Honesty Pays*. It pays, I don't know how much? Whether up to your expectations or not but it does pay. I think my honesty will also pay me one day." And at last it really paid him full.

And now.........introducing not so happening poet in Nandini-

Not an ordinary love.........

It was not an ordinary day but the most special one,
He was standing alone like an ordinary person,
When I came close to him he just kept on looking at me,
He said nothing but I saw tears in his eyes,
I know this declared the end of his pain,
I made him lie down on my lap.
He said nothing and fell asleep,
He woke up as my tears fell on his face,
He didn't say I love you and neither did I,
Our eyes talked on behalf of our words,
I held his hand not in an ordinary way and was lost in his arms,
At last I can say that
I am in love and my love is not ordinary but special,
The special person in my life is Rohit, my Rohit.

Man, Rohit should have kissed her but the two just kept on looking into each other eyes all the day. I wonder if this poem of Nandini should be named as 'not an ordinary nerd couple' instead. But man it feels great seeing them together. I saw Rohit dying out of pain called 'Nandini', but now he is the happiest person. After Nandini came in his life, Rohit stopped smoking and drinking, and is transformed into a Super Nerd (next level to nerd).

27

The Coffee Point, Writing Pathetic Ends And...........

I got only those things in life which I never wished. I was never able to achieve those things which I dreamed of. I went to the edge of my limits to achieve what I desired, but the door closes on me the moment I am about to grab it. I know this is not a new story as this happens to many other persons also. But fuck others, I am concerned about myself. As I don't want to be someone who keeps on repeating his failures in front of others for mere sympathy, which more than 99% people do.

Strange that I didn't love any of the three girls; Kamana, Shefali and Nelisha.

If I really loved Kamana then why did I refuse to go to meet her, when she asked me through Shefali. Actually I used to like Kamana the most at one point of time. You may call it a strong infatuation. This feeling lingered in my head under the wrong heading of 'love' until the school was over. I used to see her daily in school which acted as a strong misinterpreted feeling of love. But when she went to college, I started loosing that feeling.

Shefali was very good friend of mine. After Kamana case I was feeling very low and to revive myself I went for Shefali. I know it sounds cheap that to come out of my 'Kamana's Dilemma' I used Shefali but trust me I didn't have any other way out. So our breakup was obvious. Still Shefali is one of my best friends and the true treasure of mine.

Nelisa was someone which made me feel like a stud. For the first time in my life, I got a gorgeous girl as my girlfriend. But in her case also I never fell in love because I never got a chance to spend time with her alone. She always came to meet with her so called bodyguards Ruchi, Tanvi and other girls of her class. You can never fall in love until you spend time together alone to know each other better.

So I have no option but to write the end.

I am sitting at The Coffee Point and writing the last chapter, i.e. Chapter 26

But it's not Manas' fate which makes him loose in the case of Nandini. But it's somebody's honesty which paid him. Rohit once said "Honesty Pays. It pays, I don't know how much, whether up to your expectations or not but it does pay. I think my honesty will also pay me." And at last it really paid him full. Hats off to Rohit and Nandini.

At last Rohit got his true love. After looking at the marks it is Mr. Aadarsh, who won with a total of 50. Now a days Aadarsh is busy in consoling his one and only upset girlfriend Tania. Don't worry he too succeeded in doing so—thanks again to my guilt theory. Manas is looking forward to his dream i.e. finding a new girl for himself. Vicky too is happy in his world of prostitutes. Buzz of the day is that he started taking drugs, also. May be to kill the loneliness in his life. Lastly me myself I....

Suddenly somebody standing behind closed my eyes. At last I got the end, in the end Mr. Rehaan became the murderer. I am already frustrated with writing this pathetic end and some asshole is playing 'Guess Who Is The Asshole Behind You?' game with me.

"Who the hell wants to get screwed by me?"

"Amulya!"

Amulya lifted her hands and came in front of me. Screw me! Somebody, please for God sake screw me. How can I think about screwing the most gorgeous girl. I left her just because of an ugly fat aunty (Kamana) in my school days. What an asshole I was.

"So how are you? Must be going great."

"Yup." Great, yeah exactly great. Great in writing the great end.

"How is Kamana?

Yeah again, great. I wonder when a revolution will come in my life after which people stop associating me with my first and the last mistake of my life. And what the fuck, in four years spent in some US university, what Amulya has learned is to call everything great. But the only thing great here is that she is looking hotter than before. A total change, razor cut hairstyle tied on a high pony tail. I don't know what the shit she applied to her face, it is shining like gold. Fairness of her hands and legs are declaring the so called extra fair guy (myself) as the black beauty. And here I am sitting in an ordinary shirt, declaring that no change took place in my outdated dressing sense and in my 'champu' hairstyle, too. Actually I was not expecting any stunning diva here.

"It is a long story. Will tell you some other day."

"OK then that day is tomorrow. After coming back from USA you are the only bastard I was looking for."

"I missed you a lot, dear."

"Yeah, I also missed you. I think you are the one who changed your mobile number. I tried many times from States. Meet me at 9 a.m. tomorrow here."

"Sure. I will come."

Of course, who will say no to a dream date with 'The queen of beauty'.

"I have to go now. Bye and take care."

"Bye."

We step out of The Coffee Point. I was thinking of droping her on my bike but when I saw her car I didn't say anything.

I am already getting late for my home so fuck the end. I will write it tomorrow morning.

28

20 And Still a ~~Vergin~~ Virgin?!!?

Sometimes I wonder why I can't be like animals—today with this female and the next day with another. I guess because I am a human being. Am I really one?

Being a boy from a middle class family, I am expected to live a common life, surviving for the happiness of others. During college I have to work hard to score well, so that my mother can proudly discuss my scores with others. Then I will join some multinational, where I put my ass on a burner by working for more than 12 hours a day, to make my boss happy and proud. By the time I am 24 my parents will choose a girl for me. Parents are more interested in family background of the girl, the girl should be an ATM, i.e. earning five figure salary. She should prepare food and do other house-work. What about our mutual understanding, or what if she doesn't like my lifestyle, or what if our tuning does not match. But who cares, being a perfect son, I am expected to go by my parents choice. Afterwards one more member (my wife) is added to the list of persons with whom I have to deal in such a way so as to keep her happy. After a few years, few 'babas and babies' will start moving around me all the time. These 'Babas and Babies' will forward their list of demands. To be a good father, I will have to see to it and fullfil their demands. After that these 'Babas and Babies' will marry to a person of their choice and throw this old father to a dark corner. Like this I will die one day while giving lecture of how life sucks. If this is life then fuck it.

There is one difference between me and others i.e. I will follow my dreams. I will complete my novel and one day be something worth in this world.

'Burp.....ptttrrrrrr....pppoooooooon' fuck that Coffee Point, for the fifth time I am sitting in the toilet and declaring it as my exclusive fart-zone.

After dressing up well I look into the mirror. Suddenly old memories came to my mind. In my school days, how I used to dress up? Like a joker, but an innocent joker and now an evil one.

"You are ten minutes late." The hotties are transformed into hottest when they show anger on their face.

"Actually my train was late"

What? Train?"

"Sorry wrong excuse to the wrong girl." I started laughing at my poorest joke ever created by me in the history of poor jokes. But for my surprise Amu smiled at it. Girls!!

"So hero, today I am free to listen to your story. Darling, push your start button."

"It's a long story. Neither this place is right nor the aura. Don't worry I will tell you some other day. Tell me something about America. It must be exciting."

"Exciting my foot. Come with me." She stood up, held my hand and started moving towards exit. Man where is she going? The poor waiters didn't even get the chance to serve to the most wonderful creation of nature.

She opened the door of her car and asked me to get in. What's happened to her? It's a kidnap or to be more correct a dream kidnap. Why is a stunning gorgeous girl kidnapping a would be struggling author?

She parked the car in front of a Bungalow.

"Come in."

"Are you mad?"

"Shut up." She held my hand and took me inside her house. We went to a room upstairs.

"I am coming back in a moment." She closed the door from outside.

The room is all messed up with clothes spread all around. Resembles to a room in a Hindi movie where villain rapes a heroines. Time and time changes everything. Now a days heroes are being raped by lady villains. I am in the mid of the rape fantasy when suddenly Amulya came in with pillows, a bottle of cold drink, a packet of chips and sandwiches in her hand.

She puts pillow behind me on the bed, asks me to remove my shoes and to just relax. I lie comfortably on her bed. She sits in front of me in her black skirt. Some strictly prohibited areas above her knees are visible for sightseeing. That scene is enough to declare emergency in my 'Department of Sex'.

"Stop staring at my legs and say something. You are at the right place now and the right aura is also created."

"So how many people are present in your house." I teased her. It's obvious that nobody is at home that's why she brought me here.

"My parents are out of town. They will be coming late tonight. So just two of us and my grandparents."

"What? Your grandparents." I jumped in surprise.

"Don't worry; they are too old to come to the first floor."

"Do you smoke?"

I pointed to a packet of cigarette and a lighter kept on the table.

"No. Actually my father smokes. Now what the hell you need more to start your crap."

"OK. This is the tale of a not-so-happening-stud."

I started telling her my story. When I told about Sohail, Kamana and that deadly night, I noticed tears in her eyes. For the first time I felt some movements in my heart. But my sympathy vanished when I realised that the so called 'Irrigation Department' of Amulya is working for 'Rohit and Nandini' tale also. I completed my story in half an hour. Then I revealed about my novel, also.

"Hey, why are you not eating anything?" Amu asked me.

"No, it's just that I already had a heavy breakfast." Forget breakfast, it is just that my 'Department of Digestion' is not good. I don't want to turn your sophisticated toilet into my 'Exclusive Fart Zone'.

"What about Kamana? I think that you really loved her."

"No. I never loved Kamana."

"But I remember you liked her like anything."

"Exactly. I liked her but never loved her. There is a difference. Love happens only when you fall in love with each other. And now, I don't even like Kamana."

"So you are a Virgin?"

"Yup, I am sitting on a score of zero." I laughed "What about you?"

"I too am still a Virgin."

"I don't believe that you were in USA for four years and are still a virgin. If you don't want to tell me, it's OK."

"I will lose my virginity only to someone whom I love."

"So, who is the lucky guy? Have you found him?"

"Yup, the asshole is lying in front of me."

"What?" I jumped after hearing the biggest surprise of my life.

"I liked you, when I saw you the first time in the park, when you were still in school. I liked the way you were. When Sarah introduced you, that day was the happiest day for me. When you told me about the bet and Kamana, I didn't feel bad. That day I fell in love with you and with your innocence. I never wanted to come between you and Kamana, so I left everything and went to America for doing my graduation. I thought you must be going great with Kamana. Four years without you in my life was like a century filled with only tears. Boys did propose me but I was never able to think about anybody else. After completing my graduation I came to India just to see you. I just want to say one thing." She wipes out a tear in her right eye and continued "I love you Rehaan. I love you more than anybody in this world. I am not saying this because I want you. It's your life. But just for once I want to reveal my feelings in front of you."

"What if I deceive you, Amu? I am not the same Rehaan that I used to be in those school days..." Before I could complete my lines she put her hand on my lips.

"My love is unconditional. It's me who wants you."

"Welcome to RGS (Rehaan's Girlfriend Squad) then."

"Shut up. Don't put me in that category." She laughed.

"Right then, you are the General Manager of that squad." We two kept on laughing for about ten minutes.

"So. How is your novel progressing?"

"Although I have already finished writing about 260 pages, I am still not able to find any end of the story."

"Great! You are just on the finish line. Don't loose hope when success is just short of one step. Always remember that the last hour before dawn is the darkest hour of the night."

She smiled at me.

"What happened?"

"I love you!" Amulya said.

"Yup! I love you, too. So what's there to smile sarcastically."

"Nothing just that I am a virgin." Saying that Amu fell next to me.

"By the way you sound dirty." I smiled.

"A dirty mind always produces a dirty product." She laughed.

Man, I can't express how the feeling is like. She hugged me tight. Being extraordinary in mathematics, I don't remember how many kisses are interchanged and how many French kisses bombarded on my not so luscious lips.

"Condom?" I stood up.

She held my hand.

"Take my car."

"Obviously, I am going in your car. My bike is parked outside The Coffee Point."

I went to the nearest market. All the time while driving it's not possible for me to concentrate on anything.

"Give me a packet of condoms."

"What?" The chemist jumped in surprise, as if I have asked for a one night stand with his wife. I think he was expecting that I will ask for some boo-boo diapers.

"Condom, C, O, N, D, O and M, Condom, got it?"

"Yeah, sure." He gave me a pack.

I drove back to her house and ran upstairs in a hurry. She was waiting for me with a different outfit. She was wearing a white transparent nightgown holding a red rose in her hand.

I locked the door from inside and without wasting anytime hugged her.

"I love you, Amulya."

"I love you too, Rehaan."

This time I won't throw her on bed and fell on her. As my 'Throw Her and Fell On' philosphy ends declaring it a weired dream. I was in the mid of ambiquity, if it's a dream or reality. Suddenly she started behaving like a tigress, by moving here and there. Although I on the other hand acted like an idiot jackal. Curse my interest in Wild Life TV Channels, even in this sitution I am thinking about animals only. After numerous hugs, kisses and rolling tongues, my hands moved to her restricted areas. She jumped in excitement.

"Naughty boy." She smiled.

"It's time to go for something which comes once in your life."

"I have to prove that I trust you the most. I love you only. I can't give you anything more than this, as for a girl to lose her virginity before marriage is the biggest thing." Amulya said while holding my face. A tear trickled down her eyes.

"Trust me, Amulya." I kissed her tear.

And then, we crossed the limits. It's the most exciting moment of my life. She grabbed my shoulders and hair above the neck tightly out of pain. Tears are flowing like a river from her eyes. She is saying just one thing again and again 'I love you, Rehaan.' At last my knowledge of porn movies helped me in trying 'Not So Common *Asanas*'. Those positions were so strange that I got many slaps by her in between the act.

Sex is one thing, but sex with a girl whom you love the most is like one of the best things happen in life and that too with an added advantage that the girl is a stunning beauty.

My eyes stopped at the packet of cigarette lying on the table. I don't know what came in my mind that I took out one cigarette.

"I didn't know that you smoke?"

"Oh, it's my first cigarette and this is my second, third, fourth and fifth cigarette." I pointed out to four other cigarettes in the packet.

Amu smiled and grabed me again.

I am lying on a not so comfortable bed in a Dilapidated or ramshackle kind of a room. Cigarette smoke is all around and anything else is barely visible. My left hand is resting on one side of the bed with a burning cigarette and smoke rings are surrounding me all over. I am constantly looking at not so clearly visible stationary age-old fan, which seems like moving at its maximum. Amulya is lying with me under a blanket with her face hidden below my elbow. She is grabbing my vest with her hand, in which she is wearing a cute thin golden bangle. My right hand is moving on her back to make her feel comfortable. I crushed the half burned cigarette on the table nearby. I then kissed her cheeks again.

That makes a score of hundred out of hundred. I won the first bet ever in my history of betting.

I am blessed with a new life. A life with no problems, no bad luck, no looser like feeling, nothing. Life is full of pleasure and love. This strange feeling is making my heart-beat faster. This moment I want to freeze time, although after wearing my underwear, off course. It felt like heaven till I saw the photo of the 'Devil'. I wonder if my next chapter would be 'Devil in Heaven'.

"Hey who is she, hanging on the wall?" I jumped in surprise.

"Oh that's my mom. She was sexier when she was young." Amulya smiled while adjusting her bra.

"Damn! Mrs. Khanna is your mother? Are you Amulya Khanna?" My eye balls jumped out from their right place.

"Obviously idiot, I would also be Khanna if my mom is Khanna. Hey I remember you were in Model School, right? My mom used to teach mathematics there. You must be knowing her."

Please somebody erase the above lines 'I am blessed with a new life. A life with no problems, no bad luck', blah-blah. Before 'Mrs. Khanna' makes a re-entry in my life in the next chapter 'Devil in Heaven', let me finish it off with my final lines.

People call me with different names, some call me 'Stud', some 'Playboy', others 'The Next Super Model'.

I never expected much from life; neither had I fulfilled its expectations from me. I was not a born stud but situations made me so.

EPILOGUE

As I stated many times earlier, it's not a Hindi movie where in the end almost every character of the movie gets a happy ending. This is real life. Aadarsh told Tania about the bet but never disclosed about that night when he lost his virginity to the prostitute. So the dude is balancing over a score of only 50, trying hard to forget the not so fruitful memories of his not so perfect foreplay. Rohit is the only guy who got his school love, Nandini. Although he scored just 20 and is still a virgin, but he is the real winner. It's not about the bet but his honesty which paid him. Good news is that he got a job in Birlas and is side-by-side preparing for Haryana Civil Services Examination. Manas is trying hard to overcome his so called 6th love by pretending to be a stud. But a recent 'no' from another girl makes an end to his 'image projecting mission'. He decided to serve our country and joined Defence Research & Development Services as a Scientist and now is in Kargil doing some geeky stuff. I, Rohit and Aadarsh few days back went to Gurgaon to visit Vicky, the fourth guy who was also a part of that bet and scored just 20. I was shocked to see him taking drugs. He had joined some local gang indulging in narcotics business. Hunny decided not to involve himself in any more fightings. But the next day I saw him grabbing collar of his college senior. The earth revolved around me a thousand times when I came to know that Prashant had become a father. Man he is only 21 and a father! I just can't express my sympathy in words for him.

Loosing virginity almost changed my life. I am entitled with a new name 'A Stud'.

Finally I got something in the name of 'The End of my Novel'. I was on the top of the world till I listened to various comments of publishers and their editors. 'You call this a novel; Are you kidding?', 'It's the best shoddy crap I have ever seen', 'hmm it's a B grade novel for sure', 'I would rather publish an English book of 2nd standard than the stuff you have written', 'Please give a second thought regarding a career as an author'. At last my so called 'B grade shoddy crap' got a publisher.

Few months later

Life was never easy to me and neither this situation is. Losers always have their own advantages; at least they are always ready for the worst. Sympathy for the losers. Sorry but we three, Aadarsh, Rohit and I are not amongst them. We are sitting with Tania, Nandini and Amulya at 'The Coffee Point", celebrating the launch of '20 And Still A Virgin?!!?' Rohit and Aadarsh are yelling at me while reading my novel. Seeing that 'The Doors of my Ear Drum' are knocked by constant laughter doses of the three girls.

"Who thought that a looser like me will become an author one day? During my sleepless nights many a times I used to ask myself—Why Kamana came into my life? She was not meant to be with me as my love, then why? I don't have any grudges for the simple reason that I never loved her. I used to like her at one point of time but that was not love. I realised the true meaning of love with Amulya. So coming back to the question 'Why Kamana came into my life?' Simple answer is Destiny i.e. to make me an author. Whatever happened with me and my friends was just to make us what we are today and to give me story for my first novel. Life has its own ways of making us what we are today and what we will be in future. What I learned is to see things with different angles."

"You know honey, Kamana was right. Your philosophy really sucks like anything." Amulya holds my hands.

"It may sound weird, but I want to thank you."

"Thank me for what?"

"For everything. You gave me the real meaning of the most complex phenomena 'love'. That way you are my first love, Amu. Also for giving an end to my novel. I don't know why, but whenever I meet you the 'old sweet school Rehaan' overshadows the 'Evil Joker'."

"Rehaan I love you more then anybody in this world. And don't say thanks to me ever again."

After some time Amu fell asleep. Suddenly a new thought was raised by relaxing members of my 'Department of Brain'. What next? I will join a job after MBA, marry Amulya and live happily with her and a few new problems (Babas and Babies). So is it the end or just the beginning? But beginning of what? At least for now it's the beginning of my sleep. I hugged Amulya and we both went to sleep.

'There is crowd on both sides of the ramp, as fashion week is going on. The moment I step onto the ramp, audience applauds in excitement. I am wearing a designer black shining suit and walking on the ramp. I am the show stopper of the event.'